An Empty House

UNA CASA VACÍA

AN EMPTY HOUSE

CARLOS CERDA

*Translated
by Andrea G. Labinger*

University of Nebraska Press
Lincoln & London

Publication of this book was assisted by a grant
from the National Endowment for the Arts.

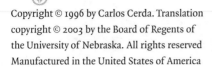

Library of Congress Cataloging-in-Publication Data
Cerda, Carlos.
[Casa vacía. English]
An empty house / Carlos Cerda ; translated by
Andrea G. Labinger.
p. cm.
Translation of: Una casa vacía.
ISBN 0-8032-1524-X (cloth : alkaline paper) –
ISBN 0-8032-6425-9 (pbk. : alkaline paper)
I. Labinger, Andrea G.   II. Title.
PQ8098.13.E668C3713 2003   863′.64–dc21
2003047306

To *Mariana*, for her counsel. To *Carlos Orellana*, for his encouragement and enthusiasm during the initial stages of this book. To *Marcelo Maturana*, for his accurate observations on the final draft of this text. To *Marcela Gatica*, For her unwavering solidarity. To *Magaly Villalón*, *Verónica Rojas*, and *Claudia de la Vega* for their contribution to the graphic design of the book. To *Carlos E. Ossa* and *Editorial Alfaguara.* To the *Fondo de Desarrollo de la Cultura y las Artes* (FONDART) for the grant that made it possible.

CONTENTS

An Empty House

PART ONE

The Restoration

They've all gone, the house is empty.
And when you open the door there's a mirror
where you see yourself full-length and feel a chill.

Pablo Neruda, *Ceremonial Songs*

1

The afternoon when they saw it for the first time, they wondered how such a lovely house could have stood empty for so long. Now at last they could truly speak of a once-in-a-lifetime opportunity, an offer they would have to be crazy to turn down. This is the opportunity, darling, Cecilia told Manuel that night, and the man rediscovered a forgotten tenderness in his wife's words. Lying in bed in the narrow bedroom of their apartment, they remembered the imposing architecture of the house, the solemn spaciousness of the empty living room, the solid shutters, the staircase whose fine wooden banister had already begun to gleam in the couple's imagination. The girls would have plenty of space for playing, not only in the enormous garden, rather neglected, really, but also in the two second-story rooms whose windows faced a vista of typically Ñuñoan backyards, with vines that had recently begun to turn green again, grottos alongside the brick walls, and doghouses for languid, harmless dogs. Manuel's memory lingered on the magnificent spread of the backyard, overgrown with weeds and a few leafy trees, probably walnut or plum, perhaps an avocado, and on the fresh fragrance of orange trees. There was plenty to do, of course, considerable expense before the house would recover its majesty. But my dad promised to leave it looking like new, Cecilia remarked encouragingly, already thinking about a room for herself, that little drawing room next to the bedroom: there she'd be able to spend entire afternoons reading, preparing her classes, mending the girls' clothing. Yes. It would be insane not to take advantage of an opportunity like this one.

That night they settled, spontaneously, into a routine that had seemed forgotten. They spoke about the days to come and about matters that had always caused conflict between them, this time without producing even a hint of a quarrel. They calculated expenses and invented savings that would guarantee them the money for the many repairs they needed to undertake. Cecilia said they could paint the entire downstairs first and scrape the wooden floors: they look sort of stained, did you notice? And the following month they'd do the second floor and finally, with new savings, the garden; an idea Manuel rejected, although this time avoiding what Cecilia called "that nasty, pontificating tone that makes my hair stand on end." He explained that doing everything piecemeal would come out more expensive because the price of paint, wood, concrete, was always going up, and besides, with that approach you can't negotiate a good price with the contractor all at once. It would be best to visit the house the next day with Cecilia's father, get him excited about it – your daughter's right, Don Jovino, another opportunity like this one won't come along, such a pretty yard for the girls – and he won't have any problem lending us whatever it takes to make the house look wonderful, darling; I can see myself already, in the summertime, reading in the shade of those trees – what do you call that big, leafy one? And they even considered not going to the beach that summer: if they rented out the house in El Quisco, they'd be able to pay for part of the remodeling, Cecilia's father would help them, they were sure of that. But, let me talk to him, Cecilia: I want him to know we'll pay him back every dime, and they recalled that, in spite of those stains on the floor and on the walls, new plumbing had been installed less than three years ago, that's what the guy at the realty company had guaranteed them, and he had also said that the wiring had been upgraded, two very important things, darling, because houses in Ñuñoa are very lovely, but they're old, very cold and damp, and besides, you have to realize that nowadays people use so many electrical appliances . . .

The idea of the barbecue came to them with their first yawns, after recalling the foliage of the trees once more. Cecilia leaned over Manuel in order to speak to him with a tenderness he couldn't ignore. Manuel discovered renewed youthfulness in his wife's eyes, now so close to his own.

"And when we're all moved in, we'll celebrate with a barbecue, over there, under that big tree, and we'll invite Marcela and Cristián, he'll understand that it's our way of thanking him for giving us credit, and Julia Medina, of course, and maybe by then even Andrés will be back home, poor guy."

"You really think we ought to invite him? I mean, we haven't seen him in two years," Manuel said, not very comfortable with the idea.

"Well, yes, but remember, he was the owner of the house!"

"And your dad?"

"What about him?"

"Should we invite him?"

"Did it even occur to you not to? Well, anyway, just don't start talking politics with him. The old man may be a nuisance, but he has his good points."

"Listen, your dad's the one who always starts . . ."

"You know he never stays long. And speaking of tension, do you think it's a good idea to invite Marcela if Andrés is going to come?" Cecilia asked, yawning.

"What difference does it make? Those two have been separated for something like fifteen years."

"Maybe I should ask Marcela first."

Manuel placed his hand on Cecilia's waist, feeling the warmth of her body through the soft fabric of her nightgown, caressing her, what does it matter if they were married once, Miss Propriety, they've both got their lives sorted out now. He sought Cecilia's lips with his own, and the long kiss conquered the coldness they thought had become forever ingrained in their bodies, slowly erasing time and distance. Cecilia stretched out in the bed and brushed Manuel's ear with her lips, moaning softly, "Let's go dancing under the grapevines, darling, to Frankie Lane and the Platters . . ."

Later on, in dreams, Cecilia saw the leafy foliage of an enormous tree, shaken by a gust of wind, knocking against a windowpane.

2

In the days following, everything the couple had imagined came to pass without a hitch. Don Jovino raised some minor objections, which were ineffectual against the overwhelming determination of the couple, who wanted to live in the new house as soon as possible, and in the end he contributed the additional sum that would allow the restoration to take place. The repairs accentuated the spaciousness of the rooms and the sober elegance of the house. The stains disappeared from the walls and the floor, the former achieving an impeccable whiteness, and the parquet acquiring the warm simplicity of recently polished wood. Only in the children's room, despite meticulous scraping, did the faint trace of a burn persist on the floor. The garden was raked, and the rosebushes, liberated from weeds, displayed their perfect blossoms, framed by the lawn, which filled in quickly. The tree pruning exposed a tranquil expanse of patio, and the sun, which hadn't warmed that earth for years, now penetrated full force, making the long grass and clover bud in a few days and allowing the gladiolus, which Cecilia had ordered to be planted against the brick wall, to bloom. This wall, a pure, limestone white, illumined a milky-blue horizon on moonlit nights, beyond which the trees in the neighboring yards loomed like the shadows of peaceful giants. Cecilia's yard no longer resembled a green tangle of uncontrolled weeds and shrubs, cobwebs, toads, insects, that aberrant, fearsome thing, that foliage thrashed furiously by the wind, crushing against her window, scratching the panes, moaning, as she had begun to dream about again for the last few nights.

The modest miracle-worker was Maestro Barraza, freed by Don Jovino from his responsibilities in the realty company so that he could devote those weeks exclusively to the restoration of the house. A mason whenever he could be one, a gardener during slack periods, a forager with no secure job in really bad times, and a schemer to boot, although this derived more from

8

experience than from malevolence, Maestro Barraza offered his services for an amount the new homeowners considered a second bargain, one that almost miraculously combined with the first, since the final cost of the property seemed more and more convenient as Maestro Barraza's labor made their rooms shine. When he had finished applying the second coat of green paint to the metal door and had sanded the peephole cover to eliminate the squeaking it produced whenever it was opened, he deemed his job completed to perfection.

During the three weeks it took to finish the repairs, Cecilia and Manuel solidified their rapprochement, stimulated by the positive changes in the house, which they observed every afternoon, whenever they stopped by after work to monitor the progress and reward the Maestro's exhausting efforts with a monetary advance or a couple of generous words of praise. Sometimes, however, they relapsed into squabbles and misunderstandings, which Cecilia had thought were a thing of the past. Eager to avoid them, she preferred to explain her husband's overreactions as a consequence of the natural tension that she supposed settling into a new house entailed. At times, though, when, as she pretended to sleep, she would hear Manuel slip carefully out of bed and sit down with a glass of wine in the kitchen, distractedly reading the headlines, like before, she thought that the promise of better times, so obsessively linked to the new house, was just a lie she stubbornly insisted on believing. At times like those, she remembered how Marta and Felipe, shortly before their separation, had decided to have their third child, and how Alicia had unexpectedly decided to marry Antonio, only to live through a few weeks of happiness, two or three months of uncertainty, and four years of unbearable confrontations, from which she finally had to recover with a sleep cure in a private clinic. Silently she listened as Manuel returned to bed, knowing he was as awake as she was, and so as not to annoy him with repeated questions, she tried to think of something else – again, the color of the little room that would become her retreat: she had seen a soft lavender that afternoon, very soothing, especially suitable for relaxing. Tomorrow she would discuss it with the Maestro.

In his escapes to the kitchen, after the second glass of wine and a few cigarettes, Manuel began to recover a certain serenity; he savored the gradual taming of his demons; he had become addicted to that overdue encounter with stillness. In the midst of so many frustrations and peremptory duties, of so many things dying and nothing being born, he assumed that in the solitary space of his nights, the new house was opening one of its doors to hope. It would be easier to be alone there. He'd have his study on the first floor, in the room facing the terrace; he'd put his old records in order, he'd listen to music again; maybe he'd go through those photos that had gotten lost in abandoned folders. He could set up a darkroom in the basement for developing pictures, that modest passion to which he had devoted himself during his first years with the realty company. Yes, after a while, after they'd dealt with the expenses, he'd put in a nice enlarger, he'd buy it secondhand, everyone was selling things cheap these days. Nevertheless, he was worried by Cecilia's insistence on reconstructing their relationship exactly as it had been in the past. Why didn't she realize that the past was dead and no one could revive it? Their mutual agreement with Don Jovino, when a separation had seemed inevitable, wasn't to salvage their lost happiness but rather to save the marriage. In the new house he had given them, they had to make all the efforts and sacrifices – those words frequently came from Don Jovino's lips – in order to avoid conflicts that might lead to a breakup. To Manuel, as to Don Jovino, the couple's new life looked much more like a future made up of controlled distances than like a past composed of a now-impossible intimacy. And that was precisely what Cecilia refused to accept. For her the new house was synonymous with a new beginning; for Manuel, under the best of circumstances, it was the acceptance of a less unhappy ending. For Cecilia the restoration and adornment of the house were accompanied every day by chores that restored her, too, to the splendid grace of her youth. She changed her hairstyle, eliminating the first gray hairs that had cast fear upon her solitary nights in front of the vanity mirror, at the same time Manuel was losing himself in the smoke and wine of his equally solitary after-dinner hour. She started working out again; she chose more vivid clothing and determined to display a banner of perpetual harmony in her expression: a smile that was difficult to sustain after noon, but which reappeared later in the day, whenever they showed up to watch the progress in the refurbishment of the house. Thinking of that smile and the new hairdo to which he hadn't yet become accustomed, trying to understand Cecilia's stubborn persistence, Manuel lit another cigarette and poured himself one more glass, feeling as though everything was losing density. The radio sounded faintly from the maid's room. Berta could go all night without sleeping, or maybe she slept till morning with the radio on. It was all the same. In the long run everything was the same. At that point fatigue was his only source of solace. He heard the soft cadences of the music, leafed through magazines without reading them, paused over one photo or another. Yes, in the basement, with a few pesos . . . Tomorrow he'd discuss it with the Maestro.

His return to bed didn't disrupt the continuity of that solitary night. There, next to him, Cecilia's wakefulness – whenever he noticed it – weighed on him like a silent demand, a call to fulfill the only duty that had failed to be peremptory.

In the afternoons, though, everything seemed different, as if another Manuel and a different Cecilia visited the new house before nightfall. She would arrive excited, eager to find out if the soft lavender, now dry, captured the same tone on the walls that she had liked so much in the catalogue; she wanted to see how Maestro Barraza overcame obstacles in building his miracle. The round window in the bathroom opened effortlessly now, and Manuel was pleased to confirm that for the last three days, the Maestro had worked exclusively on the basement, and that was why you couldn't see those ugly stains that began on the concrete steps anymore; he had applied a coat of whitewash to the walls and added some wooden shelves in the smallest compartment. And, as though it were really a miracle, the final shade Cecilia had chosen was identical to the sample, the clean basement perfectly matched what Manuel had constructed in his imagination: the tiles on the terrace shone with their waxy patina, and every day the garden became greener, happier, with butterflies and open buds.

More than once they asked themselves why they had found the house in such a calamitous state. Manuel argued that Andrés had been away for twelve years, and you know all too well that some renters don't care, especially if the owner's not on top of them. The people who lived in it for those twelve years had been careless, maybe older people, that's what I think, yes, old ladies. And they continued the fantasy and the game through the cocktail hour: old ladies who smelled of mothballs, Cecilia said, making a face; old ladies straight out of a Donoso novel, Manuel added, like characters from The Obscene Bird of Night. Yes, horrible, decrepit old ladies, letting such a lovely house go to ruin. No doubt they practiced witchcraft and burned incense in the girls' room – that explains the burn marks on the parquet. Of course – the brazier for practicing sorcery, now I get it. Cecilia raised her voice: now I understand, and now I know why there are those ugly stains all over the house. Witches awaiting the squawking of the owls beneath the trees in the yard; no, better yet, old lunatics who, by the light of the moon, filled the house with cats and ghosts, with stains and burns . . .

Manuel laughed at his wife's literary imagination. Laughing, they got into bed that night; laughing, they began to make love, and later, with the image of a limestone-white house framed by the shadowy profusion of the trees, they fell into a deep sleep. They slept without pills for their nerves or for their irritable bowels. The best tranquilizer was having witnessed Maestro Barraza's efficiency once more. He had completed the last day's task flawlessly, restoring the space that from then on would be a stimulus for the couple's new life.

Husband and wife decided that the inaugural barbecue would take place the second Saturday in October, a few days after they moved in.

2

3

Don Jovino was looking over his stamp collection when he received his daughter's phone call inviting him to the barbecue. He accepted without any great enthusiasm, inquired about the girls, said he'd arrive after the meal because he had an appointment and he didn't think it necessary to advise her that he would leave right after complying with the formalities. Soon after becoming widowed, his visits to Cecilia's apartment had become habitual. He'd show up at tea time on any given day of the week, amusing himself most of the time by playing with his granddaughters, helping the older one with her history homework and secretly regretting that she wasn't a little boy whom he could excite with descriptions of uniforms, marching bands, exercises, and stories of heroic battles. If for whatever reason he appeared at the apartment on a Sunday, Manuel would politely offer him a cocktail and then, using some appointment as an excuse, leave him alone with his daughter and granddaughters. And since Don Jovino knew that his granddaughters would be asleep for the barbecue and that he'd have to tolerate the rest of them, this time it was he, in response to his daughter's invitation, who offered the excuse of a dinner with some old army buddies, something that had been planned for a long time, something he himself had been responsible for organizing.

Marcela, on the other hand, was delighted. She responded to Cecilia's call, speaking as one does in the morning – with that eager tone, that enthusiasm that always comes with the beginning of something – the dash between coffee and the shower, slices of toast next to the bath towel. She sat in bed, as if in a forbidden place, naked beside the breakfast leftovers, covering her legs with the sheet as she lit the first cigarette – because hearing a voice on the telephone is all it takes to trigger off a series of almost automatic actions – and then nervous fingers pulling a cigarette from the pack, cast aside during the night, where the hell did I leave the lighter, Marcela? – and now it's Cecilia's voice, she recognizes it immediately, Cecilia? – and Cecilia hears the disturbing sound of a match being lit.

"I'm going to love seeing your new place. Just imagine! I suppose you'll invite Andrés," Marcela says to her, deeply immersed in her cigarette and the conversation.

"Andrés? Don't tell me he's here already!"

"Yes, dummy, he just got back. Tomorrow he's coming over to see Matías."

"Well, if you have no objection . . ."

"How could you even think that? Imagine how happy the poor guy'll be. Besides, he's got a new squeeze. Some German chick – probably a real bore. But you won't see her at the barbecue because she's not arriving till Christmas."

That night, "poor Andrés" was the topic of conversation between Cecilia and Manuel.

"And what's he planning to do here?" Manuel asked.

"Marcela says he might be able to get a scholarship, that money they give to returnees, three hundred dollars a month. Not bad, right?"

"And what if he wants to live in his house?"

"I doubt it. Sergio would've known about it. Besides, the house has been bought."

"Have you seen the deed?"

"How could I ask my dad for that? If someone gives you a gift, you don't ask to see the sales slip, too."

"This is different. We ought to have that deed."

"Okay, okay, later on I'll ask him for it. Do you really think he'd do something like that to us, knowing how much money we've invested?"

"Your father?"

"How could you even think that? I'm talking about Andrés.

He'd never ask us to tear up that deed. Besides, the house is enormous for him."

"Don't they have kids?"

"What planet are you on when I talk to you? I told you they haven't gotten married yet."

That same night they called him at his parents' house to invite him. Andrés greeted them with enthusiasm; he'd be glad to see Manuel after so many years; every day he got another invitation; my liver's going to be ruined. Cecilia told him about the innumerable repairs they had to make in the house and how run-down it was, all the while giving Manuel winks of complicity. Andrés said he was happy for them; it was better than having strangers buy it; he'd move to an apartment, something small, the scholarship wouldn't last long, and with the money in the bank from the sale of the house, he'd be able to get along for the first few years. Yes, of course, he was having dinner with his brother Sergio tonight, he'd tell him about the barbecue.

She spoke to Julia for at least an hour. Her friend's verbal diarrhea amused her, that machine-gun burst of sarcasm and irreverence that she blasted out without a pause, perhaps fearful that danger, the dropping of the mask, lurked in the cease-fire of silence and that a single shot of reality might be the coup de grâce, the end. Of course she'd be delighted to come to the barbecue, provided they didn't spend all night asking questions about the Vicaría – that damned topic really gets on my tits and knots my bowels all the way up to my throat. Yes, I'll come. Of course I'll come. You want me to bring Andrés? The poor guy's without a car. Well, sure, he arrived only three days ago, how could he have a car? All right, have him come over to my place, his driver awaits him. I hope Ramón gets invited to a party this Saturday, because as far as grandma's concerned, forget it. Last night, in my Michèle Morgan–style raincoat (that's my new look, honey), I took my offspring to his paternal granny's house. She just got back from a nice little two-month jaunt to Europe. She was clucking her tongue over exiles of all stripes, which is a lot of tongue-clucking, I can assure you. Poor old lady came back looking more like a 1930s police chief than ever: all serious and pontificating. What a pain! My poor son will have to depend on me as his only source of affection, because with that icebox of a grandma he'll never get anywhere. But I'll work something out with Ramón so I can go to the party. Besides, I'm so anxious to see Andrés – listening to the returnees really lifts your spirits, you know? It's like reading the last chapter of *Amerika* – I listen to them and I feel like I'm in the Oklahoma Great Natural Theater, the face of the world etched in a smile from ear to ear like you wouldn't believe. The poor things are so lost; they think if they don't come home, they'll lose what they call "the critical link" – you know? They keep on singing the same old tune, poor things, *El Caballero* will fall this year, . . . The decisive year, they call it. All right, to be fair, those poor dears aren't the only ones who are completely out of it. Did you see today's newspapers? This country is so demented that the only thing anyone talks about is Arrau's bowel movements. The poor maestro tastes an *humita*, a sausage, or even mere Chilean H_2O, and his whole Anglo-Saxon intestinal flora literally goes to shit. What do you think of that? Hey, remember to have lots of mineral water and applesauce on hand; it seems like my colon has decided to turn me into pure skin and bones, and now, of all times, when I'm starting to get senior discounts, I mean, just when you'd give what you never had in the first place for a figure which probably wouldn't even . . . Well, what can I say, my colon is just like our dear little country, seems like there's no cure for it.

4

What's a reunion, Andrés has been asking himself for months, long before landing, while still strolling along the frozen paths of the Berlin winter. A frustrated trip in Jules Verne's time machine? A delirium that promises you something identical to the past, and in which you discover only deterioration, loss, the punishment of time? Or is it the unobstructed view of this new stage of your journey? The mirror in which you rediscover your own wrinkles in others, your hair almost gone, your own fall, but also the tremendous desire to bring back the warm summer that can only persist in your memory? A discovery, perhaps? And if that's what it is, what does a man discover in those muted words that resound like an echo, a reply, a parody of what was said back then? What can be salvaged from that emptiness? What does the remembering eye discover?

His emotions, on arriving, exceeded those he had imagined, going even beyond the intense feeling of sanctuary that touches those who return to the end of the world after a long time away: flying over the mountain range, the white immensity that Andrés connected that afternoon, without knowing exactly why, with his childhood bed, an association that made his throat close up for the first time. Imbued with the sentimentality of losses and leave-takings, the reunion with his mother, sister, and brother at the airport, and later with his father in the house on Calle Condell, left a definite bitter taste in his dry mouth. A long, drawn-out moan from the old man and, even more pathetic, his ill-concealed weeping, called Andrés's attention to that crumpled body in a wheelchair, a body he now saw for the first time; yes, for the first time after a long, lost time, with an eye that once again discovers and ends up making everyone tremble. What does the remembering eye discover? He tried to soothe the sudden dryness in his mouth by smoking one cigarette after another and gulping down the *pisco* sours that his brother Sergio compassionately kept thrusting into his hand as soon as he had chugged down the last one. His sister Irene tried to distract him, reminding him that they hadn't bought the drinks yet. Someone cracked a good-natured joke that no one understood, but which nonetheless served as a pretext for the fake laughter that belatedly brought a shaky smile to his father's face, still brimming with tears. Yes, they needed to go out right away and buy those drinks, and let the men go because they'll have to carry back two heavy boxes, Irene ordered with more desperation than energy, and Sergio added, you come with me, Andrés, so you'll get reacquainted with the neighborhood. Out on the street, as soon as they had slammed the smaller door lodged inside the wooden front door, Sergio disguised the terrible news as a warning: it was very important for papa to avoid strong emotions; he could have a second stroke at any time.

Of all the recurring phrases he heard in the days following his arrival, of all those he heard over and over again in the dining room or out walking, it wasn't this one that assaulted him most often but rather a different one, overheard in the car just as they were pulling out of the airport. He was riding in front, next to his brother Sergio, who, taking his eyes off the road, said, ominously changing his tone of voice, "It's very important that he doesn't find out yet when you're leaving. He thinks you're here to stay. We'll figure out a way to tell him your visa's only good for two weeks."

As they cruised the supermarket aisles, Sergio reiterated his warning. During those twelve years, the old man had lived only to await his older son's return. At first he had hoped that Andrés would leave the Colombian embassy without needing to seek asylum in another country – people told him that it had happened like that in other places – or perhaps those taking asylum could remain in the embassy indefinitely: a communications system with their families was already functioning perfectly well, a routine of regular, safe visits. But one day safe-conducts were handed out; the foreign population in the embassies boarded a Colombian Air Force *Hercules*; the aircraft climbed to an altitude of twenty-seven thousand feet; and exactly fifty-five hundred miles to the north of Don Andrés's house on Calle Condell it deposited its bewildered cargo, a throng forced from that day forward to live far away, to sleep and breathe far away, to love and die far away. It was then that the old man developed the habit of taking his chair out to the patio every afternoon to wait for the postman out on the street, sitting in the doorway of his house, taking care to cover his legs with an old Castilian poncho and, on winter afternoons, pulling a tweed cap down over his ears. Waiting for the letters was the closest thing to waiting for his son. And when the stroke came, it was the whole family's opinion, but especially that of Doctor Oteiza, who always made a point of it, that the greatest impetus for the old man's remarkably quick recovery, considering his age, had been his desire to sit once again at the doorway of his house and wait for the postman, because that's how he liked to wait for those light blue envelopes: just like that, gazing down the street, he would envision his son coming along, just like on any afternoon of any normal day, waving from a distance, his arm raised, and in his other hand a briefcase, now transformed into a suitcase in Don Andrés's afternoon reveries. And even though the hoped-for letter didn't come that afternoon, the vision of the arrival, the suitcase, and the wave materialized more forcefully before his eyes. Don Andrés went up to the dining room, ate his warm soup with his eyes fixed on something that no one else at the table could imagine, and then went calmly to bed, because there he could dream his single dream more comfortably. The stroke, which had laid him low that last winter, left in its wake not only a state of semiparalysis, which confined him to a wheelchair, but also another, less obvious but more serious, effect: the total loss of the use of one kidney and only the partial use of the other. Under those conditions, the family imagined that the day so yearned for by the father would never arrive. But the announcement of the amnesty and Andrés's permission to make this trip – which he had demanded since the very day of the attack that felled his father – had an almost miraculous effect on the old man's recovery. Spurred on by a single thought, that of minimizing the visible signs of his misfortune to avoid causing his son greater pain, he persevered as never before in his rehabilitation therapy, to the understandable astonishment of the nurse, the therapist, and the entire family. Since the partial recovery of his left arm and the somewhat uncertain movement of his hand had seemed inconceivable until then, and in order that he might recover as completely as possible, they decided it wasn't a good idea to tell the old man that Andrés, in his calls from Berlin, had spoken of visiting for only two weeks. Everyone agreed that the visit would have a therapeutic effect, and Doctor Oteiza concurred, indicating that they would indeed have to be very careful when they finally told him the truth. Most assuredly, he had no objection to a merciful lie. And everyone understood that this lie referred not only to the undisclosed length of Andrés's visit, but also to the business of announcing his new departure casually, without any drama or fuss, nothing more than a transitory departure, a quick trip to Berlin to work out his commitments with the university and the travel plans for his new German wife, with whom he would return permanently to Chile in a matter of a several days. Andrés had to understand that this was a question of life and death for the old man, and that he needed to enjoy those two weeks without letting bitter topics of conversation cast their shadow over his magnificent recovery and the entire family's incredible reunion after so many years. Yes, that's it, he heard Sergio's voice again: the most important thing is not to let the old man find out you're leaving; later on we'll figure out a way to tell him.

Andrés thought that his family's wishes were the cause of the tense theatrics that darkened his reunion with his father even more. This playacting would cast a dark shadow on the party that night and on everything that might happen in the days to follow, and it would inevitably darken the faces of all those who played a role in the farce.

He stood rapt, staring at the seafood stand as he waited for his brother to fill up the boxes with beverages at the other end of the aisle. It was predictable that the nostalgic, sybaritic Ulysses, recently arrived from the austere socialist paradise, would unabashedly fix his gaze on the maritime carnival that heaped the salty bounty of the ocean together on the crushed ice: *cholgas* hidden in their hermetic shells; sea urchins displaying their lasciviously fleshy tongues from the depths of their warlike carapaces; *picorocos*, those imperfect, petrified phalluses; immodestly hairy mussels; swordfish aspiring to whalehood; conger eels like gigantic clitorises, dangling calmly from iron hooks; fishes ready for the pot, hanging victims, proud in their gaudiness. Lost in contemplation, Andrés discovered that only fish can retain their beauty beyond death. Yes, there it was again, death, that she-wolf, staring at him this time from the seafood stand. Perhaps that was why he suddenly avoided making contact with his brother's teary eyes. He felt that he, too, was at the breaking point. And the truth was that the very idea of embracing him there, among all those people, and crying on his shoulder for all those years and those losses, for the old man who was slipping from their grasp and for the old lady, even farther gone, locked inside her muteness like sea creatures in their hermetic shells, yes, to cry for all the good things that might have happened and never did . . . That was why, when he sensed the howling of the she-wolf, the dampness in his eyes, and the tightness in his throat, he took two or three steps backward, turned away from his brother, and stood motionless in front of the fish. They were right: it was necessary to keep quiet about his imminent departure. And then he realized something that had just recently become clear to him: the return to Berlin, that definitive distance, that loss of everything that was his, was the only thing that deserved to be called a homecoming.

5

That evening, as she waited for Andrés to arrive, Julia went over some files she had brought home from the Vicaría the night before, not because she enjoyed carrying that cross home with her, but because she had promised to turn those depositions over to the archives by Monday morning. A strange anxiety drove her into the shower, although it was much earlier than the time agreed upon with her companion for the evening. She always said "my companion for the evening," and that slightly lewd tone concealed a simple, brutal truth: she was one of many widows, women without partners, who spent their days in courtrooms, jail waiting rooms, churches, and even houses (their own houses, or those of their peers, or of their protégés), where sadness and neglect, clinging to each object, pointed out someone's absence. Yes, Julia was one of those widows, but in her case it was also a question of a widowhood that she could have verified with legal documents: her husband wasn't one of the contingent of the disappeared, but rather one of those who had been shot. Nevertheless, as in the case of the disappeared, here too, in spite of the documentation of the shooting and the death, the burial place was unknown, if you could call that now-forgotten place in the desert where the body was hidden a burial place. One way to bear the pain, perhaps a way to bear it with pride, like a mark on her forehead, was to accentuate it with that irreverent tone that made her say "my companion for the evening" as she applied her makeup before the mirror. But this time she said it to herself very quietly, in a thread of a voice, and with an impish tone that suggested hope.

Her anxiety – a frequent state of mind for her – as well as the demonstrable punctuality she attributed to her "companion for the evening" – a punctuality forged in snowy timetables and with more demanding hostesses than his friend from Santiago – forced her to be completely ready an hour before the time she had agreed upon with Andrés the night before. She told herself it would be a good idea to take advantage of that hour by going over the depositions, so she spread the files out on the dining room table in order to reread them, label them, and put them in some kind of order.

The excitement that possessed Julia all day and explained her dream, filled with threatening images but also with pleasant sensations as she stretched out her legs toward the cool portion of the sheets, began to settle down just before Andrés's arrival, and again with his presence in her doorway, handing her the flowers, lighting the first of many cigarettes that evening, inflicting on her those well-worn tales of exile over their second pisco sour and repeating them again during the drive to Cecilia's house, her friend's new house, which had been Andrés's old house. Why was he visiting her for the third time, and why now, on a Saturday night, in order to go to a party together? He himself had told her about his encounter with Sonia, which Julia wanted to understand only as a nostalgic relapse on Andrés's part for a place now occupied by someone else. For better or for worse, Julián had been there for ten years now, and there were two children, with all that might mean in terms of a shared life, commitment, and even compassion. She couldn't help thinking that it was the third time they had gotten together that week, the third time Andrés had come to her house, given her a bottle of cognac, an Italian silk scarf, a bouquet of flowers, according to the sequences of gifts and visits, according to the order of the moment. Then he handed her his light-colored raincoat, a bit wrinkled, before walking over to the sofa; he told her amusing stories: "elusive," she thought later, already on her second after-dinner whiskey.

The first time was at dawn, after returning from the party organized for Andrés at Lucía's house. "A dinner dance in honor of the returnee," as Julia had defined it in her telephone invitation, telling him that Lucía, "now really into her clandestine-Bolshy-Stalinist thing, doesn't make any distinction between inviting you to a little party and calling a party meeting, especially if they're right in the middle of a fund-raising drive." Julia repeated this comment amid general laughter during that evening's dance, between pauses in the music followed rather apathetically by the five or six couples, of whom only Lucía, the hostess, and Diego, her newest beau, were really a pair. And then, woven into the laughter, gazing into each other's eyes that way for the first time, and later, along with the laughter and the gaze, that hand warming her shoulder, concentrating on the dance, sticking to her blouse, running down her spine as if in a casual, affectionate gesture, like part of the movement of everything and everyone, and later remaining there, firmly, securely, with a pressure that joined the gaze, all that, of course, within the framework of that lingering joke, that dinner dance in which they kept on twirling and laughing, seduced by something stronger than the wine; all this, hand and embrace, laughter and kiss, all within the permissive framework of the dance, naturally. Conceivable only within the framework of the dance, and then, sitting on Lucía's sofa, their faces very close together as they light another cigarette, and later in the car, and afterward in the armchair in her house, his strong hand on her waist, another cigarette, another kiss, another drink, another pause, see you day after tomorrow at the barbecue, at the great première, sweetheart. What time shall I pick you up – eight? Andrés asks. You're crazy, this isn't a Berlin-style *Abendsbrot* – you've really turned into a Kraut! Pick me up at ten, there's no point getting there any earlier, she says, wrapping her arms around his neck in the front yard, and asking him, "Is it true there's nothing going on with Sonia?" Very, very close to his ear, in a different tone of voice, impassioned, quiet, don't let him notice it, you fool, in a different tone that makes her voice tremble and casts that sad glimmer in her eyes as Andrés feels the blow, something hurts him somewhere, that broken little voice is terrible, and those shining eyes, supplicating, hoping; it's terrible but it's also lovely, that break in the endless amusement, that dropping of the mask, that defense of the soul that renders any meeting impossible between Julia's constant pain and any sign that would betray the sadness darkening her inner sea.

Yes. Somewhere inside him, it hurts to realize that he too is casting his net upon that sea.

"Saturday, then. Ten o'clock. *Ciao.*"

3

6

Andrés, poor Andrés, the one who's talked about from early
morning on, in telephone conversations accompanied by coffee
and toast and the first cigarette of the day. Andrés, recently returned to paradise lost by an institution with mysterious initials.
Andrés, landing suddenly in the world he had learned to recognize as his own and that today he thinks of as the only absolutely
alien territory on earth. At this point, he's frightened by the con-
fusing way things have been happening, the promise made to his
brother in the car on the way home, even before returning home;
a tacit promise, because he very clearly recalls never once opening his mouth, and nonetheless it's clear: he mustn't mention
that this trip is only for two weeks, his father mustn't find out, it
could prove fatal. More worried than surprised by the way these
coincidences, no matter how serious, have occurred, pondering
that alarming concentration of coincidences, his encounter with
Sonia in the same old supermarket from back then, from before – those terse euphemisms in order to avoid saying before
what, back *when* – Sonia, lost among the aisles packed with merchandise, as if just emerging from the sea, that last summer . . .
or from the first sun of the summer after that, her skin tanned,
her white tee shirt like a second skin, Sonia's phone number now
burning against his side where he holds it. Reflecting also on the
meaning of that concrete yet unreal thing that surrounds him,
enfolds him, suffocates him: the multitude of hermetic faces ad-
vancing along Paseo Ahumada, their gazes fixed on the dirty sky
that forms a dark horizon of smog out there where the block
seems to end in a scream; he walks down the boulevard, thinks
about the boulevard, thinks about that story he had promised
to write one day and which awaits him in some corner of that

throng, on that gray street. The story was right there, much more violent than anything he could have imagined. Before, of course, long before the knives appeared:

The knives . . .
. . . the ones that keep falling,
never growing still,
their brilliant points spinning
on the ground, but always
falling, because they keep falling,
Will those knives ever stop falling
in his memory?

Before that night, when the blade hadn't yet entered his wound, Andrés used to walk along Ahumada mulling over the plot of his story. How could he not tell one of the stories that take place in the promiscuity of the Paseo? How could he not plunge his hand in and pull out one of those stories by the ears, even if it hung kicking and screaming in his grasp? Andrés walked along the Paseo, hunting it down, admiring the proliferation of merchandise that seemed to burst forth from the ground and the multitude of exhausted faces, his ear attuned to the chaotic offering of useless objects.

What he never could have imagined was that it was going to be a story about death. But was that so hard to predict? Wasn't the she-wolf prowling there, barely concealed among the night-stick blows? Wasn't it licking its poison into the wounded man's head? Didn't the co-ed see it as she was being kicked in the aisle of the green van? Couldn't they anticipate its blade, as lethal as a knife?

The story overwhelmed him, and he grew tired of pursuing it. He gave up walking along the Paseo.

That night Andrés stopped at his parents' house – his house, these days – in order to rest a bit and put on warmer clothing. In Santiago – he had forgotten this, too – warmth and the after-noon depart hand in hand. He was just getting dressed and was on his way to the kitchen in search of the white shirt that Teresa had just finished ironing for him, when all the lights went out. Sudden darkness paralyzes, resembles fear. From his parents' bedroom, he heard a muffled noise, the sound of clothing, the cautious movement of a body in a bed. He himself stood motionless, the hanger in his hand suspended at his side, and the shirt, an invisible white flag of surrender, suspended as well. After a while he proceeded gingerly, hoping his feet would brush against the edge of the coffee table so that, moving within his paralysis, he could reach the end table where his mother kept candles, matches, a flashlight, a battery-powered radio. Sedate objects that now formed part of a disturbing routine that ended up seeming normal to them: a blackout every week, some new act of violence every day, every hour the possibility of fear.

His hand groped for the objects that would restore the light. He left the shirt on the armchair, ran his fingers along the rough length of the candle, and rescued the matches from their own shadow. He picked up the candle and lit a match with difficulty. After the initial glow, the waning flame reintroduced the sadness of yellowish walls, dingy with shadows and silence, as if those shadows and that silence had been the most obvious reality during his twelve years of absence: progressive poverty, inevitable old age, incurable illness. Now some coughing, as muted as whispered phrases, came from his parents' room.

On the battery-powered radio he heard that some incidents were taking place at that moment on Paseo Ahumada.

The total darkness – like Borges's unanimous night – hadn't disheartened the warring factions, however. According to the metallic voice that seemed to emanate from the tiny light in the little radio, in the street shadows the battle had ignited like a blaze. Blind scrambling, blows that guessed at the location of their targets' shoulders, a scream, the dull report of a gunshot. And then the brawl, too, became extinguished.

When visibility returned to the house and the ocean of lights reappeared in the windows, the announcer reported that during the incidents, in the middle of the blackout, a policeman had been stabbed in the back.

The she-wolf walked there then,
parading her scythe along the Paseo
Did anyone hear her scream
in the depths of the double night?
Was the knife unsheathed in the light,
awaiting its dark accomplice?
Who saw the blood?
The living red hidden in the blackness?

Suddenly he felt tired. His neck hurt, he was tense, he didn't want to go out into the street, afraid that another blackout would paralyze him against the elements. He returned to the kitchen, took a beer from the refrigerator, and hung his shirt back on the hanger from where he had taken it. He turned out the living room light and silently passed by his parents' room. He could no longer hear their muffled voices, but rather a murmur of clothing and moans, a few hoarse coughs and the rising spiral of agitated breathing. He went into his room, hoping to fall asleep as soon as he turned off the light.

He slept uneasily, and at dawn he went back to the Paseo in a new attempt to penetrate its elusive mysteries.

He saw children fighting over the abundant remnants of garbage, and the start of the day in the hurried strides of office workers. He saw the metal curtains rise on storefronts like a final yawn; he saw the beggar woman arrive with her brood, and those who never emerge from their night: the true and false blind.

mutes playing guitars
guitar players begging
beggars carrying signs
sign-carriers hawking products
laid-off workers
fooling their useless hands
the useless trafficking in foreign currency
traffickers drinking their coffee
smiles collecting tips . . .

Suddenly that stretch of the Paseo changed color. The menace came along garbed in green, taking over like a whip. Uniforms multiplied, and multiple too were the mass exodus and the furtiveness of those who hid their wares in packages hastily assembled from the same paper that had been their display cases. They disappeared behind the kiosks, sticking the bundles under their skirts or hiding them with their bodies against the passageway walls, in the chaotic course of that imitation guerrilla war that stretches from morning till night.

Those who were taken by surprise in furtiveness or flight suffered a new defeat in this war, lost before it began. The humble treasures of forbidden goods were left scattered on the ground.

Andrés ducked inside a building and, after verifying that the green deployment had taken over the street, stepped into the elevator. The door was about to close when a very thin man slipped inside, barely hanging on to his clandestine package. Andrés recognized the coarse paper of those itinerant display cases. The man's face was pale; it looked like a continuation of his shirt. They started to ascend. The man grew paler; he was drenched in sweat. The ride seemed interminable to both of them. The man looked at Andrés from the depth of his fear. Finally his arms gave way, and the package slowly fell. The paper opened up, and the knives gleamed through. Something like a lighting bolt flashed across his consciousness: through its brilliance, Andrés saw two small, frightened eyes, the sum total of imaginable hatred concentrated in two pupils; with familiar pain, he remembered another whiteness, the long snow of his exile, as those long, sharp knives kept falling.

4

7

Shortly before the move and the celebration, Manuel hinted that it would be better not to press Don Jovino too much, not to call him to remind him of the barbecue, I mean, and Cecilia, in a tone somewhere between resignation and annoyance, a tone that had become solidified through time and repetition, assured him brusquely: my dad accepted out of obligation, but don't even dream he's coming.

"I just mean, to avoid tension, that's all," Manuel replied half-heartedly, heading for the kitchen, in that practiced way of avoiding nighttime conversations that might degenerate into arguments.

Cecilia, in the bedroom, lights turned out in order to enact fully the farce of being asleep, and Manuel, working on his second glass of wine, that search for another kind of feigned plenitude, unwittingly shared the same question: What role has my father/father-in-law played in our marriage? How has Don Jovino influenced the life of his only daughter, so different from her father but at times so like him? Manuel wondered. How has the old man affected Manuel's life, tolerating him at last without ever accepting him? was Cecilia's question. What part did he play in the crisis, and what was his role in the couple's shaky reconciliation?

For Manuel, the word that best summed up his relationship with his father-in-law was *insecurity*, and the more he thought about it the more he felt that the insecurity was something that closely resembled a mixture of capitulation and shame. For Cecilia, on the other hand, everything connecting her to her father had to do with what was "proper." Of all the words she was learning to reject and even despise, none was as detestable as "proper." Proper meant seeing things in a particular way, always in the way he had determined. It isn't proper for you to think such-and-such a thing, it wouldn't be proper for you to do that other thing. The old man, not her mother, had taught her to correct her schoolwork, and he kept on correcting it her whole life long. Hadn't her existence been reduced to a school notebook full of erasures, badly spelled words and unfortunate calculations that he had corrected for thirty-five years?

From childhood on, Cecilia learned that the principal sign of the corrector was the exercise of haughty disdain. She began to think that correction could be the opposite of an act of kindness. One corrects in order to demonstrate superiority and to exercise power, since the corrective measure puts the wrongdoer in her proper place, from which not even correction can remove her, since its function is to plunge her even more deeply into the error, to outline her defective, imperfect, inferior condition through that new inaccuracy. In a word, guilty.

Cecilia pondered this while drifting from her feigned sleep to the equally false reality she was assembling of voices and images from long ago, intimidating memories that fluttered around her like decrepit ghosts whose mission was to make her fall into the well, push her into a heavy lethargy inhabited by the recurring images of her nightmares.

A few steps away from the bed and from Cecilia's fitful sleep, Manuel now has the courage, after another glass of wine, to recognize that Don Jovino had never really accepted him, and he dares to think that, from the old man's point of view, he was the only mistake Cecilia hadn't managed to correct in time. Was it proof of her love, perhaps, that Cecilia had so willfully resisted her father's equally stubborn opposition? Or proof of her lack of love? Then he considers that Cecilia, perhaps in order to avoid acknowledging her mistake, had waited much longer than was convenient to make a correction that became necessary – one that surely she, too, felt was necessary – practically since their marriage began. Yes, that could be one reason for the prolonged languor of their relationship. And proof of Cecilia's lack of love and her deliberate calculation, her awareness that this would be the most decisive and also the most dangerous decision of her life: the one her father had instigated not just *with* her, but *in* her. That would have constituted a confession on Cecilia's part, Manuel thinks, of her greater error, and with it an acceptance of her ultimate defeat in her father's eyes. Wasn't this stubborn persistence in wrong-headedness, this suicidal resistance, the most direct cause of the couple's present misery? Wasn't this kind of revenge against the old man the source of all the bitterness that had accumulated over the years?

Cecilia, now on the brink of sleep, and Manuel, on the other edge, the edge of inebriation, forgot about the obvious facts, the meticulous display of disdain the old man spun around them, separating them from him and from each other through a labyrinth of emptiness and pretense. Then they began to see that chaotic past in a single tone, a borderless, amorphous gray, harsh as a concrete wall.

The long routine of misunderstandings between the old man and the couple hardly improved when Don Jovino was widowed, when Cecilia's mother's death made everyone (including Don Jovino) think that after the mourning period, things would get better, because for all of them there was a before and an after to that death, which had been as uncertain as it was desired. They knew that with the old man's widowhood, all their lives would finally change; no one knew, however, exactly how.

Cecilia suspected that the legitimacy of the correction derived more from the power of the corrector than from the importance of the rectification. And she even knew – she learned this over the course of the years and with her father's increasing prosperity – that the element conferring this power was money. Without it, that flood of corrective zeal would have been impossible. For that reason, when the money turned out to be useless and no amount could prevent Doña Leonor's death, Cecilia suspected that she was standing on the threshold of a change that would affect her life positively, putting an end to the game of error and reparation, of lapse and repentance, once and for all. Her mother's death – her father's painful widowhood, the first indications of the limitations of his power – was the last page of that school notebook she submitted to Don Jovino until the day – the very day – when Doña Leonor was buried and Cecilia turned twenty-five. The notebook was in the trash at last. She would begin another one, a new life in which changes and corrections would be nothing but a manifestation of her own desires and her freedom. Yes. That's right. One has to begin, she thought that night as she drifted into sleep – that other night, the one after the funeral. Begin? Will this be the new beginning? she asks herself now, thinking of Manuel and of the final repairs on the new house; she asks herself again, thinking also of her father, and then she rolls over again in bed, can't sleep, has to turn over the warm pillow, seek out the coolest corner of the sheet with her foot.

For Don Jovino, Manuel stopped being that skinny kid who came over to study for philosophy tests with his daughter when he noticed that gradually the boy was staying later and later. The nights before exams, he would stay for tea on the terrace overlooking the swimming pool; and during the coldest months of autumn, he would have his tea in the girl's room, which intensified Doña Leonor's uneasiness and annoyance as she lay in bed in the room next door; and in the dead of winter, there would be tea in the dining room, a preamble to the first formal dinner in early spring, a harbinger of the first family party during that second summer, because I don't know who to go with, I don't like to go alone, papa; and that first wedding party, which caught the old man's attention when he noticed the bouquet being tossed by the bride into his daughter's hands; could it be that one of these days we'll have a wedding of our own with this guy in the tuxedo? This was followed by a long period when neither he nor she appeared in the house: there were a few little parties here and there, some meetings of who-knows-what – but it soon became clear what they were – shows in theaters and art house cinemas, photography exhibitions, meetings of the Student Federation, some item or other that they watched on the news with sudden interest and inexplicable silence, holed up in the library. And later, at the end of this story, the very culmination of the premonition, which had weighed on Don Jovino two years earlier: the skinny kid, Manuel, in Don Jovino's own house, in a groom's outfit. A tuxedo, which the old man gave him, because he thought it would be unthinkable for his son-in-law to get married in rented clothing. Everyone – including Doña Leonor, who was decidedly sympathetic toward the alliance – interpreted the long, unremarked, and involuntary suspension of Don Jovino's corrective zeal as a kind of paralysis. Evidently, things were happening on the fringes, bordering dangerously on the margins, tracing a clandestine course. Thus they were able to circumvent that imaginary school notebook with Cecilia's collected mistakes, allowing her to escape becoming the target of criticism, and flouting Don Jovino's ever-weaker opposition, they pulled off a formal engagement and a wedding at last.

His corrective zeal, however, was reactivated when the alliance he had wanted to avert was consummated. If all his son-in-law's traits annoyed him, he could undertake the task of changing them, exercising his corrective passion in an indirect way. Since he could no longer reverse his daughter's decision, he decided to modify the son-in-law's characteristics meticulously. The squabbles preceding the formal engagement had to do with the skinny fiancé's wretched financial state, which, in everyone's best judgment – not just the old man's – would only grow worse when he began to practice his ridiculous profession of philosophy in the classroom of a public high school. One month before the wedding, then, Don Jovino offered him a position as publicity director with an agency of which his real estate firm was one of the most important clients. With this problem resolved – the main problem, in his estimation – he devoted himself to connecting him with institutes that had been created during the dictatorship, specifically to combat what Don Jovino always thought of as his son-in-law's "foreign" ideas. Later, and more generously, he decided to secure the new couple's basic creature comforts by presenting them with an apartment in which they lived for all those years without paying a cent, always quite aware of the source of that privilege. They never signed a rental agreement or any kind of deed to the property. They simply lived there, assuming that the dwelling was part of Cecilia's father's property, or that it belonged to the real estate firm, or that someone was paying the monthly rent according to the old man's explicit instructions. Needless to say, in the months before the wedding, they both imagined what their ideal house or apartment would be like; they fantasized about what part of Santiago it would be in and even about what the streets and the neighborhood where they wanted to settle down would look like. To be fair, they recognized that the old man had heard their wishes many times and that his decision, ultimately, came quite close to what the newlyweds were hoping for. Once a decision concerning the son-in-law's job and the apartment in which they would live had been made, Don Jovino felt calmer, and for a while he gave up his role as corrector of those worldly sins of which no one was free and which had penetrated his own home at last.

Don Jovino always suspected that this decision on his daughter's part would be the only circumstance in her life that wouldn't be subject to eventual correction. That was why – Cecilia and Manuel think now, twelve years later, after the couple's first great crisis had ended, or now that they were more deeply submerged in it – Don Jovino hadn't played all his cards trying to prevent or postpone the wedding. What Manuel recalls about the old man in that area was the vexing tone of indifference that evolved into a sort of icy cordiality.

By the time the date and place of the wedding had been decided, Don Jovino had already made a great deal of progress in his alternate strategy. The truth is that he had begun to plant the seeds of this strategy long before the first word even remotely alluding to an engagement had been uttered in his house: instead of preventing his daughter's wedding, instead of correcting a decision that seemed immutable, he chose to correct the fiancé, to file down and polish each one of the rough edges of his personality. Tossing and turning in her sleepless nights, Cecilia recalls that expression which she had heard so often during the first years of their marriage: "That boy needs polishing." "He won't be such a diamond in the rough once he's polished." "See how nice and polished he's becoming?" The old man had determined to turn his son-in-law into something absolutely different from what Manuel really was. He wanted to manufacture a son-in-law to his specifications of his daughter's needs. And naturally he was the one who decided what those specifications and needs were.

According to Don Jovino – and according to his state of mind – the change could be a matter of making obvious modifications or perhaps just giving him a light once-over. According to Manuel's fluctuating interpretation, it sometimes was a case of his absolute defeat and other times a reasonable submission to a higher power that allowed him, yes, him, access to a limited dose of that same power. For Cecilia, however, from the very first it became the most serious evidence of her father's corrective mania, a kind of roundabout way to end up correcting her again, once more scratching out and rewriting the rough draft of a life that would never manage to turn out proof-perfect.

The first change Cecilia observed in Manuel was the rapid abandonment of his most instinctive defense mechanisms, that guarded, mistrustful attitude toward his future father-in-law, which had been his most solid source of strength for more than two years. The few minutes the old man, whisky in hand, standing by the fireplace in the parlor, had devoted to listening to him talk about the importance of philosophy, and the few others, sometime later, that he devoted to him privately in the library, where they spoke of Manuel's future profession and goals, were enough to knock down walls of conflict that until then had seemed to be made of more resilient stuff. This period of interest, or what Manuel mistakenly interpreted as Don Jovino's interest, in his philosophy studies was followed by a few vague offers, the convenience of getting a graduate degree abroad, let's see if something can be arranged, and on another occasion, the offer to combine philosophy with a more concrete, better paying activity, perhaps a managerial position that might fit in with the corporate image of the realty firm, with its publicity, with its presence in the media, something that had been in the works for quite some time and that sooner or later needed to be addressed. He could accomplish this in just a few hours a week and devote the rest of his time in earnest to philosophy. Or did he plan to spend his life teaching forty-eight hours a week just to earn one-sixth of what he could get in half a day at the company?

So it was that at the beginning of his career there were no forty-eight hours a week of classes, but there was an assistant manager's position with a corporate image – a very vague thing, Manuel thought – but one whose deliberate vagueness didn't seem to bother Don Jovino.

Cecilia, on the other hand, never looked favorably on these offers. At first, Manuel's weak resistance to her father's propositions made her nervous, and then the obvious seduction that the long-awaited, tangible, and stimulating presence of money exercised on the insolvent young man made her more nervous still. Once they were married there was no doubt that Manuel's income allowed them to handle expenses that would have been impossible to contemplate during their courtship. Decorating and keeping up the apartment on Pedro de Valdivia, when this street was the most important one in a desirable, peaceful, residential area, cost three times the amount they had once jotted down next to the word rent in a notebook propped open for calculations and dreams. Calculations and dreams, of course, come together without friction only in the early stages of fantasy, but very soon expenses exceed even the most timid imagination, and the dream is crushed by columns where figures and realities are written down.

The assistant manager's position, then, allowed them to settle comfortably in the apartment, which, for the first two years, seemed very spacious and cozy, on a stately, tree-lined street of solid reputation and dignified beauty. There they could indulge in other fantasies as well. Manuel discovered an interest in photography that hadn't been fully explored until now, when he could buy sophisticated cameras and lenses, light meters, wide-angle and zoom lenses, tripods and reflectors, and he thought this long-hidden interest might also be masking a vocation and maybe even a talent.

But Cecilia also benefited from the assistant manager's job. And although this benefit was more indirect, that didn't make it any less tangible. Soon the hours Manuel spent at the real estate firm exceeded those required by his contract, and he preferred devoting his few remaining free hours to his emerging passion rather than to philosophy. As Manuel set up a complete photographic studio in the room set aside for the children who hadn't yet arrived, the living room and bedroom became filled with Cecilia's books, incurring bills that were payable thanks only to the income provided by the assistant manager's position. At first Cecilia landed an assistantship in the Department of General Philosophy, later another in Ancient Philosophy, and two years after that the title of adjunct professor, sufficient stimulus to devote all her time to that passion. She began to participate regularly in faculty seminars and study groups that met alternately in various colleagues' homes. Together with her new friends, she began to frequent the few theaters that still were operating after the military coup. After that late afternoon tea with an amphibious name – onces-comida – she would lock herself in the dining room for hours with her books and notebooks and a typewriter she took from the old man's office one day when she determined that his secretary had learned how to use the new electronic Olivetti. Indifferent to that ambiguously named tea, Manuel immersed himself in the lenses and cameras in his photographic studio while his wife devoted herself to metaphysical perplexities. Cecilia often saw him emerging from the darkroom into which he had converted the guest bathroom, with printing paper shining between his fingers, his childlike enthusiasm lending his eyes an intensity resembling that sparkle. It seemed to her that the peaceful coexistence that allowed them to throw themselves into their private passions was not just a more mature form of closeness, but also something very much like happiness.

And yet a destructive virus, which neither Cecilia nor Manuel perceived, was undermining what little they had been able to build, silently extending the cracks their inattention had left unsealed.

Living all those years in the same apartment, sleeping in the same bed – probably dreaming similar dreams – Cecilia and Manuel grew more distant day by day. Perhaps this isn't the best way to describe it. It wasn't that the breach grew hopelessly wider every day. In fact, there were moments of closeness, and sometimes, in that closeness, they even recaptured those signs of their first infatuation, gestures of tenderness in which they both sensed the wholeness of the person they'd once loved. That feeling of togetherness brightened the days that led them inexorably, although without their knowing it, to the next crisis, as if an outside force compelled them to explore newer and more serious differences.

Cecilia, whose wings had been broken since childhood by the phantom of correction and guilt, now clearly understood, as an adult, that the rupture that had taken ten years to show up had its origins in the change that mutilated Manuel's life. With every passing day, he became more embroiled in the old man's business dealings, more removed from that generous, poor, dreamer with whom she had fallen in love in those long-ago days at the Pedagógico. She understood, of course, that the change – the mutilation, as she saw it – was probably the smallest, although the nearest, stone in the mountain that had crumbled. And whenever, in the middle of the crisis, she thought about its causes – sipping coffee in Los Cisnes after class or in nervous conversations in Marcela's apartment – she couldn't help associating Manuel's transformation with everything that had befallen them. At the same time, she understood that her father's permissive conduct, without which she would never have been able to carry out the wedding, had a great deal to do with the exclusive, almost maniacal, attention the old man devoted to his work during those critical years. As the study sessions by the swimming pool or the fireplace evolved into a romance and an engagement, concerns about the disastrous course of his business prevented the old man from devoting himself to his corrective mania with his customary perseverance.

And tonight – a night filled with insomnia and loneliness for Cecilia, far removed from sleep and from Manuel, who mulls over his own memories at the bottom of the bottle – those distant days when the waters parted and the paradoxical miracle occurred seem unforgettable. On the one hand, everything was conspiring nicely to make her dream come true. Not just the marriage, but also the unexpected convulsion that made it possible to realize her dream. Yes, it had been that blessed convulsion which forced the old man to devote all his time to planning the rescue of his business affairs. He was hardly ever home, and he often appeared before her eyes on the TV screen. At those times, they would abandon their privacy in the parlor, or in what Doña Leonor still called "our little girl's room," and its weighty silence of kisses and embraces, to concentrate on the words of a stern, often agitated, Don Jovino, who publicly lamented the government's actions, announcing a grave crisis of the entire system of production, "with the deplorable consequences that the nation is experiencing." For Cecilia, in her understandable and self-interested naïveté, the same earthquake that was reducing her family's wealth to rubble was also destroying the barriers that had impeded her courtship with Manuel. In the midst of the great hostilities of those days, a oasis of peace opened up, paradoxically, within the home of one of the spokesmen of those very hostilities, granting them perfectly serene afternoons in the library, by the fireplace, under the branches of the avocado tree. Afternoons that culminated in a different kind of fever, in spasms quite unlike those that tormented the convulsed city. Amorous temblors that worried Doña Leonor as she lay secluded in the master bedroom, in a depression that might have been attributable to the extreme tension in the air, but also to her daughter's moans, which ascended unobstructed from the library, or to the first symptoms of her imminent illness.

At that moment, Cecilia thought that reality had suddenly cleft in two, that it had two faces, like Janus, and that everything was turning out to be absolutely contradictory. The problems that overwhelmed her father made her relationship with Manuel less problematical; the uncertainty the country was experiencing made the couple's alliance more secure and peaceful; the decisions the old man had to make every day in order to avoid bankruptcy helped ripen a romance that Don Jovino would have liked to avoid. The more visible the chaos became, the more freedom they had to dream about the wedding.

Manuel in the kitchen, about to uncork a second bottle, and Cecilia in her bed, ready to feign sleep, haven't stopped thinking about the old man. Perhaps because he realizes this, Manuel isn't surprised when, on returning to the bedroom, he hears her say in a voice that now sounds completely heavy with sleep:

"Let's not invite him, then."

But restored by the effects of solitude and wine, not weighing his words and already far removed from all this, he's still capable of contradicting her so he can fall asleep in peace:

"I didn't say we shouldn't invite him. I said you shouldn't remind him. But you're right – we need to phone him. It would be much better for him to be there."

"It's not worth it. Even though I think he'll try to get out of it, it's better if we don't call him," Cecilia says, exaggerating a final yawn.

5

8

Shipwrecked in the torpor of one who arrives in a city where he has nothing to do, Andrés tolerated the day's emptiness by getting ready for his evening engagements: he called up his former friends, sometimes receiving evasive responses and at other times such effusive ones that he was able to fill his nightly calendar. In the morning, he slept. After lunching with his parents, he looked for pretexts for staying home: he enjoyed being with them; a boring siesta in a family atmosphere was better than wandering aimlessly in a noisy, hostile city, plagued with beggars and strange vibrations. He sought excuses to take refuge in the tranquil house, enjoying the peace of the backyard, fragrant with orange blossoms; he played poker with his father, trying to handle the time-worn cards; and he offered to do errands for his mother like a good boy, stirring up in the old woman's mind, and in his own, memories of those distant days when he would head off, grumbling, to the corner grocery for oil, bread, the old man's cigarettes, some overlooked ingredient without which lunch wouldn't be the same.

Slipping into the game evoked by his memory, he picked up a basket, placing in it as many bottles of soda and beer as its size permitted. He shouted in the direction of his parents' room that he was going out to buy beverages, knowing they hadn't yet dozed off for their siesta. He arrived at the supermarket whistling, for the sun that afternoon and the coziness of the lunch had left him feeling happy. Like someone with plenty of time on his hands, he walked past shelves that seemed familiar to him because he discovered labels and brands he imagined were long since forgotten. He had thought everything would be predictable and routine, until suddenly he was assaulted by the most unexpected and precious vision his return could have bestowed on him.

Sonia was that apparition emerging from the crowd, framed by the shelves, jars, and packages of all sizes and labels, items that accented the motley abundance of the market, its green, symmetrical continuity. It was a memory that came from another zone of his life, from a remote, buried existence. And that exercise of memory convinced him that time seemed to have dissolved into its intangible substance, and at that very moment, as he regarded Sonia – who was as yet unaware of his gaze – in profile, the last twelve years suddenly disappeared. At first he didn't recognize her in the slender, attractive, jeans-clad girl who caught his eye, the eye of a mature animal, but when she turned around after placing two packages of spaghetti or something like that in her cart, it was as if a zoom lens had brought a beloved face back into focus, one that had been losing definition in his fragile memory. And there was that same face, coinciding with the now-perfect focus, recovering that warm October day; that smile again, and those dark eyes, and the tiny mouth, and that funny little ant-face which he recaptured with a single stroke of vision and memory.

What had become of time, then, if the only difference was in her hair, slightly shorter than in his sudden recollection? Sonia's delicate image matched the figure before him, with youthful breasts, fuller but still firm, forming a perfect contour under her tee-shirt like a second skin clinging to the first tan of summer. At that moment it occurred to him that, compared to this apparition in the fullness of the present, the substance of memory was so fragile that it filled him with instant fear, a void into which a wave of images tumbled, returning from the strange death which is forgetfulness.

He recalled his last nights with Sonia before the exodus. And the afternoons prior to those nights, when the longed-for presence of his student in one of the first-row seats or on the more comfortable, bucolic benches of the Pedagógico's spacious patios became a mandatory reference point for him, the factor that determined whether or not he had a good day amid all the agitation in which everything seemed to be immersed. Walking into the classroom on Tuesday afternoons and Thursday mornings, he knew that Sonia would be in the first row, her long hair falling carelessly over the notebook or open text that lay on the wooden arm of the university desk, covered with slogans and initials of political parties and movements. The same slogans covered the walls, the pavement, the hard notebook covers, with arguments as hard as they were, as harsh as the surfaces of the walls, as defiant as the red blood shouting its violent language up from the paving stones. Sonia's straight hair fell over those lines carved into the wood of her desk, her eyes rested on them, without seeing them, probably: in those minutes before class, the only thing that happened was the wait: she'll be here soon, the class is already full, it's time to start, what if she doesn't show up? And he, walking alongside the trees that frame the row of flagstones leading from the library to the Philosophy Department, knows she'll be in the classroom, because he doesn't see her on the benches by the trees; he's sure she must already be in class, as usual, in the first row, reading the book lying open on the arm of the desk, flicking her hair from the wood with a quick, brisk gesture, regarding him intently with dark eyes glowing like tiny bits of coal about to turn red and ignite.

But one afternoon she wasn't there, punctually seated in the first row. Andrés began his class by fumbling for preliminary strategies that would delay the beginning of his lecture. More than providing an introduction to the lecture, he was marking time waiting for her. There were one or two empty seats in the row closest to him, the row she preferred. Outside, the winter sun was sunnier than ever. What was interrupting that unnerving foolishness that was becoming a habit? Perhaps it was Sonia's burning-coal eyes, sparking a different blaze.

(In those days the nation, too, seemed like a house that was burning on all four sides, a house about to crumble upon its own embers. Burning barricades blocked roads along which only disoriented protesters now walked, shouting aggressive slogans

45

and fierce threats, which were contradicted by the very arms they carried: a few pathetic brooms contrasting with the provocative excess of their military displays, gestures that seemed like ludicrous copies of other copies, gestures that would have been laughable if they hadn't already been on the brink of disaster.)

Andrés waited for Sonia to arrive that afternoon with wounded hopes that quickly degenerated into despair. He suspected that her absence was the beginning of an emptiness that would persist, changing a habit to which he had become too naïvely accustomed, because in those days, unexpected changes were more likely than repetitions. And, in fact, the empty seat on that sunny winter Thursday afternoon was there again on Tuesday morning, and again the following Thursday afternoon, although on that occasion with a nasty prologue: just as he arrived at the classroom after having coffee in the cafeteria, he noticed Sonia walking quickly down the flagstone path toward the library. She didn't see him. But he saw her approach one of the benches, and he also saw a young man in a blue parka who was waiting for her get up and walk with her toward the Avenida Grecia exit. So she hadn't been absent because of illness! On entering the classroom, he realized that for the past few weeks he had been speaking exclusively to her, and that the rest of the class was nothing but a chorus, unaware of that duo of intense glances and hidden tensions. Once again he saw a couple of empty seats in the front row, and after clearing his throat he asked those sitting in the back please to come forward and occupy them, he was losing his voice and could hardly speak. Chapter closed. There were so many unsettling things going on in those days – it would be easier to turn the page and put an end to the anxiety once and for all.

As he put his notes in order, he noticed a summons in his briefcase and remembered that the following evening he would be on guard duty. He'd have to sleep in the department during one of those vigils intended to prevent either a takeover by one of the more extremist left-wing groups or a military break-in and weapons search. He folded the summons and stuck it in his pocket, figuring he'd still have time to get out of it. He had a cold; nights in the Macul district were frigid; and he wasn't up to making patriotic gestures.

Nonetheless, the next morning he procrastinated in preparing an excuse, and that afternoon he decided it would no longer be responsible of him to avoid the commitment. He reported for duty around 10 P.M., when Macul was like a wolf's maw, ready to snap. Walking along Irarrázaval, toward the Pedagógico, he heard the distant sound of pots and pans, growing closer. It was always like that. The noise, which ultimately spread throughout the city, perhaps throughout the entire country, began with a distant metallic hum, a monotonous rhythm that grew as new hands joined the first protesters' call. At first they banged pots and pans with wooden ladles, so that the objective of the protest coincided with the metaphor it expressed: our pots are empty; we're hungry; there's nothing left for the ladle to scrape from the bottom of the pot. Later, however, other noise-producing objects were added to this symbolic pairing, making the noise more intolerable by intensifying both the protest and the annoyance of those who didn't join in. They used frying pans to bang on the iron-barred balconies; they struck buckets with hammers or stones; anything that would intensify the feeling of chaos and intolerable clangor, anything that would make the nonprotestor next door feel defeated was welcome at the hour of the pots. The organized din reached its peak after twenty minutes and suddenly lessened, leaving a sensation of rage, frustration, hate – and in the final days, fear – hanging in the air.

When Andrés entered the faculty lounge, the noise was about to reach the height of its intensity. Mattresses were already piled next to the fireplace, and a few blankets were heaped neatly on top of the big mahogany table. Although hardly anyone ever slept, the security staff worked out a way not only to provide food and drink, but also that somewhat superfluous amenity; those who preferred to sleep never made it to the Pedagógico to stand guard in the first place.

In the semidarkness, he recognized two of his colleagues making bologna sandwiches on the section of the table that wasn't covered with blankets. He was about to take off his raincoat when he decided it would be better to smoke a cigarette on the patio, despite the noise of the pots and pans. He advanced along the main path and watched the rather foggy sky, which nonetheless revealed a few stars that seemed to twinkle to the rhythm of the utensils. He walked to the cafeteria, filled with kids preparing the night's activities: not only was it necessary to follow the logistical plan he saw posted in the faculty lounge, but also, in the case of the students, to organize activities that would help them keep their eyes open and their energy high all night long. Bonfires, songs, skits, forums, long speeches, information gathered from the radio in the student center – including the latest news reports or special broadcasts announcing police roundups here and there, strange movements, rumors of troops being quartered in the north, suspicious navy maneuvers outside Valparaíso. He left the place so he wouldn't be seen, as the students enjoyed inviting their teachers to these nocturnal vigils, which had become commonplace and much more important than their dwindling daily classes. Then he walked toward the philosophy section, and as he was taking a final drag on his cigarette, he saw, sitting on the bench closest to the vine-covered building, an immediately recognizable shadow. His heart leaped. In spite of the foggy darkness, he recognized the vague silhouette, leaning slightly forward so that her long, straight hair fell over the imaginary left armrest of a chair that would have been impossible there, although right there, on that night, a greater miracle was occurring: the appearance of Sonia, wrapped in and sheltered by her own shadow, by the black light that summed up in its purest silhouette that body he recognized, that gesture he missed, that desperately desirable presence, and the enormous, painful absence of the past few days.

He stopped next to a tree, a few steps away from the bench where Sonia remained as motionless as a sculpture of herself, or as if she were posing for an Andrés who didn't dare mold God-knows-what strange material to recreate her.

"Sonia?" he uttered softly, without moving, afraid that any

movement toward her might break the spell and startle the girl from her intense immobility.

"Hi," Sonia said in a jovial tone that didn't match her solemn stillness.

"Are you on guard duty too?" Andrés asked.

The din of the pots and pans had grown softer, dissipating into a distant hum. Then the silence filled up with more proximate things. Now both of them could hear the faint, rhythmic murmur of dew dripping from the foliage.

"No. No, I'm not."

"What are you doing?"

Sonia turned her face suddenly in order to look intently at the dark silhouette speaking to her from the nearby tree.

"I was waiting for you," she replied, exploding with laughter.

9

Twelve years later, the night before her reencounter with Andrés, Sonia was startled by something that reminded her of the night when she had sat on a bench at the Pedagógico, confident he would show up there – she had found out when he'd be on guard duty – probably guided by the hunch that his erratic steps on that foggy night were connected to a search, were related to the only thing he had been searching for lately, were all about her, and that finally they would lead him to the place where she had chosen to wait for him. Twelve years later, the experience of another foggy night – different trees weeping their dewdrops upon the path and another shadow next to a tree – suddenly enveloped her in memory and fear.

It all began with that dark mass, intensified by the shadow of the tree. There it was: that blot, her shock, the suspicion of danger, although this time without a burst of laughter to hide behind. The quarterly parent-teacher meeting had ended a few minutes earlier; she had answered a few relatively unimportant questions, left her class roster in the teachers' lounge, and headed for the exit, avoiding a run-in with two mothers who were walking a few yards ahead of her. After eight hours of Thursday classes and the horribly tiresome parents' meeting, she wasn't in the mood to exchange another word with anyone. And yet as she advanced hesitantly along the path, which was darkened by the lush foliage, she spied that shadow partially hidden in the lengthened shadow of the tree and thought it had been a mistake to leave school alone and try to walk to her Citröen, which was parked a block away, without the easy, natural company of the two women who had gotten into their cars and were no longer ahead of her.

It was then that the mass moved toward her, slowly detaching itself from the shadow that had hidden it. Sonia intuited that that man was hesitant, too. Instead of continuing directly toward her, he now waited for her in the middle of the path in order to intercept her. He had tossed his cigarette butt far away, and the arc of that minuscule light restored Sonia's confidence.

"Good evening. Are you waiting for me?" Sonia steadied her voice, making it firmer.

"I was at the meeting."

"Yes?"

"I'm Angélica's father."

"How do you do."

"I want to talk to you."

"Come back tomorrow. I'll be in school all day."

"Can we talk now? It's urgent."

"What is it?"

"It's not easy for me . . ."

"What is it? I've got my children at home, alone."

"Well . . . you spoke to us about having faith . . . and, you see . . . there's a problem with my daughter."

"Yes?"

"Can't we talk somewhere else? Can I buy you a cup of coffee?"

"I don't have time. Tell me what this is all about."

"Do you know which one my daughter is?"

"What's her name?"

"Angélica Salas."

"You're Angélica's father?"

"Yes, ma'am."

"All right. Tell me."

The man remained silent. Sonia knew he was searching for the most delicate way to say something that would displease her, and once again she felt the wing of fear brushing against her. Her children were waiting for her, she thought, and it was dangerous to stay here with this man, in this pitch darkness.

"Well. If you'd like, we'll talk tomorrow. As I told you, I'll be here all day."

"It's just that I promised her I'd talk to you today."

"I'm listening."

"Angélica is a very good girl. I don't know if you . . ."

"I know. She's a very good student."

"She wouldn't want to drop out of high school for anything in this world. Besides, she's about to graduate."

"I don't understand why she'd have to drop out."

The man stopped short, looked at a vague point in the only spot of brightness in that fog, and Sonia now saw that his eyes were shining, reflecting the faint light of the streetlamp.

"Because she's pregnant," he said, swallowing hard.

"Come back tomorrow, please. I'll be here all day. Come whenever you want. I don't have time right now for something this important."

"I won't be in Santiago tomorrow. I work for the railroad. Tomorrow at this time I'm going to be in Valdivia."

"Well, have her mother come see me, then."

"She doesn't know."

"Your wife doesn't know that Angélica's pregnant?"

"No, she doesn't know. And we don't want her to find out yet."

"Well, look, there's a café on the corner there. I'm freezing."

The café was a pathetic soda fountain joint with a tile floor as cold as the outdoors and with an annoying noise that came from an enormous refrigerator next to the cash register. The girl who served them the two steaming cups looked at Sonia with a trace of complicity. They knew each other, as Sonia often went there with her female colleagues to have coffee during their breaks; it was the first time she had seen her with a man. That discreet, conspiratorial tone, that air of making a difficult, final decision, was odd. She stood there looking at them furtively from behind the counter.

"I'm so sorry, believe me," Sonia started to say, flustered. "I'm not saying these things never happen, but I wouldn't have thought it of Angélica. That's not a criticism of her. But it irritates me that these girls are such airheads, so immature, so . . . irresponsible with their own lives. That's what I mean."

"Regardless, we have to do something. She can't manage by herself. And she has a lot of faith in you."

"Why didn't she tell me herself?"

"I asked her to leave it to me. She's too upset. She's destroyed. That medical excuse I gave you at the meeting? We got it from a doctor who's a friend of the family."

Sonia leafed through the papers she was carrying in her briefcase and pulled out the certificate. She read it carefully, perhaps to avoid the man's eyes. After taking a sip of coffee, she said, as though it were a simple comment:

"Duodenal ulcer. Two weeks."

And, as the man remained silent without taking his eyes off her, without even paying the slightest attention to his cup of coffee, she asked him suddenly, in a tone that was supposed to be objective but which turned out harsh, instead:

"And what exactly do we gain with this?"

"Two weeks, so she can pull herself together . . ."

"I imagine you're aware of the rules."

"I am. That's why I'm here."

"How far along is she?"

"Two months already."

"Are you sure?"

"Two months, yes. Maybe a little more. But not much more than two months."

"Plus the two weeks of medical absence. She'll come back to class three months pregnant, isn't that right?"

"That's right."

"This is October. Supposing I don't say anything . . . No, it's worse than that! Supposing I conceal this and find a way for Angélica to take her finals . . . It's practically impossible. The whole month of October, then November . . . and finals are right at the end of December! She'll be five months along by that time."

"I've figured it all out." The man took a piece of paper out of his jacket pocket and opened it up on the table with his thick hands, lined with such deep wrinkles that they looked liked crevices. He lifted his gaze and looked her in the eyes.

"Would you be willing to help us?"

"It's not a question of being willing or not. It's a question of not being able to lie. I can't help you with this, if that's what you're asking me to do. If you want to continue talking to me, come see me tomorrow. I have to go now."

"I'm not asking you to lie. Listen to me for a second, please," the man said, about to break down, but also at the edge of annoyance. "I'm thinking that if my daughter still isn't showing at all in November, she can complete the attendance requirement she needs to take her exams. I've looked into it: in that case, she could take them directly at the Board of Education. Just as long as no one finds out. It's just two more months. Do you understand what I mean?"

"If it were just a matter of not finding out . . . why did you come here to tell me about it?"

"Because this can work out only if Angélica confides in you and if you help her."

Sonia left a bill on the table and waited for the girl to come over, in order to make the good-byes even more impersonal.

"All this has been very hard on us," the man said. "It's been hard to keep up a family life; you see, my daughter can't confide in her mother. It's been hard to provide the money to keep her in school. It's been hard for her to confide in me, but at least I've managed that, I think. It's been hard . . ."

Sonia interrupted the litany with a question that had been perturbing her for a while:

"How did she tell you?"

"Well, it was the night before last. She was very, very nervous. She'd been keeping to herself for days, although her mother hardly notices those things. So that you'll understand, I have to tell you about the canary. Just one more minute. Okay?"

"Tell me."

"Do you want another coffee?"

"No, thanks. Tell me how it happened."

"In one of the train stations, I can't remember if it was Temuco or Los Angeles, I saw a boy, a very little boy, couldn't have been more than six, with a birdcage, freezing on a bench on the platform. It was very late, and the platform was deserted when he came over to me and asked me to buy his canary so he could get something to eat that night. He was a child with large, very alert eyes. I handed him a bill, I don't know, five hundred pesos maybe, and told him I didn't want to take his canary. He followed me and said that if I ever wanted a canary, I could find him selling them in that station. Then I understood that what he wanted was to sell canaries, not to beg for money, and I thought about how sad Angélica had been those past few days and how nice it would be to buy the kid's canary and give it to my little girl; unfortunately I'd been coming home from my trips empty-handed for a while now, you know how rough times are, so I gave him a thousand pesos and took the cage. That night, when I gave my daughter the surprise, I felt like something was wrong, something much worse than what I imagined was happening right under my nose and I hadn't even noticed . . . although, not really: I had noticed it in Angélica's eyes when she took the little bird in her hands, those eyes that looked so much like the little boy's at the station. I mean, it was much more than just noticing it: I knew exactly what it was that I had noticed, I knew what my daughter's suffering was about. My daughter is the person I love most in this world, and to be honest with you, she's the only thing I love in this world. And when she took the canary, she began to shake; she wanted to say something; her lips quivered; she was trembling all over. Without letting go of the canary, pressing it closer to her body, she ran from the dining room and locked herself in

54

her room. When I went to see her, she was crying, and she said to me, "I don't want to, I don't want to." She repeated those words, just those, for a long time. After her body stopped shaking and she caught her breath, she looked at the canary between her fingers and stroked its belly gently, saying: "I don't want them to kill it. I'm going to have it."

The silence that followed seemed very long to Sonia, but she didn't dare interrupt. She had been concentrating on the remains of the coffee at the bottom of the cup, and for that reason, she seemed to hear the man's voice from a great distance explaining to her what a child feels when she takes a bird in her hands.

"That heartbeat in your palm, something so . . . I don't know, so fragile, almost impossible, and yet the pulsing keeps warming your hand. That's what my daughter felt. And later she told me that she thought such a tiny gesture would be enough, it would be enough to squeeze her hand a little and then, no more heartbeat. Not even one. That's what she was thinking sprawled out on the bed, crying. She stopped crying when she was sure I wasn't going to do it."

"Come see me tomorrow." Sonia stood up. "Say hello to Angélica for me. Take good care of her."

"You don't know how much I appreciate it," the man said, smiling for the first time.

Back on the street, feeling the dewdrops falling on her face from the leafy trees again, stepping hurriedly on the worn cobblestones and the darkest shadows, she asked the man if he wanted a lift to somewhere closer to his house. Angélica's father thanked her, but he said he needed to walk a few blocks; he wanted to smoke, and his bus stop was just a little farther down. Pulling her car out of that pitch darkness, turning on the headlights, turning on a bit of sanity. – What a fool I am! The same thing always happens to me; I get myself involved because I'm an idiot; I get caught up over and over again! – Sonia said to herself as she drove home through the lonely streets, everyone locked up behind closed doors, everyone afraid, and me, stupid jerk that I am, I should've told him what my obligation is as a lead teacher, I should've acted firmer, I should've explained to him that what he's asking me to do is impossible; I can't lie to my own colleagues, please understand; I can't do that even if there's a valid reason – and she repeated over and over what she should have said and didn't, and especially, What a fool, I should never have suggested having coffee; as soon as we went in there, I was already sentenced for my stupidity. Ten o'clock! It's almost ten o'clock! And poor Estela, still waiting for me. I won't see the kids, again. What a moron I am! What a moron! If only I had left when I told him I couldn't help him, another dark street, another desert in the middle of the city, distant barking, another tense night, go home and lock the door, kiss the sleeping children, listen to the news on the Cooperativa, find out what happened today, and close all the doors, double lock them, slide the deadbolts, make sure the bolt on the front door is locked, I hope Julián's home, I'd like to tell him, I'll feel better that way. Julián? Tell him? Really, what I did, what I just did a half hour ago is a promise: I won't tell anyone; his daughter can come back to school confident that no one is going to know. That's what he understood. You don't know how much I appreciate it. I can't tell anyone. I'm going to have to live with this, and when she comes back, even though I don't mean to, I'll be watching the schoolyard during recess, seeking her out with my eyes, over there, in that corner, surrounded by a group of girlfriends. Is she the one talking? Yes, that's her. And now they're laughing. What are they laughing about? Did they see me? Yes, they saw me; they're looking at me, whispering: could she have told them herself? Are they laughing at me? How can I find out? Next recess I'm going to get closer; I'm going to walk past them, pretending not to notice; that way we'll find out; that way I'll find out. I'll find out? Not in that far corner of the school-yard, over there, where they're looking at her, whispering, but there, on the corner where her house stands, we're almost there, it's past ten, Julián's car isn't there, Julián isn't home, one more day, we're almost there.

"I got held up, Estela. Go home, scoot. Did anybody call?"

"Don Julián phoned and said he'd be late."

"Okay, don't wait any longer, go home."

"And Señora Cecilia called."

"Did you write down the message?"

"Yes, señora, here it is."

Sonia picked up the top sheet of the pad the nanny handed her with an alacrity that emphasized her obedience. She read the large, uneven letters of a humble handwriting.

"*Señora Cecilia called. Wants you to call back. Señor Andrés came back. They are having a party Saturday in the new house.*"

"No one else phoned?"

"No one else, señora."

"Go home, Estela. Thank you. It's very late. I want to see the children now."

6

10

"Andrés!"

Yes. It was his name he heard that afternoon in the supermarket, amid the specials, discounts, and raffles that overwhelmed customers as they busily filled their carts, besieged by announcements cleverly muffled by the background music. There, outlined against the profusion of jars and labels that compounded the assault from the shelves, Andrés spied Sonia, like an apparition, an instantly familiar figure, as immediate as if time had never passed, as beautiful as the memory he had frivolously cultivated all those years, and he felt a belated pang of guilt on seeing the tremulous smile and excited appearance of his friend.

"Whew! Let me catch my breath for a minute. Just look at me, I look like . . . I don't know what. Look. I've got gooseflesh," she said, laughing nervously, happy, startled. Turning her face to hide her blush, she added, "No, no, not like this."

"Not like what?"

"I come here to buy something for tea, and just like that, without having any idea that . . . I bump into . . . no, no, it isn't fair – you have to give me a little time."

"All the time you'd like."

"Where are you staying?"

"In my folks' house, right here, around the corner. And you?"

Sonia hesitated for a moment before taking refuge in a question that barely gained her a few seconds.

"What about me?"

"Where are you staying?"

"In my house. Right here, around the corner," Sonia said, and her eyes no longer had the same guileless sparkle. A sudden cloud had darkened her enthusiasm.

"Don't laugh. It's true."

"You're the one who's laughing. What are you laughing about?"

But Sonia didn't feel like laughing. She wasn't laughing, really. She was simply thinking about how to tell him. Wondering, rather, how she had gotten to the point of what she needed to tell him now; how her life had reached a point where she had to tell him something that seemed so unreal, almost a lie.

"What are you laughing at, mama?"

". . ."

"Is this your son?"

"My son, Julián."

"Hi, Julián. My name's Andrés. How're you doing?"

"Mama, let's go. I'm tired."

"How can you be tired at four in the afternoon, sweetheart? Go look for some chocolates. One of those little chocolate trains you like so much."

"How old is he?"

"Five."

"Is he your only one?"

"He's the younger one. I've got a seven-year-old girl. Go ahead, Julián. Don't be such a pain. Go find the little chocolate trains."

"He's cute."

"Kids here practically live in the supermarkets. It's amazing he even listened to me. Whenever he sees me with a stranger, he clings to me and won't let go for anything. He's really jealous."

". . ."

"And you?"

"What about me?"

"Are you single? Married? Did you come back with your wife?"

"Who-o-o-o-a! I'm going to need a long time to answer that one. Your kid would have to go as far as Mendoza, at the very least, for his little chocolate trains."

"So, then, . . . you're married."

"No."

"You *were* married."

"Yes."

"Did you come by yourself?"

"Yes."

"Look, he's coming back. He didn't have to go to Mendoza after all," Sonia said, recovering the enthusiastic sparkle in her eyes and her fidgety happiness, her nervousness, her trembling.

"Ready, sweetheart? He brought back four! Don't you think that's too many? Let's take two, one for you and one for your sister. Okay?"

"And for you? And him?"

"No, thanks," Andrés interrupted. "I'll buy you and your sister the little trains. Okay? Oh, look who's coming – my brother Sergio. This is Sonia, a friend of mine. An old, young, beautiful friend. Life is so strange, huh? Isn't it true I made a phone call before we went out?"

"It's true," Sergio said.

"A half hour ago I was trying to locate you. It's incredible – ten minutes later we meet here by accident."

"Write down my phone number, Andrés. Call me."

"I'm ready, go ahead."

"246-66-24."

"I've got it memorized already."

"Good, call me. And come see me. We're neighbors. You're staying this time, right?"

"No. Well, yes. I'm here for two weeks and then I'm going back to Berlin, and then we'll be getting ready to return. I think it'll be soon. I'll call you as soon as I can."

"Watch it, son, stop that. He can't stand it when someone kisses me." *We'll be getting ready to return,* she thinks. He's not alone, then. He's coming with someone. He's married.

"*Ciao,* Andrés, *ciao.* Let's go, Julián, and don't do that ever again, I've told you . . ."

"Can I get you something to drink?"

Andrés stretched out on the well-worn sofa toward which Sonia motioned him after showing him the sad interior of her house – a half-empty living room, its walls darkened by dust, yellowed in the afternoon glare – the afternoon following their chance meeting in the supermarket. From the sofa, he heard her final, hesitant movements before coming over to sit next to him: closing two doors that led to the inner rooms of the apartment; opening the one to the kitchen; asking once again:

"Can I get you something to drink?"

"No, thanks."

Groping for something to say, Andrés resorted to the question mothers always find endearing:

"Where's your son?"

"I took him to my mom's. This way we can talk in peace. My daughter gets home from school at seven."

"Would you rather we went someplace else? For a coffee, maybe?"

"No. I want for us to be here, in my house. Don't you like being here?"

"Sure. Why wouldn't I like it?"

"Because you're very, very uncomfortable, looking at the door every few minutes, as if there were burglars in the next room who might show up any minute with a bag full of silver candelabras. And here, as you can see, there's nothing to steal. They already stole it all."

". . ."

"I'll tell you about that later. Want a drink? There's not much here, but, let me see . . ." She started to get up.

"The truth is, at this time of day . . ."

"Want me to make you a cup of tea?"

"I want you to stay put."

But she wanted to move, to hide the redness in her cheeks, to channel her tremors into those familiar rituals: pouring wine into a glass might help, making a cup of tea, talking to him from the kitchen, raising her voice to make it sound firmer, asking him questions that, from over there, would sound different than if they were asked right next to him, and she felt his breath, and she looked at each dark hair on his hand that lay there on the sofa, so close to her leg.

"Let me look at you."

"..."

"You haven't changed."

"I've got some gray hair now."

"And a few little wrinkles, which are what I like best. And your eyes are filled with everything you've seen. I could stay here talking to you for days and days."

"We'll have to do that, Sonia. We'll figure out a way."

"There's not that much figuring to do. I'll take care of it."

"What are you doing tomorrow?"

"I've got classes till one thirty."

"And then?"

"Then? I was hoping you'd take me out to lunch."

"Where would you like to go?"

"Where would you?"

"To one of our little dives from before."

"Ching Peng. Do you remember?"

"Are you serious?"

"..."

"Are you serious, Sonia?"

"Yes, completely serious. I thought I was the one who kept everything locked up here inside. Why didn't you ever call me? Why didn't you ever let me know how you were?"

"..."

"Your hands are so warm. They were always nice and warm. No, no, let me hold your hand. Nothing else. Just that. Please. Let me hold that hand and nothing else. Doesn't it make you want to cry out loud?"

"..."

"Last night . . . I didn't sleep a wink. Julián got home very late, and since I was very quiet, pretending to be asleep, he thought I was pissed off because he got home so late. He started getting defensive, explaining, making excuses for himself in such a pathetic way . . . It was all so sad. I had been thinking about you all night, and there he was, asking me to forgive him, and all the time he was explaining, the only thing I could hear was a ridiculous little tune, because the only thing still in my ears was your voice saying 'I'll be here for two weeks; then I'm going back to Berlin.' So I stayed quiet, because if I had said a single word, I would've started crying, and I had a pain in my chest, not just a vague pain, it was something physical, and I bit the sheet so I wouldn't cry, and the sheet was soaked with my saliva, or with my tears, although I'm pretty sure I didn't cry, in spite of the fact that everything seemed so . . . I don't know what word to use that wouldn't sound ridiculous, but it was very, very sad . . . and there he was in bed, still asking for forgiveness, friendlier now, and he told me I didn't have to be jealous, that I'd always be the only one for him . . . and I was thinking about you and wanting to hear him say he had met another woman that very night and had fallen in love with her, because that way it would be like a tie, we'd be even, something more like justice, but very, very difficult, of course . . . that sort of thing never happens . . . it never happens . . . it would be as if your watch and mine had stopped at the same moment."

"I was thinking about you all night, too."

"Oh? Really? But I had to say it first, right?" Sonia tries to be jolly and lighten up a situation that has grown too dense, like the darkness that has finally enveloped the walls, the house, the shadows of things.

"We have a lot to say to each other. What difference does it make who says it first?"

"Maybe there's not so much, maybe there's nothing to say. Maybe after a good nose-blowing and some Peking duck and a few drinks, we'll discover that the flight will take off without turbulence, and you'll be back in Berlin again, and I'll be back in this house that makes me want to cry out loud. Did you notice I have no furniture? And my husband swears he loves me more than anyone else in the world, even though he'd rather be with his friends until four in the morning. And do you know what the most terrible part of all this is? Do you know?"

"No."

"Well, say something. Let's see. What can it be?"

". . ."

"The most terrible part is that it's true. The most terrible thing is that that man, who's embarrassed to be with me, is the person who loves me the most in the world."

"Good afternoon. Would you care for an apéritif?"

The following day was also very sunny from early morning on, clear and warm. Andrés waited for Sonia a block away from the high school, just as he had waited for her that night a block from the Pedagógico, in order not to pique the other students' curiosity. They walked along Marín toward Vicuña Mackenna, as they had decided to have lunch in the same Chinese restaurant where they had dined the night of September 10, their first night together, as well as the last one before those twelve years of not seeing each other. So it was that they found themselves there again, sitting at the same table or in the same place, in a corner far from the windows that faced the street, far from the entryway and the other rooms. Huddled in the corner as on that other night, they surrendered to the game of timid caresses and shyness, wisely guided by Sonia and clumsily dissembled by Andrés. The waiter addressed them politely, as if embarrassed to be interrupting that intimacy of squeezed hands, smiles and whispers that surrounded the couple like a halo.

"What do you want to drink, Sonia?"

"I don't know. You decide."

"Well, I'll have . . ."

"I know! Let's celebrate with champagne!"

"Fantastic. A bottle of champagne, please."

"Any particular brand?"

"Something dry. Brut, please."

"I'll bring you the wine list."

So there they were, already fully immersed in the game they had so daringly invented: trying to place their feet in the footprints, tempting time, measuring each other with a treacherous yardstick. The place was the same, but logically it wasn't, couldn't be, the same. They were the only customers at an hour when, years before, it would have been filled with patrons having lunch. It wasn't just the neglected condition of the place that dis-

65

turbed them, but also the barrenness and deterioration, which added to that sensation of solitude and emptiness. Something smelled stale, like unventilated space, like lingering poverty. The tablecloth revealed a few dark stains that had survived countless washings. The flower that languished in a small vase – a green glass vase – was yesterday's.

Andrés made a stinging remark, which he immediately regretted.

"This flower – it's like us, isn't it?" he asked suddenly, pointing to the vase.

"How?"

"It's from yesterday. Haven't we turned into yesterday's flowers, into leftovers, survivors?"

"I live from day to day here. It's very hard for me to understand what you're saying. I suppose you're right."

And she said it in such a bitter tone of voice that her words barely matched the false continuation of that sentence through which not only her present, but her entire past flowed, the previous day she had lived through like an endless detour, ever since that night when they had discovered both meeting and separating simultaneously.

"After our first toast, I want you to tell me more about your marriage," Sonia said, trying to clear her throat.

"All right, let's have a toast. Do you think we should toast to the last night?"

"For me, it's more like the first," Sonia said, raising her glass.

"To the night of the tenth, at the Pedagógico?"

"To the night of September 10, and not just at the Pedagógico," Sonia emphasized, fixing her gaze on Andrés's eyes. "Cheers!"

"Is it true you were there that night because you had gone to look for me?"

"Absolutely true."

"I went there to look for you, too."

"I know."

"How?"

"Because you were walking along toward the bench where I always waited for your class to begin."

"And what else do you remember?"

"Everything. You sat down . . ."

"First you laughed. Hysterically."

"I was so incredibly nervous. I wanted to seem like an experienced woman. And I was trembling all over. Well, you sat down at my side, and I took your hand . . . like this . . . and then I put my head on your shoulder . . . come closer . . . yes . . . that's good . . . that's how we were that night, dreaming it would be the first of many nights to come, and that we had all the time in the world, just for us, to get to know one another, to love one another, and what seemed like the beginning was already the worst kind of ending, without our knowing it."

"The beginning is now."

"Don't kid yourself, Andrés. You know it's not the same. How they fucked us up! Or did we fuck ourselves up? Cheers! Anyway, there's nothing to be done anymore."

"But that bench has another story, too, one you never wanted to tell me."

"What story?"

"You know."

"I don't know what you're talking about."

"One afternoon I saw you sitting there with a boy. You walked away with him toward the field and the Avenida Grecia exit. Do you remember?"

"Yes. Now I know what you're talking about."

"Who was he?"

"A friend. No, the truth is that he wasn't even a friend. He was a comrade. I had to give him the address of a house where he could hide in case what actually happened, happened."

"You didn't tell me about it that night."

"I couldn't. I wasn't supposed to, rather."

"Did you see him again?"

"No. Never again."

"Like me."

"No. It's different. They killed him."

The presence of the waiter relieved the tension of that silence, which lingered over the table like the smoke; the nervous mouthfuls lent a blue tone to the glare of the sunlight. After a long pause, they resumed the game, the innocent attempt to recapture.

"And later we came here."

"But first you did something dramatic with your famous guard duty, you wanted everyone to see you, to notice that you had fulfilled your duty, that you were a good boy, self-sacrificing, militant, like everyone else. I waited on the quad for you for about an hour, freezing. Later you told me it would be better if you left alone, that you'd wait for me at the corner of Macul and Irarrázaval. We were so good, so nice and decent, such comrades, such Bolshies, such . . ."

"Don't make fun of it; you did guard duty, too."

"That's why I'm saying we *were*."

"And that night you wanted to come here. It was your idea."

"Because I had just read in a chapter of Simone de Beauvoir's memoirs that she and Sartre ate at a Chinese restaurant. And you used to tell us about Sartre in class, and about Camus, and about the *Grundrisse*. You said it in German, because you were so pedantic, like all of us, the owners of truth and the world. And you would say *Grundrisse* instead of Marx's *Foundations of the Critique of Political Economy*, never imagining that before the month was up, you'd be studying German for real, up to your knees in snow and with your sweet soul even more frozen than your shoes."

"If we're going to be so meticulous in the art of remembering, I hope we'll recap everything that happened that night."

"That's what we're doing, isn't it?"

"But not just verbally," Andrés said, taking her hand again, which seemed as limp as the yellow flower languishing in the green glass vase.

"Not just verbally, of course. We're in the same place as that night. I suppose we'll eat the same things. If you really think about it, we're even talking about the same thing." She paused, lowered her gaze, still not altogether recovered from the unfortunate comparison Andrés had made. Looking at the flower, she added, with a sad smile: "It even seems like that flower was left-over from that last night. And I can accept the fact that we're here ourselves, just like that flower. We've been stuck in a thick, green glass vase since the night of September 10."

"It was only a joke, a comparison that occurred to me. That's all! Don't take it as if it were one of Feuerbach's theses. I wasn't trying to explain Leibniz's idea of principle to you, either. I'm not trying to support some fundamental truth. It was a silly remark, that's all. I'm sorry."

"It wasn't a silly remark at all. That's what makes me feel sad."

"What do you mean?"

"I've felt that way all these years. Everything I've done has been in order to forget that what we dreamed that night would never be possible anymore. Sometimes I managed to forget, it's true. But the sensation of living beneath that illusion always returned."

"We always live beneath our illusions, Sonia. That's why we have illusions, after all. To try to live above what we would be without them."

There was a long silence. They had already eaten. They had drunk the entire bottle of champagne while they waited for their lunch, and the bottle of white wine that had accompanied the meal was empty and musty, a translucent green, like the vase, like the glare that filtered in through a filmy, greenish curtain, like the reflection of that glare on the pale nakedness of Sonia's arm, extended so that her hand could continue to rest beneath the firm pressure of Andrés's hand.

"How do you feel?" he asked cautiously.

"Better."

"You want to order more wine?"

"Are we going to stay here much longer?"

"I don't know."

Gradually, they both began to laugh, or rather to hide the laughter that implied they were both thinking the same thing, and that double pretense, pretending they were trying to suppress their own laughter, that language of mirrors – because it was identical in both of them, and it was double and false, as well – although it was also the truest thing that had happened to them in a long time, finally burst forth in a decision to leave right away, to continue placing their feet in the footprints of that long-ago night.

"You'll have to pay up front for the room and the drinks," the desk clerk said, avoiding their eyes as she extended her hand for the money.

They had wandered out into the sunny afternoon toward the shadowy room of a hotel on Calle Marín. Sonia left her jacket on the bed, then went into the bathroom, ran the water in the sink, tested the shower, fixed her hair as she looked in the mirror, bided her time. Something told her that the final step in that footprint could be much worse than the loss she had initiated that long-ago night. She was afraid. Her heart was pounding. Anything she might say now would sound false anyway, and so she returned to the room without looking at Andrés, without saying anything, shielding herself with the cigarette she lit nervously, and then with a deep inhalation, and finally with the long, sustained wisp of smoke that tinted the shadowy room blue.

Andrés had hung his jacket in the closet. He made two drinks, a great quantity of *pisco* and a splash of Coke, and looked for the switch that would raise the volume of the subdued music he heard, as though it were stuck to the walls and couldn't be removed. Yes, they would need that music, especially if Sonia wasn't going to say anything, if she stayed much longer in that bathroom from which he hears the sound of running water and the shower; she said nothing, and the silence weighed on both of them. He doesn't know if it was a good idea to follow through on the impulse, to round out the shape that would close the circle, the movement that would make that afternoon end up the same way it had ended up so long ago. When Sonia had smoked half her cigarette, seated on the bed, Andrés approached her with the glasses, kissing her on the forehead.

"Do you still think I'm pretty?"

"Much prettier."

"Prettier than your memory of me?"

"Prettier than any memory I could possibly have."

The afternoon has ended and it's already well into the evening. They leave the hotel room, the trap, for the hurried, noisy tension of Calle Marín, full of footsteps, headlights, and shadows; they cross Parque Bustamente in silence. They see couples kissing, sheltered by the foliage of the trees, clinging to the dark trunks just as they clung to that night lost in the darkness of time. Could it have been a mistake? And if it was, what would the consequences be? How will she sleep tonight? Will Julián be home? Sonia wonders, as she walks with her head lowered, concentrating on the cobblestones, the sound of her heels on the cobblestones, the noise made by the cobblestones, bearing witness to that silence neither one of them dares break, because anything they might say now will be remembered by both of them, will cause solace or pain. Andrés figures: it's on the next block. Two minutes. In two minutes we'll be at her house. What should I say if she asks me to come in? I wouldn't want to see her husband for anything in this world. Sonia tries to think; it's all so hard. Will they see each other Saturday at Cecilia's? He had told her he was invited, they said he couldn't miss it, they hadn't seen each other for ages, after all, man, it *is* your house, you've got to see how nice it turned out. Will she dare go? Will she be able to stand an evening with Andrés and Julián sitting at the same table? They're approaching the house. Sonia, as always, instinctively looks up at the windows on the third floor of the building. The light in the living room is turned off; the one in the children's room is on. Julián isn't there.

"Want to keep me company for a while?"

"I don't think it would be good, Sonia."

"Not good for you?"

"Not for anyone, I think."

"For me it *would* be good. I don't want to be alone right now. We'll have a cigarette and you'll leave. I want us to talk about Saturday. We're invited too."

"The children are in bed, señora. May I leave?"

They were back in Sonia's apartment, which, by the dirty light of the single bulb, seemed as desolate a place as the hotel room. Andrés thought that by smoking and uttering a few elusive phrases about what was really happening to them, they wouldn't escape from the trap, but Sonia brought over an ashtray, smiled at him, and kissed him on the nose, making an effort that was even sadder than everything they had experienced that night.

"Once it was lovely here. We had nice furniture and this looked pretty good. One day, they arrived with a court order and took away everything, even the juicer. He's still paying for what he squandered with those damned credit cards. Eventually he paid for things with them in the stores and ran out to sell what he had bought for half the price. He was playing "bicycle," as they call it here: you start out by paying with new credit and you end up with a repossession order on your door. But don't think I've always lived like this. Before, it really looked like a home."

There was a sudden commotion that grew closer and louder, like a wheel.

"Don't be frightened. It's my son. He comes downstairs like that when the doorbell rings. He knows his papa's arrived."

"Hi, sweetheart. Did your mama get home yet?"

The man's voice, from the entryway, sounded free of tension, warm, affectionate.

"Hi. I want you to meet a friend, Andrés García. He's just back from Germany. He was my professor at the Pedagógico. Andrés, this is Julián."

"Nice to meet you."

"Pleasure."

At the door of the apartment, Andrés felt Sonia's hand trying to squeeze his, as he heard his words of farewell resounding like an echo.

"I was waiting for you; I wanted to meet you. But I have a dinner engagement, and it's very late already. You know how it is with returnees. I don't know what to do with my liver anymore."

"There'll be other opportunities for us to get together. Good night."

When they were out in the street, Sonia hugged him, and after kissing him, she asked when they would see each other again.

"I'll call you."

"When?"

"Saturday."

"What time?"

"At night. Can I?"

"On Saturday we're going to Cecilia's. You're invited too."

"Do you think I should go?"

"I'd love it!"

"You're going with Julián, I suppose."

"So?"

"It would be better for me to go with someone, also."

"Who are you planning to go with?"

"Cecilia asked Julia to bring me."

"If it's better for you . . ."

"Sonia, let's be careful."

Sonia hugged him again, giving him a long kiss on the lips. Then she ran back toward her apartment.

PART TWO

The Flaw

when
it rains
in solitude
perhaps the drops
sound
like a human voice
as if someone there
were crying

Pablo Neruda, *One Hundred Love Sonnets*

7

"Let's go inaugurate the mansion, prodigal son," Julia said to him, rolling up the car window and taking her purse from the back seat.

"Recognition of place," Andrés added, rolling up the window on his side and emerging from the car into the street.

Like the damp breeze that had stuck to his arms as he exited the plane into the temperature of the tropics, he feels the hot breath of the nightmare, the recurrent dream submerged in the depths of his nocturnal panic. In his dream he's walking around in a city he recognizes, and it's as if the street corners, the red-tiled roofs, the grass-bordered paths, were at once part of the density of the present and the condition of remembrance, as if they shared the substance of reality and the vague material of memory. But in spite of everything, this recognition makes him feel happy. He doesn't feel the weight of the suitcase dangling from his hand. In the other hand he's carrying a stack of letters. Light blue envelopes, opened, dampened by the sweaty hand that clutches them. He walks down an even more familiar street in that city reconstructed by his dream: the corner grocery store is still there, and the twins' house, and the widower's house, enormous and overrun by the weeds that have taken possession of the garden; the priests' house (two old priests live there, along with a few young seminarians who alternate with the changing seasons); the Martínez house; and then . . . ah, then, in the dream, there's a wall with an iron gate. He doesn't remember that wall, or the gate either. There once was a wooden fence there leading to a wider door, also wooden, which used to serve as the goal post for their soccer games. That was the gate and the fence of his house. But they weren't there anymore. Between the Martínez house and the long wall that extended from it in the dream, he discovers that his house has disappeared. It's not there anymore. Then he retraces his steps, begins the journey again, returns to the beginning of the block; the grocery is there again, but this time someone waves to him from behind the counter, raising his arm; after that everything is repeated until he reaches the iron gate defeated by rust. And where is his house? On that identical street, fragrant with flowers and fruit stands, where is his house? The suitcase of his return grows heavy in his hand. He's returned to his neighborhood, his block, to what is his. But he can't find his house. It's disappeared. Between the Martínez house and the garage door, there where it should have been . . . there's nothing. The Martínez house, the wall, the garage, and so on . . . the rest of the block. Just as he's recalled it so many times. The same warm color of the roof tiles, darkened by last night's rain. The same yellowish tone of the window curtains. Everything's the same. Only the house is missing. Between the garage and the Martínez house, his house is missing. Disappeared. And it stays disappeared in that recurring dream.

Once outside the car, Julia slowed her pace to look at that neighborhood corner that now seemed more typically Ñuñoan to her than ever, especially if she tried to see it through Andrés's eyes. The first thing she noticed was that all the houses were low-profile, single story. The dark sky accentuated the luminous contours of the whitewashed brick walls and cast shadows on the tiled roofs, dampened by the mist. On the opposite corner, her crosswise gaze took in the silent, wide expanse of a schoolyard. On top of a precarious wooden tower, the outline of a bell, motionless and still, hung above the playground and the swings like the corpse of a hanged man. She felt a chill growing from a place chillier than the coldness of the night. She bundled up in her jacket without moving away from the car. The trees and the many wires crisscrossing them began to drip. The sidewalk picked up the dark, shimmery light of the streetlamp. Everything seemed to be pulled in by that growing mist. Across the street from her car, which she had parked next to those of the other, more punctual, guests, was a small grocery store. The third corner, opposite the school, was an unpaved area closed in by cement blocks gathered from here and there, revealing a wide, empty space, covered with weeds, garbage, neglect.

"That's were we used to play soccer," Andrés said with sudden enthusiasm. "But it wasn't enclosed. It was a vacant lot that we took care of as though it were a stadium."

"Now you see they even closed the vacant lots, my boy. For those who don't believe there's been a complete shutdown."

He was still waiting for her next to the car, amazed by the observations that were relatively faithful to his memories, somewhat foggy, but more or less in keeping with the visions that came to him in his dreams.

She approached him silently, and when she reached his side, asked him in a tone that he found more ironic than his friend intended, "Is that how you remembered the little streetlamp on the corner?"

"That's how I remembered the corner."

"And what's changed?"

"Practically nothing. Or practically everything. I don't know. Everything was bigger then, I think."

"I imagine the only thing that hasn't shrunk is the size of the houses. And if everything seems more cramped, it's not because the houses have gotten narrower. It's what they call nostalgia. When houses, or things in general, grow in your memory."

"You're right. Everything seems so small to me. I remember this place as being enormous. And the street – it was much wider. You can hardly fit two cars in here."

"The street's the same, but your eye has grown. You're also going to find your old digs a lot smaller," she said, pointing to the only two-story building on the block.

"No," Andrés said, looking with amazement at the place Julia was pointing to. "My house has grown."

"Grown?"

"Yes, it's gotten bigger. It was only two stories, without that extension from the attic. Besides, there used to be a low wall with

81

a wooden fence. Not that wall. And there was an ordinary door, not that gate. From the garden, my mom used to be able to watch us playing in the street. The only thing that's the same is the tree in the front yard." He pointed out the peaceful swaying of the foliage hanging over the highest portion of the wall.

"The only thing that's grown is you. I didn't think you'd find anything the same after fifteen years."

"You're right. It's just that I've been remembering it like that all this time."

"Want to take a walk around the block before we go in?"

"No, I'd rather just go in right away. I want to see the house, and my friends."

"Liar. What you need right away is a drink." She gave him a quick kiss on the lips.

Then they headed toward the wide, iron gate, and Julia peered in through the peephole.

12

They're exploring the house in little groups, marveling at how well it's been restored, could it really have been as run down as Cecilia says, Marcela wonders, not believing that this miracle could have been accomplished in one month by a single workman. Because it is a miracle, isn't it? And they all agree, yes, Cecilia, it's incredible, and Manuel tells them that here, in the living room, which looks so spacious and cheerful, now painted a winter white, which accentuates the warmth of the beams – yes, mahogany, of course you can tell, mahogany is unmistakable – well, as I was saying, what you're looking at was unimaginable a month ago: not only were the walls dirty with years of accumulated dust, but also with stains. Lots of stains, Cecilia emphasizes, and in the strangest places. Would you believe, even on the ceiling? As though they'd thrown food at the ceiling – I'm sure the previous tenants had animals. So, Andrés, next time you'd better think twice before you decide to rent a place out, someone says, and Cecilia replies: But the poor guy didn't even know the house had been rented. Who rented it out, then? My brother

Sergio, and he never said a word to me; it was enough for me just to receive the dollars he sent to Berlin. And they let you receive dollars in the GDR? Of course not, they went to the Deutsche Bank on the West side, and they sent me a payment order every three months; that's how they worked it out so I wouldn't have to pay for the cost of the order. And could you bring that money into East Berlin? Marcela asks, and he says no, of course not, that was a serious crime for a resident on that side of the Wall. So I left it in the bank. That's how I did it, and I was able to pay for this trip with those savings. Oh, look, just come see how nice and wide the staircase looks from here. What fantastic wood, Julián says, this house must've been built by people with money. People with money in Ñuñoa? Cristián asks. Sure, there were merchants in this neighborhood, small businessmen who got rich, and since they weren't well regarded by the smart set in the fancy neighborhoods, they stayed here and built their magnificent homes; haven't you ever been in Macul, to the south? Haven't you seen those fabulous two- and even three-story houses? Yes, yes, we've seen them. Some of them have towers with little windows, like medieval castles, others look like houses in Seville, Arab taste, of course. The Moorish heritage, my good man. But those same merchants and manufacturers who were rejected by the stuffed shirts were the ones who dared to invest and they got rich. Remember Yarur? – they didn't even let him into the Casino. And so this staircase reflects the nobility of those days, when the most important thing was to have a nice house and no one worried about expenses if they had the wherewithal, that's the reason for the finest quality wood, the best finishes; that's why it's so infuriating that they turned it over in that condition. I think there was a rest home here. Why? Why a rest home? Because it's impossible to think that a single family could have done so much damage. And you think a few poor old folks could have done it? No, I'm not saying it was the old folks, but whenever I visit my mom in the rest home at San Miguel, Marcela says, my heart breaks, I see the kind of neglect you're describing, everything gets irreparably dirty, it's hard to believe because you see how the poor employees do what they can to keep the place clean; the old folks, naturally, can hardly feed themselves with a spoon, you should see what that dining room looks like after lunch, and not only the dining room, I mean, they eat in the living room, in their own rooms, everywhere, and everywhere there are food stains on the floor, on the walls, all around that horrible odor mixed with the smell of cauliflower soup coming from the kitchen, and the smell of the three dogs who live there in the house, to guard it and to give the old people something to play with, the ones who can still play with anything. Come on, let's go upstairs, Cecilia breaks in, and they climb the winding staircase. Come and see, here's the girls' bedroom, and here's ours, and Manuel's desk, now that he's finally going to write, he has an idea for a novel. Be quiet, Cecilia. He didn't like that business about the novel; it was the most recent thing he had confided to her, and he felt it was a sort of confession, something private; she couldn't just shout it out like that, as though his idea were a handful of crumbs you toss to pigeons. Come on, come look, and we're in the middle of the staircase, on the curve. Julia advances to the narrowest section, not wanting to push anybody, then trips on a step, she's about to fall, Andrés manages to place his hand on her shoulder and saves her, knowing that Sonia is looking at him, and that look is an inspection, she wants to know what's going on there, why did he come with Julia, why didn't he call her last night. Or did he? Was that the call she didn't dare answer while she and Julián were debating whether or not to go to the party? Did what happened when Julia was about to fall down the stairs have something to do with that? Well, here's the girls' bedroom, I don't have to show you, let's let them sleep, it's identical to this one, Cecilia says, showing them the little room with its walls painted an odd shade of lavender, the soft lavender she dreamed about in the apartment on Pedro de Valdivia when this house and this room, her room, were still very far from being a fulfilled dream, the dream we're now treading upon, looking at, touching. How do you like this soft lavender? And her friends say, Cecilia, darling, I swear it's gorgeous, and they keep looking, see how the ceiling, the walls, and the moldings are so white, they make the lavender stand out, even though it's so pale, see? And since everything's freshly painted, you can still detect that paint smell that won't go away, even through those walls, and Cecilia proudly tells her friends that she chose the color herself, she's already seen a sofa and a little armchair, just the right size, and she's chosen the fabric already, you won't believe how perfectly it matches that soft lavender on the walls, my desk will be over there, and my philosophy books over there, but I don't want it to look like a library, it doesn't go with the ambiance, I want something warm, cozy. A private place, she tells her girlfriends in a confidential tone, it's a girl thing, something only they can understand. I'm going to nestle in here to read in the afternoon, to be alone while the girls are in school or playing in the garden, which – you'll see it in a minute – is a real garden. But let's not get ahead of ourselves, when my lavender room is finished, I'm going to invite you all, we'll have a special inauguration ceremony, without the men, and they laugh. Julia finds the situation silly and the pretext for getting together without their husbands phony; she, who is alone, is annoyed by these ladies-who-lunch occasions. We're not that old yet, she thinks, and I like dinners and parties with men, someone to escort you, pick you up and take you home, someone to share special schemes with, different from everything that's being planned here, someone to invite in, or not, for a cup of coffee when he walks you to your door, but well, it was a joke, it was a really dumb idea to issue an invitation without the guys, don't count on me for that one. What? What are they talking about over there, all quiet as mice, all whispers? Thinking about that nonsense, she's missed a comment of Cecilia's that has them all plunged into that secrecy, their heads stuck together, crouching over, observing the circle that Cecilia is tracing with her finger on the wooden floor, tracing it around, like this, this size, it was burned, we had to replace that section of the parquet, polish it until it was the same color as the rest, but the incredible thing is that someone must have used a brazier or who-knows-what, so carelessly, I don't understand why it didn't cause a fire. And the funny thing is that we found the same burned circle in the girls' room, the same carelessness, and I'm telling you it was just about in the same place, right in the middle of the room. Strange, huh? And now we come to the master bedroom. Julia and Sonia look at each other, or rather cast two simultaneous, oblique glances at one another; she doesn't say "our bedroom," she says "the master bedroom," a fabulous, wide closet occupies the entire wall facing the window, and Cecilia opens the curtains, revealing the robust foliage of a walnut tree, a foliage that quivers in the wind beneath the streetlamp that illuminates it from the street. Look at the lovely tree, it's the first thing I see when I wake up every day, and very soon it'll be covered with walnuts and we'll pick them from the garden to perk up our breakfast. Marvelous, everyone says, and Manuel, spurred on by the unanimous applause his bedroom evokes, goes over to the light switch, flicks off the light, and then the surprise of finding themselves in the sudden darkness. Another blackout? Andrés asks. No, no, Manuel says, I did it, it was me, look at the light from the street, and what they all see, astonished, is the perfect, trembling beauty of the leaves illuminated by the streetlamp and the moon. On nights when there's a full moon, Cecilia says, you can't imagine what it's like to fall asleep looking at that tree, isn't that true, darling? It's true. The foliage is compact, the leaves glow, and that glow is another sort of light entering through the window, because what we see isn't the direct light, you understand? The foliage occupies the entire width of the window, so that the light that comes into the room from the street and from the garden, the light from that streetlamp, really, or sometimes from the moon, Cecilia insists, yes, that light reaches us only through its reflection on the treetop, there are hundreds of tiny sparkles falling on our bed from each moving leaf, and that's when everyone is amazed, not just by the tree in the Ñuñoan night, but by Manuel's forgotten poetic gifts, why isn't he writing his novel, he's described the feelings the tree evokes in a way that moves everyone, isn't that right? Julián asks. Didn't he give us all gooseflesh? Ah, my boy, if you really want to feel gooseflesh, Cecilia says, just listen to what I'm about to tell you: I swear it's the absolute truth.

13

The first afternoon we came to this house, when this was a kind of witch's hut, a weed-covered owl's nest, with the patio taken over by dead leaves and the scrub that had killed off the flowers and covered everything until there wasn't even a single space left to step on, and with puddles and toads and crickets and rats, and here, as I mentioned, with the floors all dirty and with huge burn marks, and with odd stains all around, I thought I would die. But then I started to use my imagination, as Manuel told me, you had to look at the house, its structure, its spaces, all cleaned up and painted, because there wasn't a single structural flaw; it had survived the earthquake very well. This most recent one and the others, someone said, and Manuel said sure, this year's and the '71 quake, this house is at least forty years old, and in those days they knew how to build well in Santiago. Well, Cecilia says, let me tell you a story that will really give you gooseflesh. I had convinced myself that the house was a once-in-a-lifetime opportunity that would be crazy to turn down, but when I came and saw how it looked, it bothered me, I thought it was a disaster, sorry, Andrés, I'm not talking about *your* house, I'm talking about the house we found, the one we saw that afternoon that I'm telling you about, and if you'd seen it, I swear you would've died, especially you, who knew it under different circumstances and played in that yard when you were a kid and slept in one of these rooms, just like the girls are sleeping now. Listen, it was a disaster. And, well, let me tell you. When we returned to our apartment on Pedro de Valdivia that night, we had a little drink and thought about what we should do; my dad had insisted that the real estate company had other houses that were in much better condition, but Manuel kept saying we should concentrate on the main thing, the structure, the problems could be fixed, and then we decided and we called him that very night, it wasn't too late, I thought he didn't sound very convinced but finally he says congratulations, it's a deal, he'll give us the house and send over a master craftsman from the real estate company who'll make it like new in a couple of weeks. We hugged each other, popped a bottle of champagne, we got a little tipsy, we ate, and that night (I had collapsed into bed, totally knocked out, exhausted), and there, right in the middle of the deepest sleep, I had an experience which, I swear to you, didn't feel like a dream but something different, I was aware that I was sleeping, and just like that, asleep, I heard a very strange noise, something I had never heard before in my life, how can I describe it? a sort of moan coming from very far away, and I couldn't move, all bundled up in bed, and the moan went on and on, gradually changing into something like a hinge creaking, and that hinge sounded like rubbing, like something being scraped; after a while, but very gradually, changing almost without your noticing it, it became a human voice again, a moan, something dragged out very painfully that sounded like it was about to die or disappear into the most complete oblivion. And then, probably in a second dream, something I remember on an even deeper, more buried level, deeper within myself than the first dream, I discovered that that moan, that anguished voice, that hinge, that slow, constant gnawing, an agonized gnawing in slow desperation, was the sound of a tree being pushed against the bedroom window by a strong wind. Now listen to this: in our apartment on Pedro de Valdivia, there was no tree anywhere near our bedroom window; that's why it wasn't, let's say, a natural or real experience turned into a dream and relived in a second dream or immediately on awakening. No, it wasn't that. Where could I have gotten that experience from? Well. The first night we slept here . . . no, I'm lying, it was the second night, because we'd finished moving, only a few little details were still left, I went to bed as tired as I was that night I told you about, knocked out again, dead on my feet, and again, I had a dream, the same dream . . . but it wasn't! It wasn't the same dream; it wasn't even a dream at all. I thought I was asleep. Manuel was downstairs looking for some photos, and I'm falling asleep, and suddenly I begin not to dream but to sense the same sounds, first that one that sounded like a prolonged moan, an agonized, slow, continuous pain, but at the margins of my senses, and then that hinge noise, and I look toward the window, and what's happening is that the tree you're looking at here is knocking against the window, pushed by the wind, but its branches and leaves are sort of stuck against the window, and then the wind, pushing them against the window, drags them along the glass at the same time, and that rubbing, that scraping against the window, that movement of the branches, seeing it that night reminded me of the effort of a body, an arm, something human, something that could be saved only by finally opening that window; that's what was transformed into a moan, a plea. That slow, continuous squeaking hinge, a strange cry that could only come from a human voice.

This happened to me right here, just a few days ago. The tree I dreamed about in the other house was this tree. The noise I dreamed of was the same one I heard here without dreaming. And I'm sure I'll keep on hearing it on winter nights, whenever the wind is strong.

14

But really, we have to show you the rest of the house. They were all so stunned by the dream of the tree, its foliage shimmering outside the window, its brilliance multiplied in the thousands of splinters produced by that sort of explosion, thousands of leaves sparkling, rocked by the breeze. And with that image, and their expressions of astonishment, they now investigate the second-floor bathroom, small, nothing out of the ordinary, a pink curtain separates the minuscule tub from the equally minuscule space into which the toilet and sink are crowded, it's not the master bathroom, obviously, Marcela thinks, the master bathroom is part of the suite; this one's for the girls; they have two bathrooms on the second floor, not bad, they think, descending the staircase. And that's the end of the tour . . . or is there more? It seems so, because at the bottom of the staircase, Manuel tells them that there's more house down below; beyond the spacious living-dining room and the mirror facing the bottom of the stairs, there's more, something very important. And then we continue descending, between the bottom of the staircase and the door to the kitchen, there's another door. Cecilia opens it, motions them through, saying, Manuel will show you this, it's his pride and joy, what he always dreamed of: a darkroom for developing his photos, and then Manuel takes the floor: it was horrible, filthy, the most run-down part of the house. It seems the ladies who rented the house never came in here, when I say ladies, I use the term loosely, who knows if they were old women like we imagined, old witches, who demolished all this. What matters is that the *maestro* passed through here and worked miracles. Manuel reaches out for the light switch, turning on the light before opening the door that leads to the basement: be careful, the steps are very high and narrow. That's right, Julia, go down carefully, and Julia places her feet cautiously on each of the tiny, concrete surfaces, she leans against the wall, it's rough, it's concrete without stucco . . . and she counts the steps, without realizing she's counting. Almost there, Manuel says, there are only eight of them, now we're all the way down, look at those shelves: Maestro Barraza finished them in less than a week, and notice how they cover the entire wall, this isn't just an ordinary basement, it's my darkroom, no less. Look, there's the little room. He shows them a sort of cubicle, which not even one speck of light can penetrate when he goes inside to develop his photos, and he stops in front of the shelves that cover the widest wall. This is where I'm organizing my photos, at last, what I dreamed about, see? I'm not only putting my tools in each one of the compartments, but also my books and everything you see here. He spends hours here, Cecilia smiles, he goes down after dinner and that's the last I see of him. Naturally, it's very exciting when you can finally do what you always dreamed of, here's where I amuse myself with my pictures, or sometimes I read. Eight, he said, there are eight steps, and Julia's turned around, she's left the group examining Manuel's photographic material and books, and she climbs up again, step by step: that's right, there are eight, and they're so high and so narrow that she almost loses her balance, she leans against the wall, the rough texture that seems to stick to her hand, that seems to trap her as she hears, like distant voices, the comments about the photos that Manuel is showing his guests; lost at the other end of the basement, she, clinging to the rough, cold wall, keeping her memory fixed on the texture of the concrete and the eight counted steps, a count she's repeated twice to avoid mistakes, there are eight steps, while her hand feels the cold, harsh consistency of the wall. And then other voices, no longer the ones that were commenting on the pictures, they're no longer coming from the basement, but she hears them clearly, as if she were hearing them at that very moment, they speak to her of that rough wall, those eight steps, that other staircase, the spiral one that goes up to the second floor, and the noise like a rusty hinge, the strange moan produced by the foliage of the tree when it's pushed against the windowpanes by the wind. Let's go upstairs, let's go upstairs, she hears them saying now, and as if she's awakening from one of her nightmares, she sees them all next to her, once more climbing the eight steps from the basement. Let's have a drink, the tour's over, don't you agree the house is lovely? It's hard for me to imagine the impression it made on you, Andrés says, I have such a different memory of it, not the way it is now, but different from that haunted house you've described. Of course, I understand, Cecilia says, later we'll talk more about what it was like, but right now, a drink, an apéritif, and then we'll get the barbecue ready, the fire's been going on the grill for quite a while, now let's go see the patio, you can't imagine how great that patio is. Here are the glasses, the ice, and the bottles – everyone take whatever you want. Do you all have your glasses? Let's have a toast, then, Manuel says. Yes, says Sonia, let's have a toast at last. To the new house, Julián says. Not just to the new house, Manuel says, let's toast to Andrés's homecoming: this will always be your home, Andrés, you can come over whenever you like, we always thought about you, isn't that right, Cecilia? Of course. Okay, but let's not get ahead of ourselves. Did everyone fill their glasses? Is anybody missing? No, no, we're all here. But we're not all here, Manuel says, there's a glass left over. Who's missing? And they discover that Julia is missing. Yes, Julia's missing. Where can Julia have gone?

8

15

Julia ran into the bathroom because while still in the basement, she had felt like she was about to throw up. Of course, she can't recall the exact moment when she felt the nausea and that stuff emerging from deep inside her, struggling to come out of her body, the stuff her body (just her body?) wanted to expel, the stuff that could no longer be contained within the confines of her poor physical matter, so now, sitting on top of the toilet seat, resting her head in her hands, her elbows firmly planted on her knees, she tries to remember. She still feels a sour taste in her mouth, a few chills she tries to overcome by seeking a hard-to-achieve immobility, because the moment she thinks her body has settled down, she's overcome by new chills, labored breathing she can't control, shivers that give her gooseflesh. What was that ominous feeling she had the very moment she saw the house, or more precisely when she placed her eye against the peephole? What triggered that fear? Did she perhaps remember the names of those streets? Did she associate them with some revelation that might explain her trembling? Apparently, she wasn't able to associate the streets on that block with any of the depositions she heard at the Vicaría every day . . . and yet, very deep down, she felt sure about the origin of those convulsions: that house had a past, which touched her more directly and dangerously than anything her consciousness or her memory was in condition to determine. And now, after expelling the sickness from her guts, after freeing herself from the nausea that had suddenly filled her mouth with excess saliva and bile she couldn't contain, forcing her to run toward the door she guessed was the bathroom's, since it was by the door to the master bedroom and next to the little lavender room, opposite the girls' room, she headed there, twelve or fifteen feet, probably no more than that, but she knows she must have made her way through the group of friends who were listening to a description of the strange noise at the window, how could they know it came from the window, she bumped into someone in her haste, but she doesn't remember whom, it was the body of a man, yes, yes, the body of a man, and then straight to the bathroom, saliva's coming out of her mouth, bile she can't hold back because something that seems like her palate has become detached from her, doesn't obey her orders, in this case her wishes, her dramatic urgency to prevent the vomit from spilling all over the recently polished, glassy, shiny parquet, and in view of all of them, listening to the description their hosts are providing of the old house and the state in which they had found it. She reaches for the doorknob; it gives at the turn of her wrist; now she's inside; she hasn't closed the door yet, but she knows they can't see her; she's finally safe from those glances; she closes it without being able to muffle the sound; she turns the latch and raises the toilet lid; all the sickness comes out now, pouring in spasms into the clean water in the bowl, tinting it a greenish color; she retches bile; feels like she's drowning; her chest hurts; her nostrils are plugged up with that same greenish liquid, now a yellowish foam, and another spasm, a more intense nausea, and the vomit washes her stomach clean of everything. She can hardly breathe; she's suffocating. What would it be like to have your head inside the toilet, sunk into the vinegary misery of your own vomit while a man's strong hand pushes down on the back of your neck and holds you down until you're practically asphyxiated, and then lets you go, there's a sudden relief, and again the pressure on the back of your neck, again the retching, again a lack of air and suffocation that makes her faint, and again, at that same instant, nearly drowning, desperate for air, for breath, the image of the walnut tree striking the window, dragging its thick tangle of branches along the wall and the windows, making that sound like a hinge, like scraping, like rubbing, impeded by rust, like moans, like a distant lament, but also like breathing throbbing by your side, very close to your shoulder, to your ear, which moves closer to hear better, near your nose, that smells something strange and evil in the air. Once again the stench of vomit, a new wave of nausea, and now, somewhat revived, she sits on the toilet seat lid; there she is, remembering the worst part now that the worst part is over. But is it over? At least now she breathes more calmly, no longer suffocating, and when she inhales normally she feels better, although her vision is still cloudy, her eyes are filled with tears she dries with the back of her frozen hand, poor Cecilia, so happy with her new house, poor thing, when she finds out, she's taken such pains with all the details, she thinks, staring at the two towels hanging from the metallic rod within reach of her hand: one's gray, the other pink, she takes the pink one, the other one must be for Manuel, then, just as she used to have one towel for herself and another for Carlos, different colors, colors that say something about the odd chromatic correspondence that designates sex in the world of objects within one's grasp, and just as Carlos's hand for some reason would reach for the gray towel, Manuel's hand must surely reach for it now, he'll reach for it tonight before climbing into the bed where Cecilia perhaps will be waiting for him, sleeping, maybe, or pretending to sleep, as she told her. And tomorrow, before breakfast, Manuel's hand, and for many years to come, right there, they think they'll live there for a long time, the gray towel in Manuel's hand, never again in Carlos's, not anymore, she doesn't know how he dried himself in the concentration camp, what the prisoners used, what was thrown over their faces after they were killed in the middle of the desert, what was used to cover their last glance. Julia stretches the towel out in her hand in order to sink her head into it, to feel its slight dampness, the trace of other hands on the cloth, that pink bit of relief on her forehead, on her cheeks, that relief scented with soap and a woman's fragrance in her nostrils, now restored with air and confidence. The problem now is how to tell Cecilia about it, how and when. That very night? Just Cecilia? To plunge the knife into her without wanting to? To plunge it into the open wound? And all tonight? Would everything have to happen that very night? You're crazy, crazy, don't do anything else crazy, every day you get crazier, that's what they told you several times at the Vicaría, your colleagues told you that afternoon when you were crying and no one could comfort you for hours, crazy, crazy woman, and they said it like a joke, that tendency we have to say things without saying them, to reduce everything to banality and jest, but deep down, and in this case calling her crazy, you can't take everything to heart like that. What do they mean, take it to heart like that? She had been listening to those horrible depositions all morning and into the afternoon, and when she finally reached the cafeteria, without energy, without tears, without any desire to do anything except erase it all, cancel out reality, cancel herself out, they told her: you have to learn to control yourself; it's hard for all of us, but we won't be able to help if we can't control ourselves; and she didn't listen, how was she supposed to listen if that afternoon she had heard too much in her office, a cubicle that barely contained her desk stuffed with files and statutes. What good would those accusation-filled files do? What good would those statutes do, the stories by those women who had planned a meeting several days earlier to tell about what was done to them in that infernal house? In what house? That's precisely what the interviews were for, that's why the depositions were required, in order to find out in what house, where was that house that all the women entered and exited blindfolded, where was that place in which the worst happened to them, something they couldn't even have been able to imagine in normal times. A house where they arrived with a blindfold already over their eyes, and those who were able to leave, those who could eventually tell of having been there, weren't able to say a great deal about the house. But was it really a house? Couldn't it have been a police station? Could it have been something very different from a house or a barracks? A school, perhaps? Or a factory? How could you find out, if they tortured on ships, at military headquarters, in barracks, at police stations, in stadiums, in offices, in government buildings, in abandoned factories, at universities? How could you find out? And then she, Julia, with her job of hearing, listening to scores of depositions

that, once filed away, ended up occupying a tiny space in her
cubicle at the Vicaría, voices that followed her in the street, in the
café, in her car, in her dining room at home, mixed with her son's
unheeded words that followed her into the bathroom – just as
they're following her to this other bathroom where she is now –
they pursue her into her bedroom, into her bed, into her nightmares, and then the next day, when she tells them of her dream
the night before, the voices of her friends, no longer those of the
blindfolded women, warn her: if you get so involved, you'll go
crazy, try to distance yourself, if anyone reads them, they won't
know if you wrote them calmly or in tears. If anyone reads them?
Who cares if anyone reads them? Would that change anything?
Would that change the lives of those women, blindfolded, terrified, raped in this very house? And what makes her think it's the
same house? Does she have any proof? Can someone guarantee
that this was the house? One of the houses? At what point do
the memory of those voices and the plaintive noise of that window come together? Was the window weeping, then? Was it just
the wind and the leaves and the windowpane moaning? Or was
there some other moan? Another voice matching that cry, another pain, the real pain obscured by the sound of the tree brushing against the window? Could she really be going crazy? Or was
it the destiny of that night to capture a piece of truth, the point
at which Chelita's voice fused with the description of that fatal
sound seemingly coming from the window, from the branches
pushed by the wind and the threatening storm outside? Chelita
was the most miserable of the informers; she could hardly speak,
hardly separate her lips because she didn't want anyone to see
that catastrophe of missing teeth, she could hardly think after
what happened to her there, and she, Julia, attempting to calm
her down, making sure she was comfortable, that she wasn't cold
in that hovel of a Vicaría where she had to give her deposition, re-
live the panic, go back and touch the blackest moment of her life.
Would you like some coffee, Chelita? How about a cigarette? Yes,
I understand how you feel, but only if you try to remember can
we find out where that house is. Of course, I know it's hard since

they took you away blindfolded, but just the same, there has to be something you remember, a noise, something you touched, the shape of the room where you were the first few days. How many steps could you take? We couldn't walk. All right, Chelita, but you could hear – what did you hear? Nothing. What do you mean, nothing? Wasn't there any noise from the street? Didn't you sense the other women's presence in the room? Didn't they cry? Or moan? You see, that's important: you knew there were several of you in the room; how did you know? By the moaning, of course, you're right. And didn't they speak to you? They couldn't speak. Excuse me for taking notes, but your deposition will help us find out where that house is, you understand, of course, that's why you're here, that's why you came to tell us . . . so, you couldn't speak because you were being guarded. Yes, we were guarded. And did you ever see the guards? No. Why not? Because I was blindfolded. Was everyone blindfolded? I don't know, I couldn't see. And could you hear? Yes, sometimes. Why sometimes? Because I was afraid. And you couldn't hear when you were afraid? I don't know. We couldn't hear; I don't remember anything. Nothing at all? No, I don't remember anything from the times I was afraid. Did you ever hear anything? Even though you were afraid, do you remember something, some smell, some noise, something you were able to touch? I realize they had you all blindfolded . . . don't get nervous, Chelita, drink your coffee, let's take a break, I'm tired too.

9

16

Before she was "Chelita," even before her cold-reddened hands held the steaming cup of coffee Julia gave her every morning during the five days she gave depositions for the Vicaría's archive, even prior to that repeated gesture, her trembling hand taking the cup, Julia's patient caress of that hand, calming it, let's not spill the coffee on the files or on your skirt, be careful, Chelita, you're very upset, let's take a break, that's okay, drink your coffee. Before the warmth of the cup, a warmth that didn't begin in the boiling water that Julia spilled on top of the coffee granules, but rather in the glance that sympathized with her tears, long before, when she noticed how her chin was starting to quiver, she knew it was necessary to stop. We'll stop if you want to, Chelita. The warmth of her glance and her voice, very soft, as though inventing a secret, another complicity, it's very important that you don't leave out anything, I'd rather you speak to me when you're all calmed down. Yes, even before all that, she knew that her hand resting in the other woman's, that patient caress, was nothing less than the older pain of the one taking shelter in the other's more recent suffering. And it lasted, it lasted much more than five mornings, it still continues, even now as Julia, locked in the bathroom, scarcely hearing the voices coming from downstairs, recalls that morning when she heard, as faintly as these voices, two or three timid knocks at the door of her cubicle, and the person who entered when she opened the door, the person who seemed to darken the irreparable darkness of the hallway like the darkest shadow, the person who asked in a tiny voice if this was the office of Julia Medina, attorney, wasn't yet Chelita, but rather Graciela Muñoz Espinoza.

A woman like so many others. Like those who at that very moment were getting on a bus or going into a cafeteria to have a simple meal, or simply standing in the street short of breath, and one just knew that those fragile bones, that dark face framed with gray hair, held all the accumulated pain in the world.

Julia is all ears; she doesn't want to sit down at the typewriter right away. She wants to hear her, she wants her to know that she, too, has a wound that stays open from morning till night, she wants there to be some kind of bond between them. Are you comfortable, Graciela? Do you need anything? A glass of water? A cup of tea? And then a quick, negative shake of the head, as timid as the soft knocks on the door. She's like all of them, Julia thinks, not only do they drag around tremendous pain, but they're horribly afraid, too; they tremble and look around as though they were letting out an interminable moan, the way a beaten dog looks. Trust me, Doña Graciela, we're going to spend lots of hours together, I'm going to have some coffee anyway, if you'd like, you can keep me company, I hate to drink coffee alone all day long, and she says, yes, I'd like that, some coffee: before, I hardly used to drink any, but lately I've gotten used to it. I'll bet you need several during the day. Sure, and at night, late at night, when you know you won't be able to sleep. And I'll bet it's not just coffee. What? I don't understand, Señorita, I don't know what . . . You just got used to drinking coffee? Well, I don't know what . . . And Julia's hand searches the bottom of her purse, takes out a package, offers a cigarette. Oh, yes, I also got used to smoking! She smiles unexpectedly. Before, I didn't smoke . . . How'd you guess? You're pretty clever, my dear. And those are the first words that open another door, my dear, you're pretty clever, my dear, how'd you know? And Julia tells herself that she can't tell her she's been sitting behind that desk taking depositions, listening to testimonial accounts, contemplating the same pain that passes through all the bodies and the faces that tearfully look at her from that same chair. She can't tell her that that pain – which, as the first item to be registered in the deposition, has a proper name, an I.D. number, and an address – is the same as universal pain, is part of the same thing, a minimal part of the same thing.

ITEM ONE: Graciela Muñoz Espinoza, Chilean national, separated, teacher, residing at 221 Esperanza Street, Apartment A, Estación Central District, I.D. number 5.116.753-3, Santiago Office, affirms under oath that she wishes to make the following declaration.

That's how Graciela Muñoz Espinoza began her deposition, ageless, with all the time required by her pain, one late July morning at the Vicaría de la Solidaridad, on the second floor of an old building in the Archbishopric, at the southernmost end of the same block from which the Cathedral of Santiago de Chile rises, opposite the Plaza de Armas, which well deserves its name, if one observes that right on the corner of the plaza opposite the old building where the Vicaría is located, some green buses permanently sit with military police inside, armed with guns, nightsticks, tear gas, shields, and other weapons, and beyond that array of green weaponry, in the middle of the plaza and opposite the display, as if remaining stubbornly there despite the fog, are the artists who gather to find out about gigs, to land understudy parts, to get their hands on a tuxedo or a clown suit, a red or yellow wig, to offer a parrot for sale or the plates from a juggling kit, the score of an old bolero or a tango from the thirties, an offer extended by a pale hand, white from so many sleepless nights, from so much lost daylight, as white as the skin framing those blue shadows under the eyes of nocturnal singers, their listlessness like that of the regulars who frequent the opposite end of the plaza with identical punctuality, the unemployed who gather to pass around a newspaper they all chip in to buy, looking for the help wanted ad that, as they know, doesn't exist. They do it, really, to feel in their bones that there are always others who are worse off, and all of this is shrouded in the fog and smog of downtown Santiago, all this infinite sadness dripping from the trees, the cries of a baby left in its crib – a box of shoes lost among the equally disgusting odors of the plaza – trampled in the crib/box by that vertigo of gray hats, gray ties a slightly darker shade of gray, and above all, grayness itself in the glances of those who count the cracks in the duck-yellow paving stones covered with pigeon shit, and from time to time, as if all this weren't bad enough, the hard, stiff presence of a dead pigeon next to an equally dead bench in the plaza.

Yes, from the depths of that grayness one foggy Monday morning at the end of June, Doña Graciela Muñoz Espinoza emerged, resolved at last to file a report at the Vicaría.

17

It seems that Graciela Muñoz Espinoza brought something very special to the Vicaría. Something that captured everyone's attention right away, and especially Julia Medina's. Was it really something different or merely the stubborn repetition of a suffering and an integrity that appeared to have no counterpart but also no end. What did she bring with her from the plaza so enveloped in sadness and fog? What was stubbornly clinging to her hair, fixed in the depths of her gaze, in the trace of a smile that scarcely illuminated the depths of darkness? What did she bring with her that first morning, when words hardly emerged from her throat? Because they hardly did emerge from her throat. And nevertheless, in spite of that predictable difficulty, she was able to tell the beginning of the story, her own arrest and that of her two children, although you couldn't describe it exactly like that, people might think they were all taken away at the same time, even in the same car. How did it happen, then, Doña Graciela? And, back at the typewriter, we continue recording, the ITEM TWO, WHEREAS part of your sworn testimony goes like this, listen, let's see if it's exactly what you want to declare: At approximately 7:00 P.M. on the aforementioned date, my son Rodrigo and I were alone at our residence. Under the circumstances described, six individuals arrived at our home, dressed in plainclothes and carrying machine guns. My son Rodrigo, who was only ten years old at the time, opened the door of our apartment, and these individuals dispersed through all the rooms – dis-what? – dispersed, scattered through all the rooms. I know what the words mean; it's just that I didn't hear you; you read very fast. All right, don't get angry, I'll go slower. I'm not angry. They dispersed through all the rooms, reaching my bedroom, where I was in bed, ill. They quickly surrounded me, aiming their weapons at me, while they interrogated me about a person they called "Lucas." I declared that I didn't know anyone by that name. Only later was I able to find out that the person they called Lucas was the same one I knew as Alberto Martineau Hermosilla. Hermosilla, yes, that was his second surname; if you aren't sure, I have the clipping from the newspaper. No, no, I'd rather go on, tell me what happened afterward, Julia says, and writes ITEM THREE. When I replied that I didn't know anyone answering to the name Lucas, I was tied up and violently beaten, at the same time my apartment was subjected to a thorough search. During this search they found some of Alberto Martineau's belongings, as he had lived there until the previous week. My son Rodrigo was also interrogated by these individuals and by a woman who entered my residence. They told Rodrigo they would kill me if he didn't inform them of Lucas's, or rather of Alberto Martineau Hermosilla's, whereabouts. Are you sure you don't want to see the newspaper? Make sure we didn't get his full name wrong . . . No, no, later on we'll check all the names, dates, and addresses; for now just keep going, and she removes the sheet of paper from the old Smith Corona, slips another legal-size sheet into the roller, and once more the click-click of the keys can be heard, Doña Graciela's words translated by Julia into the stiff, starched language of reports. ITEM FOUR: My son Rodrigo was taken into a bedroom, and I, tied up with rope and with my eyes Scotch-taped shut, was removed from my residence. My son Rodrigo remained behind, guarded by two men and a woman. In spite of being blindfolded, I could determine that there were more people posted outside my apartment building. Before they loaded me into a vehicle, I heard the voice of an individual shouting instructions to others to remain there, standing guard. Here there is a hesitation on Julia's part and her finger pauses before landing on a key. How shall I put it? She said: shouting instructions to *others*. Not *the others*. If I write *to the others*, it will sound like the others she had already seen and recognized, like she knows *which* others. Shouting instructions *to others* suggests she doesn't know who they are, she only knows they have to do with the people she sensed without seeing, stationed around the building, keeping watch. I need to put *others*, then, not *the others*. The omission of the article makes all the difference, a different feeling, incomplete, the amputated experience, the blindness imposed by the blindfold. That's when a door to the darkness opens, from that moment on, and for many days thereafter she would be able to see absolutely nothing. They took you out to the street blindfolded, then? Did they blindfold you in your own house? Yes, that's where they blindfolded me. Once out in the street, I couldn't see a thing. I just recognized some of my neighbors' voices, very quiet, but I recognized them just the same. And what were those voices saying? They're taking Chelita away. Chelita? It can't be! Again, the noise of the keys. ITEM FIVE: I was placed inside a vehicle, and five other individuals got in. After driving around and around, we arrived at the place where I would be subjected to torture and interrogation. When I arrived at that place, I could tell that the vehicle had stopped and they honked the horn, after which I sensed that a metal door was opening up, which closed again after the vehicle had passed through. They made me get out of the vehicle and took away my personal belongings, later taking me to a room where they instructed me to keep my eyes closed while they proceeded to replace the Scotch tape with a cloth blindfold, all the while keeping a weapon against my temple. In spite of finding myself deprived of sight, I could perceive that there were other detainees in the room where they had taken me. I remained in that place for several hours, until I heard the door open and another person enter. ITEM SIX: Once the new detainee had entered, they gave me a hand to touch with my own, asking me if I recognized it. A woman's voice told me: "This is your daughter." I understood that the hand they had put in mine was that of my daughter Loreto, who was only sixteen at the time. My daughter spoke to me, saying: "Mama, we're all here," by which I understood my whole family had been arrested; I even thought they had arrested my son Rodrigo, who as I stated earlier was only ten years old at that time. Only later did I discover that my daughter was referring to the arrest of my son Pedro and of Alberto Martineau. Let's take a break here, Graciela. Let's have a cigarette and rest a little, okay? Whatever you say, Señorita. No, no, I don't give orders. We're both in the same boat here. We have to find out where that house is. If we file a deposition, they'll have to close it down, and during the transfer of those women, perhaps some others will get free. But, well, let's not get ahead of ourselves. Tell me, during the first few hours you were there, do you remember anything in particular, some noise, something you might have touched, before you touched your daughter's hands? Yes? Very good, I'm going to take it down. ITEM SEVEN: At approximately 1:00 or 2:00 A.M. on November 21, I was taken outside to a patio and leaned against what could have been the trunk of a very large tree. As I stood there in that position, they taunted me and asked if I would cooperate. I swore that I knew nothing that could be of interest, for which I was violently beaten by two men, after which they led me to a room that was high up, since I had to climb a staircase; actually, they pushed me up the stairs, they shouted at me that I'd really talk up there. I noticed that there were several other people in that place, who stripped me, tearing off my clothes. Completely nude, I was tied to a metal bedspring, and the interrogation began. They asked me if Alberto Martineau was my boss. I understood that they wanted information about the person who was living in my house, and I indicated that he had come to me as a tenant after having read my ad in El Mercurio. I replied that I didn't know that person, for which response they applied electrical current to my breasts, vagina, teeth, and stomach. Because of the pain and the convulsions the electrical current produced, the blindfold fell off my eyes and I could see that my torturers were six persons, among whom I noticed a fat, solidly built man with black hair. Also among the torturers there was an individual with white hair and brown marks on his hands, tall and muscular, forty-some years old. At a given moment they put a hood over my head, no doubt to keep me from having another opportunity to see their faces, and they applied the electric current again, after which they took me back to the room from where they had brought me. It must have been very windy, at least that's what I heard, whistling very loud, rattling cardboard boxes and cans in the street, it seemed like some roofs had been blown off somewhere. That's when I heard a strange noise that seemed like another moan, but I knew I was alone in that room. How did you know, Chelita? Look, I don't know how I knew, but I knew. A person knows these things. You can tell if someone's breathing nearby, you're so alert to everything. But you couldn't hear anything like breathing, not even smothered breathing. It was like a faraway moan, although I knew it was coming from right there, it was like the noise a hinge makes, rusty, as if they were dragging something very slowly across a surface that squeaked. Later I found out it was the sound of the tree being pushed against the window of the room they had thrown me into; I think they themselves didn't know if it was for me to recover or to die in. ITEM EIGHT: After a few hours had passed, on the morning of November 22, I was taken from the room and led to another room for more interrogation and torture. On the afternoon of that same day I was taken out so that I could comb my hair, after which they took me out to the street for the purpose of identifying people and denouncing them to my torturers. I should make it clear that by that time I was sure that the place where I was interrogated and tortured was DINA Headquarters, known as The Sexy Blindfold, where electrical current was applied to me on a daily basis. ITEM NINE: Three or four days after my arrival at the torture house, a woman identifying herself as Jackeline arrived, telling me that she and her husband were from Los Álamos, that they were to be released, and that's why they had come with suitcases. ITEM TEN: I should state for the record that I had several opportunities to listen when they called certain other people who had been detained at that place. ITEM ELEVEN: After having been returned to the room together with the other detainees and having had the opportunity to converse with some of them, I was again removed from there and taken for more interrogation, again with the electrical current. At this point they took a written statement from me, asking me who my "boss" was, to which I replied that I had no boss, and then they raised the voltage until I lost consciousness. I awoke back in the room, together with the other detainees, but I don't know how long I was unconscious. ITEM TWELVE: In the days following I was forced to go out into the street, accompanied by my torturers, for the purpose of identifying people and declaring their involvement in political activities. I was taken to various sections of Santiago, all of which supposedly were contact points for political activities. I was taken to Villa Portales, the place where I lived at that time, for the purpose of denouncing people with leftist ideas. I was also pressured into denouncing colleagues at the school where I taught. As I didn't provide any information that satisfied my captors, I was taken back to The Sexy Blindfold under threat of additional electrical torture, but when we arrived there, they announced that there would be no electricity that day and therefore they took me to another nearby location, where they applied electrical current to me, only to return me to my customary place of detention. ITEM THIRTEEN: On another occasion I was taken to the torture room, and there, in the presence of my children Pedro and Loreto, I was tortured, after which they were tortured in my presence. We were tortured in this way so that we would provide information that we didn't have. ITEM FOURTEEN: While I was at The Sexy Blindfold, I can't remember the exact date, at approximately 3:00 P.M., I was taken to a room where there were several DINA officials and two other people, detainees. They were a man and a woman, and the woman I recognized by voice as the one who had introduced herself to me as Jackeline from Tres Álamos and who said they had been released and that's why they had their luggage with them. For a while they read us various documents, and then we were urged to cooperate in interpreting them. I immediately declared that I had nothing to contribute because I knew nothing, for which reason I was taken from the room out to the patio, where, after walking me around several turns, they told me they would give me "the treatment." At that point they asked me why "Lucas" – Alberto Martineau – was living in my house. I explained, as was the case, that I had put an ad in El Mercurio offering to rent out a room in my house, and that was how Señor Martineau had come to live in my house. Both my children and I were designated as "the Lucas group" by our torturers. ITEM FIFTEEN: One night our torturers took my daughter Loreto away to rape her, as they themselves said. In despair I awakened the other detainees, but there was nothing we could do. Approximately one hour later they brought my daughter back to the room, and she told me she had been constantly threatened with rape, and at one point they pretended they were going to do it, but that it wasn't consummated. More than once one of the DINA agents accused me of putting ideas into my children's heads; specifically, they told me I had corrupted their minds. ITEM SIXTEEN: On a certain day, they took me to a room, and there they showed me several photographs. I declared in each instance that I didn't know any of those people and that, at most, I had seen pictures of them in the newspapers. ITEM SEVENTEEN: On one of the occasions when I was taken out to the street in order to point people out, I was conducted down Calle Ahumada, also along Brasil, along Avenida Matta, through Plaza Italia. At no time was I able to identify anyone, for which reason they threw me back into the vehicle and brutally beat me several times. As the result of the blows I received, I experienced severe pains, which ultimately resulted in a terrible hemorrhage. The hemorrhage kept them from hanging me, which was my torturers' intention. Then I was taken back to the room that held the other detainees, where I lost consciousness, coming to only to find myself in a clinic run by DINA, the Department of National Intelligence. When I regained consciousness I tried to move my arm and was ordered not to try to move at all. I could tell they were giving me intravenous fluids. Since I couldn't see anything, at that moment I thought I had gone blind, but later I found out that they had placed gauze on my eyes. I started to faint again and heard someone say, "She fainted again; it looks like she's on her way out." I heard them call a doctor, who proceeded to give me an injection. There were two other people there where I was lying. The woman called Jackeline and her husband. At that point I no longer knew if her story was true or if the poor things had been tricked about their freedom and then treated as brutally as I had been treated. From the clinic where I was a patient, or rather a prisoner, you could hear the cannon on Santa Lucía Hill rather loudly, which is why I conclude that the clinic must be located in that area. On my third day at the clinic, a DINA agent came by to interrogate me. I told the torturer we had nothing to talk about, since I knew nothing. For refusing to take part in that interrogation, I was taken to one of the lower floors of the clinic, and there I received electric shocks again, leaving me in a semiconscious state, after which I was taken back to bed, and the agent proceeded to leave. I should point out that the medical and paramedical staff at the clinic constantly pressured me to give the information they supposed I possessed. After several days I was taken from the clinic, and I could determine that we were going through an underground passageway. I would like to state for the record that the clinic personnel, in their conversations among themselves, revealed that they had taken courses in different places, among which I remember their mentioning Cajón del Maipo, Rocas de Santo Domingo, Panamá. ITEM EIGHTEEN: When I was taken from the clinic, now with a new blindfold covering my eyes, I discovered that they had done the same thing to Jackeline, who was also loaded into the same vehicle. We were taken to The Sexy Blindfold, and on arriving there they separated us. It was the last time I was with Jackeline. The night of the same day when they transferred me from the clinic to the torture house, I was removed from the torture house and taken, *incomunicado*, to the detention headquarters known as Cuatro Álamos, from where I was transferred to the facility next door known as Tres Álamos. ITEM NINETEEN: While I was at Tres Álamos, whenever it was my turn to pick up my dinner, I had the opportunity to hear different first and last names that the detainees there would shout out and which belonged to prisoners in the men's section. ITEM TWENTY: From Tres Álamos, I was led to Trudeau Hospital because I still suffered from continual hemorrhages due to a perforated ulcer. While in the hospital, I requested to be returned to the camp at Tres Álamos, because it was very difficult for me to tolerate the manner in which I was being watched. I was watched constantly, inside the room, by two policemen armed with machine guns, which they rattled constantly, loading the bullets and pointing the guns toward my person. Also, despite the fact that at no time was I out of their sight, they checked my bedclothes and my nightstand. The situation became more desperate for me when, on May 1, 1975, six police officers were assigned to guard me, and no one was permitted to enter the section where I was hospitalized. ITEM TWENTY-ONE: From the hospital, I was taken to Pirque, from where I was returned that same day to Trudeau Hospital, together with a person named Delia Fuentes and another woman. We were not admitted, and they pretended to hide us on the pretext that they were waiting for a visit from an International Human Rights Commission, for which reason they attempted to have us admitted to some psychiatric clinic. They also tried to admit the person whose name I don't remember into the López Vega Foundation, on account of leukemia. Finally all three of us were taken to the Tres Álamos Camp. A new attempt was made at Trudeau Hospital, but our admittance was rejected. I should point out that their interest in not keeping us at Tres Álamos was due to the fact that all three of us were sick: I, with constantly bleeding ulcers; Delia Fuentes, who suffered continuous epileptic seizures; and the person whose name I don't remember, as I've indicated, who was said to be suffering from leukemia. In essence, it was a question of getting rid of us in the event of a visit by an International Human Rights Commission. Finally we were taken once more to Pirque, from where I was brought to the Tres Álamos Camp on September 20, 1975, and set free. The day I was freed, something happened to me that could have cancelled out my good fortune. It seems I had a pair of shoes wrapped up in a sheet of newspaper. The sheet of newspaper contained information pertaining to the Revolutionary Leftist Movement, for which reason I was taken before a captain who had just replaced the commander, and threatened – simply because of the information contained in that piece of paper – to be sent again to Villa Grimaldi and lose my freedom. Fortunately, this turned out to be no more than a threat. ITEM TWENTY-TWO: Now free and living at my new residence, I was visited by Alberto Martineau Hermosilla, who wanted to know how my family and I were doing. The last time I saw him was in November of 1975. Subsequently, I found out that his body had turned up at the Legal Medical Institute, having been brought there from the hills of Buin. His mother told me this, adding that a short time before his body was found, Alberto Martineau had been taken from his home by a group of National Intelligence agents, and that was the last time she ever saw him alive. ITEM TWENTY-THREE: Recently, on July 11, 1978, around 11:20 A.M., a group of Investigation Services agents came to my apartment, first asking who the owner of the apartment was and then asking for my daughter, Loreto Rosales. When I asked them what was going on and why they were interested in my daughter, they replied that they were investigative agents and that they had come in a private car in order to avoid making a scene. They instructed me and my daughter Loreto to accompany them to Investigative headquarters, while one of the agents searched my daughter Loreto's bedroom. We obeyed the order, and one of the agents was assigned to remain in the house with my thirteen-year-old son, Rodrigo. Furthermore, this agent who remained in the house was instructed to carefully check all the rooms. When we got to Investigative headquarters on General Mackenna Street, they showed us in, leaving me in a sort of waiting room while my daughter was ushered farther inside. They took special precautions in the room where they had left me, as a woman who came to that room was ordered to leave me alone. After a while, an agent asked me for all my identification documents and sent someone else to check them out. Later, another agent, who looked like the "boss," talked to me, explaining that my daughter was "involved," and without further explanation, he indicated that she would be detained. He instructed two agents to escort me to my residence, which would then be searched. Leaving Investigative headquarters on the way to my house, and conscious of my previous experience of being illegally detained for several months, I thought that I would have to find a way to talk to someone who might help my daughter and me out of this situation. And so it was that, taking advantage of what might have been carelessness on the part of the Investigative agents, I got away from them without their noticing. Fortunately, justice was served, and my daughter, after standing trial by a competent court, was granted unconditional freedom because there was no evidence against her. ITEM TWENTY-FOUR: I make the present declaration with the object of stating for the record the facts that have affected me, and as a way to bring out the truth concerning the situation of those people who were arrested along with me in the places I have mentioned and who currently are missing. I authorize this statement to be used as necessary. Sign here, Chelita. No, no, wait, you must calm down, you're shaking, if you blur anything, I'll have to redo the page. Do you want some coffee? No, thank you, I'm quite calm, Señorita, you're the one who looks upset to me. Yes, it's true, excuse me, I'm going to leave you alone for a little while. I don't see why you make me tell you these things if you're going to start crying. Don't worry, Chelita, I'll be right back. It's just that if it's going to make you so sad, why are we doing this, that's what I say.

10

18

The moth comes and goes, fluttering out of the darkness toward the intense glow of the light bulb. She comes and goes, dazed, bumps against the ceiling in the colonnade, descends in her futile frenzy to the first cloud of smoke from the fire, toward Manuel's arm as it lights the hawthorn branches, adds little wads of paper at all four corners of the grill, brings over a match, and then the first glow, the first sparks in the first group of coals, and the first cloud of smoke frightens the moth away, sends her off once more to pursue her erratic siege toward the heart of the radiance burning her wings. Manuel feels his persistent neighbor's fluttering around his head, brushing against his arms; he shoos her away with quick movements, seeming not only to want to brush her away, but to end the game forever. Aren't they alike, then, in their siege on the incandescence and in their flight toward those dark edges? But there's a lot of smoke – we'll have to ask Berta to bring the hair dryer; they told him it was the best thing for getting the fire started. Then he goes to the kitchen. Berta, bring the señora's hair dryer, and Berta says of course, Don Manuel, I'll be right there, and she heads toward the winding staircase. Manuel hears her footsteps climbing the stairs, takes advantage of the pause to taste the second pitcher of pisco sours that Berta was stirring when he entered the kitchen, a quick check even though it's not his responsibility, he's just responsible for the barbecue, but let's see, and he feels suddenly happy as he regards the perfect shape of the platters, the intense coloration of the salads, the red tomatoes dampening the wooden bowl, and the lettuce on three blue ceramic platters, flaunting its green profusion, its overflow, and another platter heaped with tender green beans stripped from their pods, their shiny nudity drenched in olive oil and bejeweled with tiny white nuptial flecks, the bridal veil, onion minced with that mastery only Berta can . . . and then, I can't get into the bathroom Don Manuel, it's occupied. Why the bathroom? He's distracted, in that other world conveyed to him by those platters containing another sort of possible perfection, that's where the señora keeps the hair dryer, Don Manuel. Don't worry about it, hand me a piece of stiff cardboard like that one, okay? like the lid of that box, and here he is again at the grill, attracting the idiotic fluttering of the moth, how strange, everyone's here. Andrés – the special guest – in one of the canvas chairs they had put out on the lawn, chatting spiritedly with Sonia and Julián, who has his arm around his wife's shoulder, and in the other group, beneath the colonnade, sitting in the wicker chairs at the far right corner of the shiny, red-tiled terrace, Cecilia's telling Marcela and Cristián how they had to fix up the garden and how much it cost to build this colonnade, which will allow them to enjoy their wonderful terrace on summer nights. Julia is missing, then. Julia's the one in the bathroom, he remembers, swatting again at the even more dazed fluttering around his head, fluttering that crashes against his forehead, leaving a tenuous trace of dust shining there by the light of the bulb, and Manuel feels and touches and admires its ephemeral golden splendor before returning to the business of the barbecue, before asking himself if tonight, while everyone is celebrating, or at least while everyone has a glass of *pisco* sour in hand – some people are on their third already – and occasionally laughing, and when every so often you can hear laughter coming from the Andrés/Sonia/Julián trio, chatting spiritedly on the lawn, and from the other trio, Cecilia/Cristián/Marcela, proceeding with its apparently more serious conversation at the other end of the terrace . . . yes, before asking himself if tonight, when everyone seems to be celebrating or at least in the mood to do so, is cause for celebration for him as well. Before asking himself why, here comes the moth again, elusive in her flirtation with light and shadow, dazed and tired, satisfied and sated, high on freedom and uncertainty, unaware of what follows the flight, of what awaits after that game of light and shadow – what else but pure, ineluctable shadow, everlasting darkness, the eternal nothingness that follows Manuel's well-aimed swat – and the bit of substance that had been fluttering, drunk on life, is reduced in one second to a little pile of dust that, if you really looked at it, seemed to be made of gold. Manuel observes it now, that deathly stillness illuminated by the light that no longer exists for her. He blows on the little heap of still-shiny dust, wipes his hands off with his handkerchief, waves the cardboard vigorously over the coals, and asks himself, now in earnest, what the hell he's celebrating with this barbecue. And he asks himself where he figures in this game of inauguration and feast: closer to the glow or to the dark side of the radiance?

19

About thirty feet beyond what had been the moth's final pirouette, and as Manuel continues searching for a trace of the golden remains in his right hand, Andrés, out there in the canvas chair on the lawn, his left leg stretched in front of him and the right one flexed in a comfortably insouciant pose, listens to Sonia and Julián's questions, tells them about those years on the other side; they reminisce about Cortázar, the explosion *Hopscotch* produced on the campus and in the classrooms of the Pedagógico and at the literary gatherings at Las Lanzas and Los Cisnes, and now, without realizing it, they're back on this side again, as is right and fitting for them to be, to exist, quite naturally, without tension, without fear, although after a little while the conversation inevitably touches on the topic of fear and stress, the abnormal lifestyle that existence on this side has become. Andrés detected in Julián's attitude, in the way in which he tried to focus his attention on every one of his utterances, an exaggerated courtesy designed to conceal his fear, the suspicion that something linked Sonia to Andrés, not only from those days at the Pedagógico, which they'd discussed, but something more current, much more immediate. There's a memory of a twosome here. Perhaps the most emotional way of linking two people together. And he felt excluded from that present disguising itself in allusions to the past. Now he placed his face next to his wife's, offering her another *pisco* sour and squeezing her hand more tightly, and Andrés noticed that, as did Sonia, and they communicated to each other through the fear of the man who was already beginning to suspect his loss. Sonia tries to find some topic of conversation that will focus on her husband, something that can be talked about, or at least something he can tell about, but he insists on asking Andrés the most obvious questions, like how he thinks his parents are doing, what he thinks of Chile now, how long he'll be staying, and Andrés replies, aware that these questions are a formality required by fear. He knows perfectly well that Julián is afraid he's going to be intimate with Sonia soon and that all his behavior is contaminated by that fear. What Julián doesn't know about is that the intimacy has already taken place, and not just on the afternoon they were at the hotel. That intimacy was there, it existed, even before his marriage to Sonia. What was new was this belated awakening of something that had gone dormant twelve years before; what was new was Andrés's return, a return that wasn't really a homecoming. Will you be staying for good? No, I'm just going to be here a couple of weeks. Is your wife coming? Sonia asks as if she knew nothing about it; she wants Julián to hear that Andrés has a wife. We're trying, but it isn't easy. Why isn't it easy? Julián asks. Because getting an exit visa from the GDR is a real pain. Even if you're married? We're not married. Why didn't you get married? Sonia asks as if it had nothing to do with her, as if she weren't talking about someone with whom she was making love in a hotel just two afternoons before. Well, you know I haven't been able to get a separation. Still? Still. And Sonia stares openly at the trio conversing over there on the terrace: at that moment Marcela is raising her glass of *pisco* to her lips, barely moistening them with the sweet-and-sour liquid.

Sonia asks again, this time more interested in the answer: "Didn't they grant you the divorce?"

"It's just that we've never discussed it. When you live in another country, so far away and with such different customs, that doesn't even appear on the horizon of your concerns."

"But you do want to get married, I imagine."

"I don't know."

"What do you mean, you don't know?"

"I don't know, believe me."

And then Julián: "If he's happy living with his German partner, I don't see why he'd need a separation. Those divorce proceedings are interminable, as you know."

And Sonia, looking directly into his eyes, as if Julián didn't exist: "And if you wanted to remarry, here, to a Chilean woman, how would you do it without working out the separation business?"

"I haven't thought about it."

"And how did Marcela do it? How come she's married? Or aren't they married?"

"Yes, they're married."

"Well, how?"

"Because she got an annulment, saying I was 'disappeared.' Desertion for more than ten years."

"And you went along with that?"

"I think she has the right to lead her own life."

"But you're not 'disappeared.'"

"Yes, in a certain sense I am. I couldn't be found in this country."

"And you think that's all right?"

"Yes, sure. It was the only way to end our marriage without a long, expensive annulment trial. There's got to be some advantage to living outside your country for ten years."

"What about your son?"

"I think this was better for my son. For him to have a new family."

"And also a new father?"

"Not a new one. The only real one."

"I don't understand you."

And Julián: "But I do."

And now Andrés feels a real closeness, as if the very genuine fear he intuited since their meeting has opened up a crack, and through that crack both men might communicate.

20

Cecilia noticed a couple of insistent looks by her friend Sonia, who, from the trio – or triangle, rather – chatting on the lawn, flashed her a minimal sign, something more than a greeting, more than a friendly smile, almost like an extension of the glance that was trying to capture Cecilia's attention. Now Cecilia turns her eyes toward the Marcela/Cristián group, serving them another pisco sour. She wants to ask Marcela about Andrés, yet she doesn't want to be rude to Cristián, but just as she's given up wanting to know, Marcela herself is the one who tells her.

Two nights ago, when Andrés came to see his son, Matías, she found Andrés crying. Crying? Yes, in Matías's room, that unholy mess of a room, with football sneakers and socks scattered everywhere, and his jeans, which he never takes off, because he literally doesn't take them off, he pops out of them from above, from on top of them, you might say, leaving them in the middle of the room like two cylinders, two denim circles curling around the basketball sneakers, and then someone called him: Matías doesn't have a phone in his room. Just as well, Cristián remarks, if he did, we'd be in trouble. It's true – we had to remove it from his room so he'd talk from the living room or the kitchen; that way we can monitor him. You monitor his calls? Cecilia asks. No, are you kidding, at this stage what can a parent monitor, not even the length of the calls, you know what I mean, this kid can easily spend a couple of hours stuck to the phone. Well, the fact is he went downstairs to take a call. Andrés had arrived an hour earlier, and they were talking in Matías's room. Then Matías goes downstairs, and Andrés is alone in his room . . . I went by on the way to the bathroom, saw the door open, and behind the door, I saw Andrés with one of Matías's sneakers in his hand, looking at it.

(He was sitting on the bed looking at that Adidas as if some truth were hidden in the dirty, worn-out, greenish, grass-stained leather, a truth he had expressly come to discover behind this mountain range. And that truth, at least part of it, was in the chaotic room, perhaps hidden beneath that unmade bed or in the strong odor of those sneakers imbued with some part of his son. He discovered that this was what made his soul tremble: the fact that the old sneaker contained more of his son than all he himself possessed of Matías. It had been difficult to talk with him that afternoon; subjects came out as if pulled by a corkscrew: he was uninterested in the world of commercial success that drove Matías wild with enthusiasm, while Matías had no reason to care about the little culture capsule where he had sought refuge to avoid being contaminated by the world.)

On top of all this, Marcela continues, long after I came out of the bathroom, back in my bedroom – I was getting ready, that night we were invited out to dinner and Cristián was picking me up at nine sharp – I realized that Matías was still downstairs talking on the phone and Andrés was still waiting for him in his room. One hour, because I was all ready, when, as I came out of the bedroom and walked toward the staircase, I looked again at the half-open door to Matías's room. It was late already; it was quite dark out. The truth is, you could hardly see, and that's probably why he didn't realize I was standing by the door. From there, I could barely make out a motionless shadow, sitting on the bed with his gaze fixed on Matías's sneaker between his hands. I was going to say something to him; I wanted him to know I was there; I didn't like spying on him without his noticing it, and then I was about to speak to him when I heard a strange noise; at first I thought one of the cats had gone up to the second floor, but then I realized that the noise, which sounded so strange, like a moan coming from far away but which was really right there, by my side, was Andrés crying, at last crying and really sobbing, poor thing.

Yes, Andrés too remembers that he had been crying and sobbing. There's a reason for his remembering it just now. Some twenty feet away from the Marcela/Cristián/Cecilia trio, without knowing that they're talking about him at this very moment, suspecting it, perhaps, from Cristián's sidewise glance and also Cecilia's, but especially from Marcela's non-glance, Marcela who keeps on speaking in muffled tones without even casting one look in his direction.

(They hadn't been able to talk the way he – both of them, surely – had wanted to do for a long time. The boy, now an eighteen-year-old man ready to start college, took him for a ride in Marcela's car to see the famous spiral shopping ramps and superstores in the elegant neighborhoods. He was sure he'd get into the university. Sure, too, that it would be the Universidad Católica, the only one he would attend, or at worst, another private university specializing in commercial engineering. Later you can go into teaching, Andrés had told him, to make the idea of commercial engineering at La Católica more bearable, and Matías replied frankly that that would be the last thing he'd want to do: the salary was very low, and these days no one had the slightest bit of respect for teachers, not even university professors. They returned when it was getting dark. They went up to the bedroom. Andrés began to look over his son's CDs; he was looking for some object, a trace, a hint of possible identification, something in common. This is what he was doing when the telephone rang. Matías went downstairs. A lot of time passed. First the sun and then the light disappeared from the window. Outside, the garden was growing dark. He had to walk toward Apoquindo, and he realized he didn't want anyone to drop him off there. What was he doing here? From downstairs his son's voice and laughter into the telephone reached him like a faint signal. From somewhere closer, the noise of running water in a nearby bathroom. He sat down on the bed. He took one of the sneakers from the rumpled sheets. He touched it, looking for something, brought it up to his nostrils, stuck his hand into its still-damp interior; there was a sort of warmth there that had eluded him all afternoon. He realized his father had been waiting for him, even knowing he wouldn't return until much later in the evening. But nonetheless he had been waiting for him. That shadow passing outside the door, slipping barefoot from the bathroom to the bedroom, was that of Marcela, his first wife. When did all that happen? From what geological layer of some long-lost existence did she emerge, this woman who today strikes him as the strangest of beings, the most impenetrable person, as distant and lost as a forgotten dream? What was he doing in that disorderly room in the darkness, alone, the accidental neighbor of his ex-wife, who, in the room next door, naked, newly emerged from the bath, dresses and adorns herself for another man who will come to pick her up in a little while? What was he doing in this strange country, different from the one he had left behind, different, too, from the one he had expected to find, and above all, definitely different from the one he would have liked to find? Those words, which over there had described a distant but meaningful world, a world painfully longed for but nonetheless familiar, lost the halo of unreality that made them fit into the scheme of understood things with this transitory homecoming. First wife, son, father and mother, brother Sergio, childhood home, city of his youth, were precise notions that had put his memory in order and that, just by being mentioned, inflamed his desire to return. The facts, the reality, of the returnee: *la réalité, monsieur*; reality, my dear; *Wirklichkeit oder Realität?* First wife, who now was that shadow in black underwear, carelessly wrapped in her bathrobe, daring to glance out of the corner of her eye as he stuck his nostrils into Matías's sneaker. *Son*, that young man who dreams of what the father had rejected, that reverse angel who adores what he had cast aside and who casts aside what he had adored; who regards him with pitiful indulgence, with arrogance, really; who's been talking on the phone downstairs for over an hour now. *Father*, the one who's waiting for him now; the one who waited for him for twelve years; the one who managed to survive in order to wait for him; the one who has transformed this belated voyage into a return to the seed; the one who, in his present precariousness, shows him a mirror of his own inevitable future. He was thinking about him and about all this, with his right hand inside his son's Adidas sneaker, when he felt himself beginning to tremble, without being aware of the sneaker or of the tangle of sheets on the bed where he was sitting, or of the room with posters of celebrities who weren't part of his universe, because the trembling came from deep inside, it was contained within the limits of his own limits, within his body convulsed by spasms he didn't know how to prevent, that he didn't even try to prevent because what he did then was look for his handkerchief to dry his eyes and muffle the sound of weeping that he himself didn't recognize, what if his son gets bored talking on the phone and comes to tell him, well, I've got to go out, if you want, call me before you go).

And so he was crying. Yes, even if you don't believe me, he was crying. But now he's laughing, Cristián says, looking toward the trio chatting spiritedly in the canvas chairs on the garden lawn. Yes, it's true, Marcela and Cecilia acknowledge, uneasy at the incongruity between the sentimental scene that had begun to move them and Andrés's laughter floating toward them like the uneasy fluttering of a different moth. Leave the poor guy alone, Marcela says. Yes, Cristián mimics, leave the poor guy alone; and staring at his wife, nailing his reproach into her eyes, he adds: "Don't you see he's having a great time flirting with your friend Sonia?" And noticing that Andrés is watching them, too, they raise their glasses, share a toast with the other trio, and when everyone remembers that the owner of the house is very busy with the barbecue, they direct their glasses toward Manuel to include him in the toast to the new house. The six glances catch him in his ridiculous frenzy: they catch him waving his arm in the air at the crest of a simple greeting and they register the moment he waves his hand and then clenches his fist in a victory sign. He had just put an end to the moth's annoying fluttering.

11

21

Julia felt a blow knock her over: her fear had returned. The relief of the night before felt so far away now, slipping into sleep in a different way because something at once foolish and encouraging had just happened: Andrés had kissed her. The embrace at the door as they said good night, the sudden – and yet expected – closeness of their bodies in that kind of shelter, attraction, need, which had been predictable from their first reunion, culminating in a brush of cheeks, in the quick caress that Andrés's lips wetly planted on her forehead, and later in the absolute insanity of that other wetness awakening their lips and then their tongues. She fell asleep with renewed confidence, the certainty that after so much time and so many defeats – or just one, perhaps, that no longer had a beginning or an end – the dampness of a kiss was a proximity, something approaching: touching, licking, healing. She returned to the dining room to turn out the lights and go upstairs to her bedroom. From her window she saw him walking away, clinging to the shadows of the trees, hurrying, turning around to look back, not at her but rather at the other possible shadow, the thing one fears in the dark solitude of a street. When he was no more than a blot of wavering light, Julia stood there for a moment looking at the files, depositions, accusations, and folders that had been strewn chaotically across the table, as if they were strange animals with a life of their own, and suddenly she felt, with a twinge of fear, or at least alarm, that those papers and even the voices that spoke out from them, that beseeched and wept from those repeated phrases, were the antithesis of dampness and closeness. They were aridity, perpetuated death, the opposite of the warmth she was beginning to feel again. She had the premonition that those testimonials, repeated ad nauseam, would become something very different for her from now on, no longer that sap-like thing that she had thought gave her life when in reality she had only been dying, but rather the completion of an urgent and ineluctable task. Yes, now she could see and feel that way. Tomorrow she'd go back to those files, she'd pick out what the director of the Vicaría asked her for: about twenty depositions that would serve as evidence for the existence of clandestine torture houses, houses of horror administered and recognized by a network of bureaucrats. They had suggested she give priority to cases of tortured women and that she choose paragraphs from the depositions that would point to the location or the characteristics of those houses. She spent the entire afternoon reading those depositions and thought a couple of hours on Sunday would be enough for her to complete her assignment by Monday. While she was reading she recalled on a second level of consciousness – or was it the first level? – the "dinner dance" that evening and the drinks upon awakening, the sky blue clarity awakening them from that dream of repressed caresses and furtive kisses, which was part of a cowardly game grown-ups played.

And now, locked in the second-floor bathroom, as she listens to the laughter rising from downstairs, intermingled with the first whiffs of sauces and the crackling of the coals, now, remembering the depositions word for word, she sees herself the night before, examining the files, perceiving her empty house in a different way, imagining Andrés's footsteps on other streets, tossing his lit cigarette butts on other sidewalks. Yes, that which ignites and gives life is immediately recognizable; it cannot exist without our awareness of its existence. It's the opposite of pretense or the search for alibis. It is what it is. It's what it knows itself to be. And yet despite that certainty, as though she were rowing against a current hurling her once more into the moment before the kiss, even before his visit, into the moment when she was reading the depositions just as she's done for years at the Vicaría and in courts and in the café on Paseo Ahumada and in her dining room at home and in her own bed, just like that, deposited on that side of time, carried back to the feeling she thought she'd overcome for a few hours, she finds herself listening meticulously to those testimonies once again. Not only can she smell the fragrances emanating from the garden and the kitchen, but also those odors described in the depositions, the steps, counted a thousand and one times, the sound of the tree against the windowpane, the chorus of voices constructing a house identical to this one that now encloses not just its last, violated occupants, but her as well. It imprisons her in this bathroom with all its memories, all those words resounding from her office: Another cup of coffee, Chelita? From the dining room in her house: Do you have to read all those files, mama? From the car, a little less than two hours ago: And have they discovered any house fitting that description? Andrés, skeptical but respectful of her obligation, that determined illusion, what she's been doing every day for the last few years. She senses that those voices, the entire chorus, not just the weeping of the tortured women but also her son's affectionate words, giving up her company at bedtime; her friends' voices admonishing, you've got to take care of yourself, skinny-bones, you seem very upset about all this, you should think about taking a vacation; the words of the director, and Andrés, too, during the past few days: all of them are part of the chorus; all of them weep; all clamor for life. How could she have thought that something decisive could change in her life, if her life and everyone else's hadn't changed at all? How could she have believed that an armistice would be signed because of her efforts? She'd even thought about buying him a tie! Worse yet: as she read the depositions that afternoon, she discovered that she wasn't really reading them but rather thinking about a tie. Why a tie? True, the idea of the gift was justified by a comment Andrés had made the night they agreed to go to Cecilia's barbecue together. He had said, almost casually, he hoped they wouldn't stay up all night because the following night he was having dinner with his entire family; they were going to celebrate his birthday. "Fortunately, family dinners are venial sins; get-togethers with friends are the worst; my liver's already a mess . . . But it's really not all that serious, over there they practice the same sport, only with German excess." It was his birthday, then, the night before the barbecue; they would go to Cecilia's new house together, and the least she could do would be to greet him that evening with a little gift, an affectionate gesture for the returnee. That's all? Yes, that's all, she lied to herself, but at the moment *then they took Jackeline and me to the basement; that meant being pushed down the stairs to the first floor and then those eight steps, so steep, it was impossible not to fall down, especially when you were blindfolded.* What? What was she reading when her mind wandered, choosing the colors of the tie? Because the best thing would be to give him a tie, it was less of a commitment, almost impersonal, almost everybody gives a grown man a tie for his birthday. Not everybody, she told herself with a reproach that lashed at her in a sort of revelation. Not everyone is thinking about ties at the very moment she reads about how two women are pushed into a basement where they're going to be tortured. But the idea of the tie was so strong, so natural: would he like it? And more than that: what would he think if she gave him a tie? The simple normalcy of things interrupted with such force, the beautiful normalcy of life without excesses, without *those excesses*, the deceptive word that signaled the crime in that way. Now she remembers that as she lit one cigarette after another, convinced she was reading the depositions just as she did at the Vicaría, where reading those terrible lines and smoking also were one and the same, she noticed that the act of smoking lacked a reason now, for the truth was that she didn't understand what she was reading, not even the fact that she was reading: she was thinking about Andrés. About his birthday party with his family the night before; about his paralyzed father; about the compassionate lie to prevent the old man from suffering a setback; all that viscous material took real pain and generous deceptions that solved nothing, and wrapped them together in the same lie. That's when she accepts the truth: she has no choice but to accept it, that's where you'll find your wellspring and the strength of your resurrection. It wasn't the kiss, it wasn't that wetness on your lips, the life you thought had been buried for good. No. It wasn't the kiss that night, the moment before her return to the folders piled up on the dining room table; it was earlier, even before the kiss, that afternoon prior to the wetness and the closeness, the afternoon when she was reading – just like at the Vicaría, but this time in her house, waiting for him – when the memory lapse occurred: she had started to think about the birthday and the flirtation of the first and second nights, and about what might await them on the third night that was approaching so slowly, filled with all the things she wanted and didn't want, things she had been waiting for, fearfully, for a long time, not knowing it would be like that, so simple: anxiously waiting to hear the doorbell ring. Come in, I'm ready, and receiving a different kind of kiss, a greeting, no longer thinking of that kiss she had been waiting for all the time, isn't your son home? I brought him these chocolates. My son's been at my mother-in-law's since Thursday. At my ex-mother-in-law's, I meant to say, but she knows he understands, perhaps better than anyone else. Isn't it late already? Andrés asks, as if looking for a reason not to accept her invitation, and she says no, nobody goes to dinner in Chile before ten, I can see you've become a complete Hun. And yet, how tender he was in the car! The way he caressed her hand when she reached over with the lighter as Andrés took out another cigarette. It was the last surprising gesture of his that she recalled. Later, what happened on the way over and when they got to the house, including that other kiss, which seemed so affectionate but very different from the one she had been recalling all that afternoon; it was lost, just as a recent event gets lost, without room for nostalgia, without time to turn into a memory. But the memory was there that night. It too was a kind of viscous material that wrapped everything up, it was those familiar voices. *Aren't you tired, Chelita? Do you want to take a break? No, I'd like for us to finish up right away.* It was that strange sound she heard now in the bathroom of the new house, that moaning that seemed to come from the bowels of the house, and so she stuck her head against the tiles and remained there for a long time, trying to hear, until yes, that's what it was, luckily, that's what it was, the clandestine noise of water in the pipes, sounding in her ears like a human voice, as though someone there were crying.

<h2 style="text-align:center">22</h2>

"And what else, Chelita? What other things could you hear?"

"The bells. It was the ringing of school bells. I got used to hearing them, and I was able to count, when they weren't torturing me, how many hours of class had gone by. I managed to figure out which one was the last bell that ended the school day. After that, it was nighttime."

"And at night . . . what voices? What noises?"

"The voices of my *compañeras* asking for water, or asking us to come over and touch their faces after a session. We were the blind mirror of the blindfolded. Why does my eye hurt so? Tell me how it feels to you. What did they do to my mouth? Is this wet spot on my blouse blood? Smell it, please! Tell me!"

"And the men? Did you hear them?"

"You mean the torturers. But don't forget, it wasn't just men. There were women too. And toward the end, when I was about to leave, I have the impression that there were many more women."

"Could you hear them at night?"

"Yes, of course. At a certain time, all the doors of the downstairs rooms were closed, because their laughter and conversations sounded less clear. But you could hear it, we heard the nicknames . . ."

"Their own nicknames?"

"Theirs and ours. We all had names they invented, but I'm not going to tell you about that. They were terribly vulgar. Don't ask me to tell you about that; I'd rather change the subject."

"Another cigarette?"

"Okay."

"Tell me, Chelita, what else could you hear that would allow us to identify the place where that house was? What else besides those school bells?"

"The street fair."

"There was a street fair?"

"Of course."

"And how do you know it was a fair?"

"A person knows that; it's a very special sound. Besides, you know it by the frequency. It wasn't like the bells that rang every day."

"That noise, then, you heard it only once a week?"

"No, twice. In general, street fairs are on Thursday and Sunday, or Wednesday and Sunday. Whenever there was noise from a fair and no school bells, it was Sunday. When the voices of the vendors mixed with calls for recess, at first we thought it was Wednesday or Thursday. But later we found out that fair was on Wednesday."

"Why? How do you know?"

"Because my son likes soccer. That's why I know that the Copa Libertadores games are on Wednesday. Whenever there were school bells, sounds of a fair, and later shouts from the torturers who were listening to the game, it was Wednesday. From that point you could count the days."

"Wasn't there any noise from vehicles in the street?"

"Yes, of course."

"Buses?"

"Buses too."

"And didn't those noises tell you anything?"

"Nothing special. Except that the house was someplace where there was public transportation, schools, a fair. It wasn't like Tres Álamos or Ritoque, which are far away from populated areas. This house was surrounded by people. They passed by all day long. What I don't understand is how they didn't hear our screams."

"Because you did hear them."

"All day long. Of course you could hear the screams. They were really loud shrieks. How is it that they couldn't be heard from the street?"

"Maybe the house is set way back on the lot. It probably has very large back and front yards."

"That could be."

129

"How much of the street vendors' cries could you hear? Could you make out any words?"

"Very few. It was more like a murmur that grew, and after a few hours it grew fainter until it disappeared."

"And what other noises?"

"The footsteps on the staircase. You heard the noise of the footsteps and the creaking of the wood."

"Did it creak a lot?"

"Quite a bit. Is that important?"

"Of course it's important. It could mean it was an old house. But there are other people investigating that. We have to supply as much data as possible."

"Then the steps going down to the basement . . . those I counted several times, because the first night, I fell on that staircase. That's why I wanted to know how many I had left going downstairs."

"And how many steps were there, Chelita?"

"Eight. Of that I'm very sure."

12

23

Out on the terrace Marcela is telling them that she had discovered Andrés crying in his son's bedroom. Cecilia notices that Sonia, with the trio out on the lawn, has raised her arms a few times. It seems like she's sending her strange signals, it could be a greeting – look what a great time we're having! – but it could also be interpreted as a call for help, an SOS that Cecilia doesn't understand, for at that distance, some ten yards away, all she can hear is laughter. It's hard to establish a connection between those hurried movements of Sonia's arm and a conversation that Cecilia can't quite hear; she decides to wait for Sonia herself to take the initiative, but once again Sonia is concentrating on a story the returnee is telling; I'd like to be over there too, Cecilia thinks, Marcela has become a bit one-note, for a half hour now she hasn't stopped talking about Andrés, poor Cristián. And Andrés, courted in the other group by Sonia, who looks provocatively into his eyes, ignoring Julián's presence, is saying something Cecilia can't hear . . .

"It's just that there can be no conditions, Sonia."

"The circumstances, I mean."

"What circumstances?"

"The ones that would make you decide to get a separation."

"But legal separation doesn't exist here!"

"Listen, everyone gets annulments!"

"Everyone who lives over here, you mean. The world is much larger than this little country."

"Is it true you've never thought of returning?"

"How could that be true! I've thought about returning thousands of times! During the first years, I did nothing else. Day and night, I thought only of returning. But luckily that illness is curable. I'll come back, of course . . . I suppose I'll come back someday."

"What if you fell in love here?"

" . . ."

"Tell me. What if you fell in love?"

" . . ."

"Can you bring me another *pisco*, Julián? The pitcher's on the table on the terrace."

" . . ."

"You can't treat your husband like that."

"Like what?"

"Come on, Sonia. Don't keep playing this game."

"He's over there with the others and he can't hear us. If I were to get a separation, would you marry me?"

" . . ."

"Answer me. Now you can't use Julián as an excuse."

"I don't need an excuse."

"Tell me, then."

"No. No, I wouldn't get married."

" . . ."

"That's the truth. Forgive me."

"Not to me . . . not to anyone?"

"What's the point of that question? I love you, but I wouldn't marry you."

"You love me? Are you sure about that?"

"Yes, I think I love you."

"Well?"

"Well, what? I have nothing to do here, Sonia. I should never have come. It's the most ridiculous thing I've ever done in my life. Here everything is tense, suffocating, sick . . . it's . . . like tonight . . . even this conversation. I think it's fear. Everyone's afraid. Maybe because they've lost practically everything, they live in fear of losing the last thing they have left, which sometimes is only the hope of having anything at all. Forgive me, Sonia. It has nothing to do with you; it has to do with everyone and everything. I can't stand it anymore."

"What if I went with you? Over there I could study philosophy, like you . . ."

"I don't know, Sonia. The situation was different . . . Right after the coup, they welcomed us with open arms. Now they won't even process tourist visas."

"It would be different if we were married."

"Ah, so that's it!"

"Naturally! I haven't changed so much, and I'm not so scared that I'd want to marry you just to avoid gossip. I'm asking you because it's our only chance to stay together. I know you're not going to stay here. I even know you're not coming back. If only you knew how well I understand you! The only thing I wanted was to dream of the possibility of our being together, far away . . . Yes, only that, maybe . . . To dream for a couple of days . . . like a rest."

"Where's Julián now?"

"He's working at another bank . . ."

"Where is he right now, Sonia?"

"Having another drink."

"Is he watching us?"

"Yes, he's watching us."

"We can discuss this somewhere else, tomorrow, if you want."

"After what you told me, does it make any sense?"

". . ."

"He's heading back here. Lend me your handkerchief. I'm going over to talk to Cecilia."

24

Julián, who seemed annoyed and even irritable to the other members of the trio on the terrace, listened to them silently at first, then filled his glass with *pisco* sour, made some remark or other related to Cecilia's comment about the loan that had allowed them to finish the decorating, explaining that according to the amount and the form, it wasn't a mortgage loan, but rather a simple consumer loan with fixed payments. When Marcela asked him to define the difference, his annoyance was obvious despite his effort to conceal it. He gave a couple of examples relative to minimum amounts for different types of loans, based on the percentage of interest, all of this more attuned to what was taking place on the lawn than to his happenstance students of financial esoterica. Poor Julián has to do this all week long, let him have some fun, Cecilia suggested, defending him and aware of how uncomfortable Julián's arrogant tone had made Marcela and her husband feel. When Julián returned to the garden to rejoin the other trio – now dangerously a duo – Cecilia, who followed him with her eyes, was surprised to see that Sonia brusquely stood up the minute Julián went to sit down in the canvas chair, extended her arm to Andrés, took something white from his hand, and ran toward the terrace. When she reached Cecilia's side, Cecilia saw her raise the handkerchief to her eyes; come here, please, come, and now they hurry across the terrace, passing by Manuel, who keeps fanning the fire and turns his back on the heat in order to follow them with his gaze as they enter the house.

"What's wrong?"

"I want to ask you something."

"Tell me."

"I don't know how to tell you."

"Do you want a glass of water?"

"Yes."

"Berta, please."

". . ."

"Thanks, Berta."

"It'll make you feel better."

"I feel better now. I've stopped choking."

"Is it about Andrés?"

"Yes."

"What's the matter?"

"That's what I'd like to know. He's acting really strange."

"What did he say to you?"

"I don't know what he said to me. But overnight he's turned into a different person. Cold, distant, even annoyed when I ask him certain things. Did you ask him to come with Julia?"

"Yes. I asked him to."

"It would've been better not to invite him."

"I asked you, Sonia, and you told me to invite him. You even told me it would be much better if he came with someone else."

"That's true. And what does that fix?"

"I don't know what you want to fix."

"Where's Julia?"

"I haven't seen her for a while. Berta, have you seen Julia?"

"Yes, señora. She's in the upstairs bathroom."

"Well, it seems like something strange is happening here tonight. Did Andrés say something to you? Something about Julia, I mean?"

"No."

"Why did you ask me about her, then?"

"I don't know. Forgive me. I'm a complete idiot."

"Berta, please go see if Manuel needs anything."

"Yes, señora."

"What's going on, Sonia?"

"What's going on is that I'm crazy, it seems."

"Julián's acting very strange."

"Strange?"

"Worried. Crushed, I would say. What's going on?"

"Nothing's going on."

"Nothing?"

"Yes. That's the worst part. Nothing's going on."

"You want something to drink?"

"No. I don't feel good. I've already had three *piscos*. I'm going to have a huge hangover tomorrow."

"Eat something."

"Yeah, I'm going to eat a potato."

"Eat a hardboiled egg instead, it's the best thing. Look, there they are, on the wooden platter. You haven't told me what happened with Andrés."

"Don't you understand nothing happened?"

"I understand a lot happened, Sonia."

"But he's forgotten that."

"You know he's leaving next week?"

"Yes."

"And?"

"And what?"

"Don't dream about lost causes. It doesn't help."

"You're right. It's just that I hadn't hoped for anything for such a long time."

"I understand, Sonia. I understand you all too well. The same thing happened to me."

"It's not the same thing. You dreamed of this house, and now we're here. What more do you want?"

25

They had to find out what had happened to Julia, of course. It wouldn't do to stand there arguing when their friend had disappeared over an hour ago. Berta, are you sure she locked herself in the bathroom? Yes, señora, in the upstairs bathroom. For such a long time? We'd better go see what's wrong with her, Cecilia. Yes, let's go see, and now they're leaving the kitchen, already at the first step of the winding staircase. Sonia follows behind Cecilia, in order to step on the wider steps, clinging to the wall, supporting herself on the banister, this staircase isn't very steady, she thinks, I don't know how the girls will handle it, and now they've reached the last step. Cecilia puts her index finger to her lips, ssshhhh . . . let's go to my room first, mustn't make the floor creak, mustn't make any noise. Cecilia turns on the light in her pale lavender room, sit over there, she whispers to her friend. They're seated on the loveseat, upholstered in winter-white chintz, the only color that goes with this pretty lavender, Cecilia had explained to all of them less than an hour ago, when they were talking and laughing out loud, looking everything over and discovering this lovely house in amazement, and in the lavender room on the second floor where Cecilia confided to them about her hours of privacy, this decadent form of being alone, and they laughed and nudged each other with their elbows and fell silent when they sensed the men looking at them. What are you women laughing about? Who's gonna tell us the joke? But now they're not laughing anymore, now the two of them are all alone in the lavender room speaking very softly so Julia won't know they've come upstairs, so she won't think they're trying to find out what's wrong with her, because that's exactly what they're after: to find out what's wrong with Julia. Ssshhhh . . . listen, and then they're not only silent, but it seems as though they're trying to achieve such a profound silence that they even stop breathing. They look at each other and then the first sound reaches them as if it were the continuation of a game in which they both start to think, without knowing how . . . that the sound is coming from very far away.

"No, it's coming from right here."

"It can't be."

"What's that noise, Cecilia?"

"Ssshhhh, listen!"

"It's like very soft snoring."

"No. Listen carefully. It's not snoring."

"It's like someone's having trouble breathing."

"Julia?"

"There's no one else here."

"What do you mean, no one?"

"Oh, how silly of me! The girls are here, of course."

"But their room is farther away."

"What could it be, then?"

"I'm going to see."

And she walks on tiptoe to the girls' room, presses her ear to the door, pushes it gently, doesn't turn on the light, stands there, barely illuminated by the bluish light of the streetlamp, that cone of cold light that filters from the street through a gap in the curtains. She remains there a while. There's nothing there. No strange noises. And that? What's that? Is it the same noise, fixed in her ear and her memory? Is it the girls? She goes over to the beds, leans over the older girl, who's asleep, and pulls the covers up; she places her ear against the child's forehead, brushing it with her lips, don't want to wake her, and then the same thing with the younger one: it's more difficult to cover her because the child is on top of the bed, uncovered; the blue light coming through the window shines on her white pajamas; her dark hair outlines an even deeper darkness on the pillow. Cecilia kisses her, rests her face on the little girl's chest, hears nothing but the sleeping child's calm, nearly indistinguishable, breathing. On tiptoe, she retraces her steps; she's at the bedroom door again, turns around to look at them once more, closes the door very slowly, leaving it ajar, advances quickly down the hall toward the lavender room within which a ray of light refracts at an angle between the parquet floor and the wall. She sits down next to her friend.

"Was it the girls?" Sonia asks.

"No."

"I keep hearing the same noise. But now it's like something intermittent. That's not someone crying. It's not Julia."

"So what do you think it is?"

"It's like running water . . ."

"The pipes?"

"Maybe."

13

26

But it wasn't just the fear returning. Although Julia was no longer crying, she still had her eyes buried in the towel, lost in the fragrance of the cologne with which she had drenched the cloth she didn't dare remove from her face. She clung to that palpable, soft, warm security blanket, fragrant now, and the only thing that existed between her and the pain that took her breath away was that blurry, pink presence. She had just vomited again a minute ago, even though she'd thought there was nothing left to throw up. And now she imagines that the recurring stitch in her side is a reflex pain related to her heart. *Matters of the heart* was exactly what her friend Cecilia thought when she became aware of Julia's long absence from the group and Sonia's lively conversation with Andrés in the garden. Matters of the heart: the doctors at the Vicaría had been warning her about it since last year, and her friends knew not only of her physical pains but especially of her breakdown when, alone, with copious tears and sometimes genuine sobs, she finished editing the reports in that impersonal, starched language, the only one that the trial sheets could bear, and which she called "the solicitor's sigh." Yes, matters of the heart, but now she's growing calmer, it's probably all a mistake, a few coincidences, an architectural resemblance between the houses, maybe I'm imagining things, she tells herself, removing the towel from her nose, leaning her face toward the faucet, which now shoots its cold stream into the sink; that's it, that's better, she feels relieved, how silly I am, any day now I'll be the one to kick the bucket, I can't go on like this, what a fright my face is, now the water's nice and warm, it's getting warmer, something's getting warmer, her eyes are pure fire, devoid of tears, two red plumes, the trace of a bird that has abandoned its nest forever, leaving that impression of empty sockets, those two pink stains the same color as the towel, the color of tears, the color of those insubstantial feathers lost in a frightened canary's wake; what was the use of spending all afternoon doing her makeup, going to the beauty parlor that morning, plucking her eyebrows, worrying about those little black spots on her skin that weren't even there anymore? If he saw me like this, he wouldn't recognize me. What a beauty! Andrés had flirted as soon as she opened the door for him, I'm starting to like that Vicaría with its lady lawyers who look like movie stars, and that little gambit before the first *pisco* sour, before asking about her son, asking her, really, if her son was home, to find out if they were alone. And just look at the movie star now, a mess with red eyes, outlined with dark misery, those other dregs that resemble the dregs of the soul. And then, when there's no reality but her pathetic face in the mirror, a slight shifting of her gaze, as minute as the hidden noise in the pipes, she's forced to look at what's behind her face: another image reflected in the mirror, enveloped in the steam of the hot water streaming from the faucet. And there, from the fog that clouds the glass, right next to Julia's ear, almost kissing her, from a barely perceptible sound of water, from that moan emanating from the pipes, she sees Chelita watching her from the tub with eyes as drained of tears as her own. Very quickly she cleans the haze off the mirror, convinced she can make her disappear: on the clean surface of the mirror, there can be no ambiguities or meaningless visions. But nonetheless, she's there again, even more clearly delineated, more present than in all the sessions at the Vicaría, more deeply submerged in the tub. Chelita? she asks in a thread of a voice that doesn't even leave her breath on the mirror, such a silent murmur, such a hushed question, uttered so as not to destroy the hope that it might all be a dream.

27

"I practically killed myself getting here, Julia. The plaza is impossible with all the tear gas. Look at my eyes. I waited in the hall for a while so I wouldn't come into your office crying."

She thinks she's in my office, then.

"Do you feel better here, Chelita?"

"Much better. But I'm still half choking."

"Drink this coffee. It'll do you good. Drink it nice and slowly; that will help you stop choking. That way you'll get rid of the effects of the gas. That's right, that's right, like that."

"I was choking when I got here. My eyes are the least of it. I know that's what happens. But not being able to breathe is awful."

"This time I won't offer you a cigarette, then."

"No, don't even mention it. I can hardly catch my breath. But I'm going to ask you for another coffee. I'm freezing."

"You're soaking wet, Chelita! I hadn't noticed . . ."

"Well, yes. Just as I was crossing the plaza, they started to douse us from the cars. I still feel like I'm being hit by the water cannon."

She thinks she's in my office. She doesn't realize she's in a bathtub full of water.

"Take this towel, Chelita. You'll get sick if you stay like that. I'll go see if I can get you some dry clothes."

"No, don't bother. Don't bring me anything, for God's sake. If they catch me with this, they'll put me on the grill."

Where's Chelita, then? Where does she think she is? Where am I?

"Well, I'm going to write down everything you tell me, just as I do every morning. But first I'll bring you some dry clothes."

"Don't leave me alone. I beg you, *hijita.*"

"All right. I'm going to look for some documents in the desk, so I'll turn my back to you. Meanwhile take off your blouse, and I'll hand you my vest."

"It's hard to believe these things happen."

"Take off the wet stuff; you might get sick. Take this, put it on. It's nice and warm. That's it. See how much better that is? How do you feel? Now you could use another cup of coffee. I'll give you one of the big cups. Do you feel better?"

"Much better."

"As soon as you feel all right, we'll begin."

"I'm all right now. What a way to drench us! I feel like I'm still in the water."

Is this what I'm hearing? Where is she? Where am I?

"Where were we, Chelita? What were you telling me? Oh, now I remember. That protest when they drenched you from head to foot."

"I was on my way over here. The water caught me by surprise."

She's stirring the water with her hand, making little waves, like a child playing in the bath.

"Well, then . . . what should we do, Chelita?"

"Well, just take down what I tell you, as usual. In case it does some good. In case you people discover where that house is."

"Let me put some paper in the typewriter."

"Why does the paper have those lines?"

"Because they're trial sheets."

"Trial?"

"That's what they're called. It's the kind of paper they use at trials. I call them the 'solicitor's sigh.'"

"That's Neruda . . . from *Joaquín Murieta*, right?"

"That's wonderful, Chelita! Oh, what a dope I am, you're the teacher! Are you ready?"

"Ready, *mijita.*"

"And then?"

"Then they took us to the bathtub. That was whenever they couldn't get a word out of us, when we couldn't tell them what they wanted to hear because we didn't know what they expected us to tell them. They took us upstairs from the basement to one of the bathrooms in the house. We had to climb a lot of steps. First, the eight steep steps, touching that rough wall, all bumpy, like concrete without stucco. Then a long landing, a few paces on the wooden floor, then some tiles, we felt them with the soles of our feet, don't forget they always kept us barefoot, and after a few shoves, they grabbed us by the arms and we knew that the next flight of stairs began there. Those steps weren't as steep, and we had already figured out that it was better to stay toward the right, because that's where the steps were wider."

"A winding staircase?"

"I guess so."

"And then?"

"At the top of that winding staircase, they let go of our arms and pushed us so we'd know which direction to walk in. When we felt the tiles again, we knew that all the bathroom business was coming."

"And what was all the bathroom business, Chelita?"

"That was one of the worst things."

"I'm taking it all down: tell me very slowly."

"They stuck us in here, in the bathroom, and they left us alone for a long time, because the fear of what was coming was part of the torture. Imagine. We knew we'd come out of here half dead. Sometimes doctors even came to check if we were dead or alive."

"How do you know they were doctors, Chelita?"

"Well, because we heard them: What do you think, doctor? Can we keep going, or should we leave this bitch for tomorrow? That's what they would say."

"And what did they do to you?"

"Well, they called it 'the submarine.' "

"They stuck your head in the tub?"

"We already were in the tub."

"Why do you say *we*? Were you ever with someone else in the tub?"

"No. I say *we* because we knew someone else would be next, and then someone else . . . And when the water was low and they had to refill the tub, it was because they had already done the same thing before."

"And what happened, then?"

"At first you thought they were going to kill you by suffocation, but after a few times we realized it was to make us suffer more."

"How many of them were with you in the bathroom?"

"I . . . I don't know. Remember, we were blindfolded. But it was never just one of them. There were several, really. I'd say two or three, sometimes more than three. You could tell by their different voices. And because they didn't all laugh the same way. And probably some of them didn't even laugh, poor things. I think some of them were forced to be there."

"They were men."

"No, not just men."

"But almost always men . . ."

"No, just at the beginning. Remember, Julita, I was there a long time. I'd say it changed, and toward the end there were more women than men torturing us."

"Are you sure, Chelita?"

"Not really. But I can tell you that some women were worse than the men. They knew us better. They knew our weak points."

"And in the bathtub?"

"They knew that we screamed more than normal."

"How so?"

"Well, a man is always moved or frightened by a woman's screams. The women who tortured us were different. They told us we could scream all we wanted, they weren't impressed."

"And you screamed a lot."

"Of course. It was a way to defend ourselves."

"How is it that no one on the street could hear your screams? The screams from the basement couldn't be heard, naturally, but how could they torture you in the bathroom without the screams waking up the neighborhood? Bathrooms need windows."

"This bathroom didn't have one."

"How do you know that, Chelita?"

"Because after the session, they would leave. You'd stay there, thanking God you were alive, all filled up with water inside . . . we got rid of it by heaving, like vomiting and choking all together, we could hardly breathe. Gradually, we got up, feeling along the edge of the tub, leaning against the wall. And that wall was continuous, I don't think there was any window."

28

Definitive proof was missing, of course, the knife in the back. How could anyone really believe that these were hallucinations on Julia's part, another way to remain entangled in the depositions she heard at the Vicaría, those mountains of folders of dubious destination – or very clear destination whenever a protection order is processed in any of the courts: useless efforts, defeats that collectively deprived her of more than sleep – fat folders with tales that could leave even the most unscrupulous gasping . . . and the chain of repetitive images every night in the darkness, unable to sleep, unable to rest, invaded, occupied, trespassed upon like a house in which the faces and gestures of pain have taken up residence inside her, prepared to remain forever. And so the faces of those women, so different from the others and from each other, go passing by, and among them Chelita with her torn stockings, the dab of lipstick now coloring her mouth, so silent, omitting so much. And then she awakens from that half-sleep to which she's become accustomed, it's not sleep, she tells herself, I don't sleep anymore, I enter the darkness and I hear voices, the voices of my women, all their voices, and she realizes that presence in the air, that other music, those words naming the darkest part of darkness, is what most resembles sleep. And when those voices appear with their faces, a hand brushing a lock of hair from a forehead, another slowly removing a handkerchief from a purse and spreading it on a thigh only to soak it in tears, then, with those images, Julia enters, not only into a sleep that isn't sleep, but a sleep that doesn't deserve that name, and so she describes it. And because she's described it for so long, since that day now forgotten in the haze of repetition, of eternal sameness, even those same faces and those same voices repeated to the point of desperation, because she's described it forever, it's surprising to find a pair of friendly eyes looking at her suspiciously, incredulously, more focused on her symptoms than on what she's telling them. Just like what's happening tonight: again she's told one of those stories that provoke inquisitive looks, veiled skepticism, pure pain . . . in essence, pity toward her. How can you get well if you yourself admit you don't sleep? How can you go on like this if you don't take care of yourself? How are we supposed to believe you when you say tomorrow you'll see the doctor, tomorrow you'll ask for a leave of absence, tomorrow you'll go to the beach for a few days? How are we supposed to believe you? How can we believe you tonight? *What about the eight steps to the basement?* There are thousands of basements with eight steps. *And how did I recognize it beforehand? How did I hear the voices again? How could I know there were eight before I went downstairs?* I don't know, I don't know, there's probably some explanation, but just because you imagined eight steps, we're not going to keep this up; you've got to get out, you've got to take care of yourself, you're not well, Julia. *And how do you explain the stains on the walls?* Because it was an abandoned house, old, occupied by old people, just like Cecilia told us. *But she never saw that for herself; that's what she supposed.* And you're supposing, too. Or do you have some proof, some evidence? *And everything I'm telling you, isn't that proof enough?* Tell us more; these things aren't proof. *What about the iron door with the peephole? Why would they install an iron door with a peephole?* Because everyone's afraid. *Would those crazy old women Cecilia describes have put in a barracks door, and with a peephole, besides, that they couldn't even reach by standing on a step? Did those crazy old women ruin the house and the yard? Did they ruin it?* Probably not, they probably didn't exist either, Julia, but the fact that they may not have ever existed doesn't confirm your suspicions. They don't confirm them at all; Manuel is right. Yes, he's right. You need proof. How are you going to file a deposition without proof . . . definitive proof, I mean.

And then the proof, incontrovertible proof, emerged. It wasn't inside the house . . . but yes, it was there, too: it wasn't the steps to the basement, or the stains on the walls, or the burn marks on the parquet floor, or the front door with the peephole, or the noises of the street fair, or the pealing of the church bells, or the shouts and activity at recess, or the punctual repetition of those other bells from the school. Someone asked a question that shifted things from the nervous, slightly offensive dismissals of one argument or another to more solid terrain: questions that would reveal how Andrés's house ended up in the calamitous condition in which they had found it and how it passed from that state of neglect into the hands of those who restored it. What was the renter's name, Andrés? Do you remember? Of course not; in all these years, I never knew how many renters there were or who was the last one; I simply received the money at a branch of the Deutsche Bank in Berlin, religiously, every month. Did a real estate agent send it to you? No, my brother did; he was in charge of the house. Is the house yours? It belongs to both of us; when our folks were left alone, we bought them the house in Condell, which was smaller, more comfortable, and in better condition, and we kept this one, and then we rented it to a couple with several children; they owned a rotisserie restaurant in Ñuñoa, and it was perfect for them because it was so close to their work. I'm sure they lived here till '73. And afterward? Do you remember what happened after that? Well, then I left, and after a while, my brother told me he had rented out the house and that he thought it was fair to send me the sum total of the rent money to help me while my situation abroad got straightened out, even though the house belonged to both of us. So Sergio rented out the house? That's right, unless he handed it over to a rental agency, but I understand he didn't. We need to ask him who rented the house from him. Right now? Yes, why not right now? Do you want me to call him, Cecilia? Of course, Andrés, call him right away, and then Andrés went to the phone in the little room on the first floor, with everyone hanging on the conversation. Apparently something was wrong; Sergio seemed to be holding back because Andrés became more animated. We're all walking on hot coals here; you've got to come over. You can still go to Viña tonight; we only need you for a few minutes and then you can go. She can wait for you, make her understand, yes, you can bring her along. All of us here want to talk to you, understand? Well, okay, one hour. But please don't take longer than an hour. And since everyone had overheard the conversation through the open door to the little room, Andrés only needed a single sentence to explain the conversation: "He's coming; it'll take him an hour because he's leaving directly for Viña from here. He's taking his girlfriend to the Casino."

147

What a louse, Cecilia blurted out in obvious jest, exaggerating the terse comment in the extreme, almost shouting, which relaxed the tension a bit, although only for a minute or so. He told me he couldn't come to the barbecue because he had to turn in an investment report on Monday. I even begged him to come, just for a little while, saying that for better or for worse we owed the house to him, that he'd enjoy seeing it all fixed up, just like new, remembering when they lived here as kids . . . But he told me he thought it was practically impossible, that he'd make an effort, anyway; friends are friends, was what that louse said.

But following the laughter everything fell once more into a silence that grew as the pauses became longer, and the same questions and the same arguments grew briefer from constant repetition. In any case the suspension of judgment, the wait of an hour or so in order to find out what had taken place in that house during those last few years and especially who the last tenant had been, created a different mood. Cecilia went upstairs to see if the girls were still asleep, since the grown-ups had become quite loud without realizing it; even Andrés's conversation with his brother had gotten louder, and Andrés, now less agitated, served himself another drink, this time a whisky that Manuel offered him, because if you're going to stick with *pisco* all night, you'll have a pretty good hangover tomorrow. And so the Johnnie Walker won by a clear majority; nothing relaxes you like whisky, Sonia said, pouring the amber-colored stream over ice. But it makes you calmer, it's a better sedative, if you drink it straight, Manuel told her. John Wayne style, Cristián added, and so, little by little, without noticing, they began to relax. Someone ventured to ask about the meat: don't worry, it's all marinated and ready, just a matter of throwing it on the grill. What about the fire? The fire had already turned into smoking embers, without heat or glow, the pathetic harbinger of ashes. It'll have to be fanned; I'll do it, Manuel said, positioning himself beneath the bulb that attracted the fluttering of the moths. Now everything's back on track, it'll all be cleared up when Sergio arrives, Cristián says, very piously. The first thing he's going to clear up is why he lied to me, why he didn't come, what does he mean by leaving town to go to the Casino tonight, Cecilia emphasizes.

Maybe he was embarrassed, since his girlfriend doesn't know us; she doesn't know anyone here, Sonia says, still standing next to Andrés, still distant and cold toward Julián, increasingly distant with each passing minute, not even cold anymore, simply nothing now, as if he didn't exist. As if for all of them, downing another round of drinks and recapturing the reason for the barbecue, Julia didn't exist either, Julia's left us again, Manuel says after a while, less surprised this time. You go look for her this time, Andrés, Cecilia says, I was upstairs with her already; I dragged her out of the bathroom once, now you try, it's not easy, and Andrés sets his glass down, goes into the house, heads toward the stairs, and turning around, sees that Sonia is following him as if she were his most recent guilt, his newest shadow.

14

29

They waited for him for over an hour. Around midnight, like an old Santa Claus minus his Christmas Eve and gifts and without the bright red outfit, but sporting a slightly graying beard, a stately demeanor, and a ring of flab beginning to bulk up his body, smiling like a Christmas vision, full of wisecracks and worldliness for the first fifteen minutes only to collapse into an alternating series of frenzy and silences, he surprised them with his belated appearance, his double-breasted white suit, his stone-colored sport shirt unbuttoned, the tongue of his magenta handkerchief sticking out of his breast pocket. This presence, incongruous in and of itself, created quite an impression against the less-spectacular ambience of the barbecue; the party-goers were dressed simply for enjoying a good piece of meat under the trees in a peaceful backyard, not for partying in one of the gaming rooms of the Casino. Yes, he was dazzling. But in truth he was much less dazzling than his blonde consort, who looked like she had just stepped out of the display window of an exclusive boutique. I'd like you to meet Ivette, you've heard me mention my friend Ivette, and the lovely Ivette smiles and nods pleasantly, takes control of the situation, kisses the women on the cheek and offers her face to receive the same kiss from the men, moving with exquisite elegance among the chairs that have piled up on the tiled terrace, far from the lawn, which is becoming covered with dew, and closer to the embers languishing in the barbecue pit. It's as though he brought her along to justify himself, Manuel thinks. So he won't have to offer an explanation for lying, Cecilia agrees, silently. So that Ivette's pure essence, her simply being there with that figure, that broad, confident smile, that self-possessed, alert look, would be the best justification for the lie, everyone thinks, after admiring her; the evidence, the in-your-face reason, the *habeas corpus* argument that explained why he would have rather spent that night with Ivette, in Viña, specifically, risking it all on roulette and cards, games that are invigorated by a bottle of champagne in an apartment bedroom, games that penetrate the most nocturnal substance of surprise, the real bounty of that lubricious night – filled with caresses, kisses, saliva, Andrés thinks, steering his imagination so the affair will end up docked at that harbor.

The questions Sergio was expecting – and had been expecting for a long time even though the bewildered faces that night may have been different from those he had imagined – sprang from all corners of the room where they gathered when Cecilia suggested it was starting to get cold out there. All the questions hinged on how the house had come into Cecilia and Manuel's hands, why they had found it in such a run-down condition, who was the first to rent it when Andrés left for Germany. Or had there been other renters later on, and was what happened to the house their fault?

Sergio answers each one of the questions, listening very calmly, although later they interrupt his explanations more often; he speaks as if he wants to disassociate himself from something that's over and done with for him – but he understands that he must explain; there are people who have taken a while to become acquainted with certain forgotten events – and now and then he directs an intense gaze in Ivette's direction, smiles at her, with coy winks and gestures that mean it won't be long now, we'll leave soon, just be patient.

The month after Andrés left the Colombian Embassy for Germany, the former renters announced they were going to move out. At that point Sergio put an ad in the newspaper, thinking the rental would provide some extra income for his folks, for whom that sum came in handy, although it wasn't much. But in those days it wasn't easy to rent out or sell property; there were too many places available, something that had evidently never happened before; lots of people were leaving, selling, renting, mortgaging their property in order to buy tickets out of the country for entire families.

For months nothing happened. No one was interested. The ad didn't even appear in the paper anymore.

Then I got a letter from you, the one where you told me how hard it was to go from East Berlin to the west side, how you were having problems getting exit visas, and that those who could pay with dollars could get permission more quickly. It was something like that, if I'm remembering correctly, Sergio says.

Andrés nods, gesturing with his head, glancing at Ivette's green gaze as she takes in this strange family reunion, baffled.

In order to help his brother out of that bind, Sergio placed a rental ad, and one morning a very respectable-looking couple showed up at his office at the Stock Exchange, both of them around thirty, people who looked more sporty than intellectual, self-employed professionals, they said, before asking a series of questions about the house.

"We met right here that afternoon. They explored the whole place, looked around many times, and I had the impression they were really interested. The next morning they returned to my office to finalize the rental agreement. They didn't ask for anything; they didn't object to the three months' security deposit I asked them for so I could send a larger amount to Berlin, because I understood you needed it more than our folks, and that's why I felt I needed to send you the whole amount of the rental, not just the share that was yours. I want you to understand that in those days I had just started working at the Stock Exchange; my job was quite different, nothing like what I'm doing now, and my income was very modest."

Andrés nods again, makes a new gesture with his head, this time indicating comprehension and gratitude; someone helps himself to a drink; Manuel goes into the kitchen, asks Berta to bring out the little bar cart with the ice, returns to his place; everyone becomes impatient at this unnecessary interruption; they all want to hear; they all have their eyes fixed on Sergio, who pauses, trying to remember correctly, wanting to be precise, smiling at Ivette.

"That's how the house was rented out. I never saw them again. They were never late with a payment. Not a single neighbor ever complained about anything."

Three months after turning the house over to the new renters, while on vacation walking along the beach in La Serena, Sergio ran across the man, but the guy didn't greet him. He didn't recognize him, or else he didn't want to. That same afternoon he saw him again, this time sitting on a bench on the promenade, watching the sunset. Sergio noticed that the man was with a different woman and a boy of around ten, and he imagined that must have been the reason for his attitude.

"But that didn't trouble me too much, since he always paid on time. The serious part happened a couple of months later, when I saw the picture in the paper. That afternoon I was at the barbershop, and while I waited my turn like everybody else, I was reading those old magazines they leave there for people who are waiting. At that time the creation of the Women's Military Police Corps in certain parts of Santiago was causing quite a stir, do you remember?"

"Yes, of course, the *Pacas*."

"Yes, right: that's the name they gave them right away: the *Pacas*."

"And do you remember how they ran those information booths right in the middle of Paseo Ahumada? Well, it so happens that in the magazine I was reading, there was a story about these women and a photo of the woman who had rented the house from me. The caption said, I remember it word for word, that she was one of the instructors of the newly created corps. Her named was included, too: a different one, of course, nothing like the one she gave me the afternoon they came to look at the house."

"So you rented it to military police?" Sonia asks, rather aggressively, annoyed by how this might affect Andrés.

"Of course, but how was I supposed to know? They know how to do these things; if I had seen them show up in uniform, it would've been different."

"But I suppose after you found out . . ."

"After I found out," Sergio interrupted, "I was very conflicted. I suspected something could happen to us, not right then, or even in the following months, but I couldn't get my mind off the house. I even had nightmares; I knew that that house had been rented in a very strange way."

"You must've wondered why, I imagine," Cecilia slips in, also annoyed.

"Sure, I could imagine why; people talked about those things every day, so one afternoon – it was Saturday, I remember – a day like today, also at the end of October, I came by to take a look and see what was going on in the house."

"How long after?" his brother asks him.

"Not long after . . . a month, if I'm not mistaken, no more than a month, anyway."

And Marcela: "What did you see?"

"Yes, could you see anything?" Manuel asks.

"Of course, I could see. I remember I was driving by slowly, frightened, to tell the truth, and I was so shocked I almost hit a tree. It was as if the house had disappeared. As if it were no longer there, you understand? As if they had skipped over it in the line of houses along the block. It was no longer that house with a half-wall and a fence and a wooden front door. What happened was they had changed the entire front wall and put in this same gate you're looking at right now, walled in with iron or whatever it is, and the door was also metal, with a peephole, and everything was very high with no openings; it was impossible to see anything inside. Then I realized that it had to be . . . well, . . . what it was, you know?" And he looks at Ivette, no longer smiling, and he runs right into the blonde's cold gaze, a gaze that emphasizes her paleness and clouds her expression.

"And what did you do then?"

"Nothing, at first. I was very frightened; I knew that it was a time bomb; I didn't get anything done. The truth is, I didn't want to know those houses existed . . . and it wasn't difficult, in those years; they didn't have any of the magazines that circulate today, so whenever they said anything on the Cooperativa radio station, right away someone turned it off or looked for some music; it's easy in the car, the radio's always within reach of your hand, and whenever the subject came up in conversation at friends' houses, I would walk away, pretend I didn't hear; I didn't want to know anything more about that business. Until one day, after receiving the rent payment, I decided to phone the number on the envelope, part of the letterhead of a real estate firm. I didn't speak to the renters in person, of course, but I left a message saying I had something urgent to tell them concerning the house and urging them to contact me as soon as possible. The next day, in the afternoon, the same couple who had rented the house showed up."

"Why do you say 'couple'?" Cecilia asks.

"Because that's what I thought they were at the beginning."

"A couple of agents, that's what they were," Sonia says.

"Of course, there's no doubt about that now, but put yourself in my position. I'm telling you about something that happened ten years ago, we're talking about '74 or '75, in any case before 1980. You collected the dollars in Berlin, and thanks to that you were able to cross over to the western side every day, work on your doctoral dissertation at the Hispanic American Institute or whatever it's called, that's what you said in your letters, remember; besides, I never touched a cent of the rent money from that house, which also belonged to me."

"And what did the 'couple' tell you that afternoon?" Andrés inquires.

"They got right to the point. They knew what my concerns were, and they threatened me."

"How?" Andrés asks.

"They threatened me because of you," Sergio spits into his face.

"They found out I was in exile," Andrés concludes.

"Don't be naïve, Andrés, they knew that from the start; if they hadn't, they would have never laid eyes on that house."

"But what did they say to you? Tell us, don't get sidetracked," Cecilia prods.

"Well, it seems they had dug a big hole in the garden. And they found your books, Andrés. They let me know about it the afternoon they responded to my call. They even made it clear to me that it would be very easy for them simply to take possession of the house without so many formalities, to use force."

You saw it coming, didn't you? they told him. Or were you blind? Fortunately, now these things are being done everywhere; no more pussyfooting, international threats have no effect, nobody has the right to interfere in Chilean internal affairs. Aren't you going to thank us for this gesture of courtesy? Don't you see that your brother has placed you in danger, that he doesn't care about your future at all? In a word: he's off living quite happily in a communist country . . . and, they added, not even that was a guarantee of impunity: we have long arms, they repeated, you know it, so if you want to protect your brother, it would be much better if we just forgot all this. Or would he rather endanger his brother? Did he want to put himself at risk?

"At first I couldn't understand how a few simple books could cause such a fuss," Sergio continues, "but then I realized that my brother's philosophy books weren't simple books . . . or rather, they were, but only everywhere else, not in Chile in those days."

And he also realized that where they had found the books, they could have found, or tomorrow they might find, something much more damning, and if there wasn't anything there, nothing would prevent them from placing, next to volumes of Marx or Che, a nice package of explosives or a few Czech-manufactured weapons, which the army possessed in abundance and displayed next to the red and black flags, hammers and sickles, and ski masks whenever an explanation was needed for "a raid in which extremist elements were brought down, fortunately without consequences for the forces of law and order." In his nightmares he can still hear the voice of authority threatening, advising, protecting him, reminding him of his brother's precarious situation, recommending that he not breathe a word of this to anyone, let's see if we've made ourselves understood . . .

"That was the last thing they said to me."

"Holy shit! The old witches were just *pacos!*" Sonia exclaims, grabbing her head, bending forward until it touches her knees.

"So then they weren't Donoso-style old ladies," Manuel concludes.

"It could be called *The Green House*, then," Cecilia jokes, not smiling.

"You're always so good at interpreting everything through books," says Manuel, taking another drink.

15

30

Some decisions are the result of an overwhelming impulse: we surprise ourselves in the midst of acting on them; we perceive them as actions divorced from reason and even from will; something overtakes us, and we can't help following through, dealing with the consequences later, climbing the winding staircase to the top without realizing it; getting there, just as Cecilia got to the girls' room that night, avoiding the light switch, the light. Was it simply to avoid waking them? Or to avoid seeing what looked like a lash mark in her memory? The stains that the burns had left in the floor, those black circles on the parquet, evidence no longer there because Maestro Barraza had been efficient in scraping down the floors. Hadn't she just boasted of that to her friends? No stains, nothing to detract from the miracle. The parquet: waxed, shiny, without history. So she doesn't turn on the light. She doesn't want to dislodge the tenuous, conspiratorial clarity, the light barely filtering in from the street, sharing the rhythm of the leaves' shadows, a motion that enters the girls' room, brushing against their bed, a motion that intensifies the swaying of the tree on the street. And in the midst of the barely moving, minimal light, she accelerates her own rhythm, walks to the closet, opens it violently, stands on tiptoe to pull out a blanket, and then another, from the highest shelf, and without closing it again – the blue light coming from the street continues to sway the tree branches on the freshly painted surface of the doors – goes over to her older daughter's bed, bundles her, still deeply asleep, in the blanket, wrapping her in that warm pelt, that second, warm skin that covers her, protects her, saves her, and then repeats the process with the little one, the one who sleeps on top of the sheets, the one whose shimmering nightgown receives the light of the moon or of the streetlamp in a kind of premature morning. Now the two of them are protected; now they're safe; now she has to go downstairs without anyone's noticing, without their discovering her in the flight that can hardly be explained, because she herself doesn't understand it. She has to go downstairs without their noticing, without waking the girls, preferably without turning on the light on the stairs, although the yellowish brightness coming from the landing scarcely reaches the steps to the second floor, and here she goes, trying to carry both of them, but she can't, it would be dangerous to go downstairs that way, she needs to grasp the banister, it's dark. Then she leaves the little one in bed and grabs the blanket bundled around the older one, advances with her toward the staircase, starts descending one step at a time, touching the next step with her toe before stepping down completely, testing the waters, her father used to say, why remember that now? testing the waters, danger, dying of fright, but she's almost there now, just three or four steps, we're getting there, she feels the child's warm breath on her cheek, like a sweet tickling combined with the soft wool of the blanket, now we're downstairs, now the voices coming from the patio sound more distinct, no single voice approaching, Manuel's is somewhat closer, chatting with Julián in front of the barbecue, Sonia and Marcela's voices are a bit more distant, wait just another second, and at last she deposits the child on the wooden seat next to the mirror on the landing. Then she quickly climbs the stairs two at a time, walks over to the closet, lost deep inside, hidden by the open doors that continue receiving the slow movement of the tree's shadows on their brand-new coat of white paint. She gropes for one of her jackets, finds it, recognizes it, feels around in it, looking for something, and finally pulls out the car keys, sticks them in her pants pocket, takes a thick suede coat from its hanger, puts it on with a despairing gesture that combines with another despairing gesture, her quick movement toward the bed so she can carry the younger girl, how light she is, she's grateful for the relief. Now she can descend more quickly; one hand around the blanket is enough, the other hand sliding quickly down the wooden banister, now she's almost at the bottom step, she hears the voices from the patio, conversing more intensely, you can tell from the sound that they're arguing, some voices are raised, a harsh tone, she's about to do it. Berta, Berta, come here, please, and now she's in the kitchen with the younger girl in her arms, suffering Berta's astonished expression. Could you please help me? Yes, señora. Take the baby to the car, don't let her wake up. Yes, señora, and the maid takes the child with a gesture that's a continuation of the same concern, the same complicity, and seeing her standing in the doorway of the kitchen not yet understanding what's going on, Cecilia indicates with a gesture that she'll take care of the older one now, and Berta understands, steps out of her way; with the child in her arms, Cecilia proceeds toward the door to the front yard, the other exit from the kitchen to the paved parking lot. Berta watches her employer walking with the girl wrapped in the red and black checkered blanket, approaching the car; Cecilia opens the front door, lifts the button, opens the back door, places her in there, careful, Berta, don't let her wake up. Yes, señora. Now the child is in the backseat, halfway across. Move her farther down; she wants Berta to leave room for the older one. Of course, señora, she's okay there. Yes, they're both okay, now go back to the kitchen and make sure everything's all right, do you think there's enough salad? Yes, señora, don't worry, I can make some more if there's not enough. Good, now open the door for me. Yes, señora. She sits behind the wheel, puts the key in the ignition, turns around to see her sleeping daughters. Yes, they're sound asleep; she turns on the motor, the headlights, illuminating Berta's blue apron, her black hair, her surprised face. I'll be back later, she tells her. If Manuel asks where I am, tell him I took the girls to my dad's place.

31

But why to her dad's house? Did she already know this as she climbed the stairs, determined to take the girls from that room and from that house? Cecilia not only asks herself if she knew then – only a few minutes ago – what her destination would be in the escape, but she even wonders if something resembling the escape, a quick departure in the middle of the night, a rejection of what was irrevocably lost, a desperate opting for her point of departure, a return to her father, to her childhood home, to the little tables with photos here and there of her dead mother, wasn't something that had been decided long ago, long before the renovation, long before the gift, a very long time before the house. Something she had wanted to do but repressed several times in the apartment on Pedro de Valdivia, on those solitary nights to which she had grown accustomed, which at first she tolerated and later desired, when she no longer heard music coming from Berta's room, and Manuel's footsteps painted their last drops of bitterness on the kitchen tiles. Every so often Cecilia would hear the noise of the refrigerator – the metallic tremor, the shiver of the motor – and hearing the door open, she visualized the white wine's return to its compartment and Manuel's return to bed. In truth, it hadn't been a marriage bed, a place of companionship and desire, for a long time. For the last few months it had been the place where Cecilia longed for company at night, but that's something different, she thinks now, stopping at a red light. This signal takes forever. Could it be broken? I have to be more careful, she thinks; I can't even remember how I got here. Nonetheless, she honks the horn, an absurd gesture because there's no one in front of her, just the red light staring at her from atop the traffic signal, impassable. How strange to be there, far from the new house, far from her home, freezing with the girls in a lonely car on that Saturday night, watching the slow red light, a light that seems determined to block her way forever. Hadn't they envisioned something very different? Hadn't they dreamed for the past few weeks of a party with friends, of a juicy, fragrantly seasoned roast, of *pisco* and wine, which would raise the temperature of the night, content in their new home, happy in that insistent pursuit of happiness that their repaired relationship represented? Another car comes along, respecting the wait demanded by the traffic signal. Now it's pulled up alongside her. She looks out of the corner of her eye and manages to see a group of youngsters. The windows of both cars are rolled up, but she can still hear the music faintly from the neighboring car. She recalls the music that emanated, equally tenuously, from the kitchen in their apartment, from Berta's room, from Manuel's solitary, unapproachable brooding. She remembers they had thought of dancing that night, retro music, a return to old times, to memory, to the only thing that was still young. The Platters, Frankie Lane. Do you remember? Do you remember, Manuel, alone now in your new house, trying to explain to your friends what you yourself don't understand? Because she feels it's no longer her house, and in some way she knows that from this night on, nothing related to the house will be the same. Finally, the green light, the kids' car pulls ahead, passing her immediately. Cecilia is annoyed by the sudden, sharp squealing of their tires, the arrogance, the noisy stupidity. She doesn't want to hurry; yes, she does, what she doesn't want is to endanger the girls, on the street you can see there's more traffic, Irarrázaval is livelier on Saturday night, there are more cafés, more bars, there are movie theaters and plazas and intersections with trees and timid streetlamps that invite embraces, caresses. She's hardly paying attention to the street, but she knows that the backdrop of her flight is Saturday night on Irarrázaval. What she doesn't want to do is hurry. Although she does want to get to her father's house soon. But what does she really want? Why her father's house? Cecilia knows that for a long time, moments and words and rejections that she can't even remember clearly, hanging over her and her marriage, even during the good times of her marriage – there's been this force, this magnet, this prolonged seduction: the idea of an unavoidable return to her father's house. That's why, when she felt the pull that compelled her to undertake this flight, to remove her daughters hurriedly from the house and put them in the backseat of the car, in some vague although paradoxically clear way, it meant that the flight that night wasn't an escape, but rather a return. A return, planned forever ago, to her father's house. A house that, when you thought about it, was her own house, her first house, the house of her childhood, the house-nest, but also the house-flight, the house where she pronounced her first no, the house of her naïve rebellion and her closely observed transgression, yes, closely observed by her own father. The house that was good to leave but not because she had ceased being good; the house it was good to return to without implying that leaving it had been bad.

32

But that wasn't the house she was thinking of. The house from which she fled that Saturday night with her daughters is the other one, the new house, the renovated one, the one they saw two months ago in deplorable condition, deplorable for reasons Cecilia can finally understand. It hadn't been a few cat-loving women and some incense that precipitated the crumbling of that witch's mansion. No, they weren't the ones, the ones she had invented with her bookish imagination, ghostly old women shackled in that dismal Ñuñoan mansion, who had ruined the spacious garden and allowed the gladiolus and lilacs to wither, who had permitted the orange trees to die and let the walnut tree end up inhabited by dark creatures who fed on its sap or on the sticky slipperiness that oozed from its arteries to the cracked scabbiness of its trunk, consuming it entirely, nearly killing it. They weren't the ones who went up and down screeching, terrorizing, from the basement to the attic, drunken with sadism and death, no; the denizens of her imagination were not the guilty parties. Not they and not the house, she thinks, her eyes fixed now on the avenue swallowed up by her headlights, salvaging more and more asphalt from the shadows, more tree silhouettes, more foliage swayed by the wind, more garbage and sheets of newspaper and packs of cigarettes and plastic bags and empty jars and beer cans and dirty rags, detritus that in the stream of her headlights achieves its final splendor, like a blinded rabbit, an instant sign of its sojourn in the world before dying in the gutter. Then Cecilia understands that the poor house had been taken apart too, that in some way it, too, had been violated, and Andrés's memory of

164

it had been betrayed, poor thing, so pale and unable to say a word since the moment he found out, such an educated European gesture demonstrating the enormity of our barbarity; perhaps the same gesture as on a Sunday morning in Buchenwald before the deserted plaza of the concentration camp, the interminable barracks, the chimney of the crematorium, as he described it to them over the first round of drinks. And then he sees that the house, the thing that is still his house, was also a victim of that barbarity, a ship that sank with its involuntary crew of supplicants tied to their beds, immersed in the freezing bathtub, capsizing toward a dark sea floor. And she, hadn't she noticed that afternoon when she saw it for the first time, that the house was wounded? It was dirty, and now she knew what those stains that looked like barbecue sauce were, the reddish trickle like burst tomatoes, not just against the walls of the kitchen, but everywhere. And also the wound in the parquet in the girls' bedroom. Or wasn't that a wound? The burn mark that keeps burning in her memory. And then she tries to discover the exact moment when the coincidence took place. A fluke, perhaps? A simple accident? Suddenly she realized that the most important thing was for her to find out how the wounded house, before it was ever wounded, had passed from Sergio's hands to the agents' and then – already converted into the misery they saw that afternoon, filthy with the most repugnant sort of filth – into the hands of her father.

16

33

The nicest part was imagining, Andrés recalls, looking at the cracked tree bark, and he transfers the glass to his left hand in order to touch the rough texture of the trunk with his right. In a way, the tree was a house, too, a structure inhabited by different species that traveled its length, penetrated it, nourished themselves on it, left a pearly trail on its extremities, a libidinous saliva, spittle that shines in the moonlight tonight, reminding Andrés of the residue of an act of love, an unwanted trace on the recently smoothed sheets.

Then he thinks, sliding the palm of his hand along the rough wooden surface, that the tree lives like a ship: it travels along with its conglomeration of captives, and like a ship rocked by the wind, it rocks its disciplined, nocturnal armies. Crickets that launch their signals from the darkest shadows; ants that extend their highways from the treetop to the green tide of the grass, as orderly and linear as soldiers of some anachronistic infantry; mosquitoes so tiny that they occupy only those spaces ignored by the wind; open trenches in the curves of the bark, secret cavities, hiding places, nooks, all of it wrapped in the protective breath that accompanies the weaving of the web; spiders in fright wigs, the queens of this masked ball, as well as their pale sisters on the fringes of nonexistence, closer to evanescence than to ostentation: humble grubs, bored bureaucrats secluded in the outlying neighborhoods of the pulsing city, silent tenants of the basement; but also birds that establish their nest in the treetops, and worms that cling to the keel from the bottom of the sea, boring into the submerged timber, rolling themselves up, lascivious and slimy, in the hungry, muscular roots. All this, the minute nomenclature of visible things, things that caught the eye and captivated the ear, and beyond that, everything that lived within the tree and with which the tree lived, that which could be seen in the light as well as in its multiple, buried throbbings. All this – he thinks, sliding his palm slowly along the rough surface of the trunk – had accompanied him and his brother since their childhood games: their dizziness from the highest branches and their hiding in the crevices nestled among the roots, a sort of initiation, the discovery of a parallel between the tree's mysterious vitality and the unknowable evidence of life.

Yes, that's how we imagined the world, that's how we discovered it, Andrés thinks, without daring to remove his palm from the bark, such a strange, unexpected way to feel safe. Then he sensed a clear whiff of alcohol and a strong arm around his throat, and his head drew close to his brother's.

"What are you thinking about?" Sergio asked him, seeking closeness.

"About this," Andrés replied, not wanting to say anything, not wanting to draw closer. And he leans over so that his brother will withdraw his arm, that strange animal clinging to his neck.

"It's not the same anymore, Andrés. It's not our house. The best thing is to leave here right away," and he speaks softly so that the others won't hear their conversation from the terrace and become aware of the proposal to escape.

"Well, we don't need you anymore. You can go to the Casino. Nothing's happened here. End of story," Andrés says without lowering his voice; he doesn't want to be drawn into the game, he doesn't want alliances; he prefers to define distances, to establish clear differences.

"Are you accusing me?" Sergio asks, stepping back a little, grasping the glass, which had begun to tremble in his left hand, more firmly.

"Is there anything I should accuse you of?"

"That's what I'm asking you."

"You know better than anyone else."

"Then say whatever you have to say to me and don't hide with that expression of victim by extension. It's hard for you to understand why I didn't file a complaint, right? It's hard for you to understand why I didn't go to the military police to ask that the house to be returned to me immediately. You would've liked to see me go to the police station, kicking the door in with my feet and dragging those guys by the lapels. But those uniforms don't have lapels. It's that simple. What kind of world do you think you're living in? Have you figured out what it means to live in this country? Sure, it's easy to shoot from the high moral road, especially at unarmed people. What you don't understand . . ."

"Why the fuck did you hand over our house to them?" Andrés shouted at last, without caring if they heard him from inside, perhaps wanting someone to notice the shout.

"I didn't hand it over! I rented it out so I could send the money to you in Berlin!" Sergio replies, stifling his shout in the hushed tones he insists on imposing.

"Why the fuck did you rent it to them?"

"I told you I didn't know who they were."

"And when you found out, why didn't you do something?"

"Like what?"

"Talk to someone who could advise you. We have friends here, don't we? Why didn't you talk to Julia?"

"I hadn't seen Julia in ages!"

"But what about Cecilia? And Manuel? And me? Why didn't you talk to someone? Why did you keep your mouth shut? Why did you hide with that information, when it harmed you, too?"

"It's not what you think, Andrés. I swear to you it's not what you think."

"What's not what I think?"

"That I kept it to myself. That I hid with it, like you say. I did speak to someone."

"Who?"

"Someone you know. Don't ask me to tell you now. Please, don't ask me to tell you here."

Andrés stopped staring at him and tried to calm down, attempting to hold in a deep breath as long as possible. He drew closer to the tree in order to disappear in the shadows of the leaves; he felt the soft earth and the peaceful blades of grass under his shoes. He hugged the trunk, which still held the afternoon's warmth between the infinite striations of its bark. And he wished he could remain there.

"What's the matter with you?" Sergio asked after a little while. It bothered him not to be able to see his brother's face, not to know what was going on there.

Andrés didn't answer.

"It's still a wonderful tree," Sergio said, immediately thinking how incredibly stupid that sounded. But he felt less uneasy when he heard his brother's voice, calmer now, but cloaked in a colder, distant tone, as well.

"It's the only thing that hasn't changed."

"It's changed, too. It was about to dry up," and he recalled how when he used to go by there every once in a while, especially when the house was already vacant, he could see from the street that the tree was dying and that the branches, already leafless, were more dried out every time, growing darker. Toward the end they were almost black; they looked like pieces of arm-shaped coal trying to raise themselves above the roof of the house.

"It's been brought back from the dead. Like you."

"Why do you think I've been brought back from the dead?"

"Because you've returned at last."

"I haven't returned, Sergio. Don't ever say that again."

"What?"

"That I've returned. I'm leaving in a few days. And that's it. *Ciao.*"

"And the folks?"

"Well, I'll try to help them out from over there."

"You know those are just empty words."

"What can I do for them?"

"A lot, Andrés. Believe me."

"What?"

"Help them. Just by being here."

"I don't think that's possible."

Sergio understood his brother's dramatic answer, and after a pause, tried to smooth things over.

"I understand. Believe me, I understand. It won't be easy for her to get used to all this."

"For her?"

"Your wife."

"I have no wife."

"Your future wife, then. They say you were thinking of coming with her."

Andrés turned toward the trunk of the tree, trying once more to retreat into the contemplation of its infinite designs. Without turning back toward his brother, he said in a muffled voice, enunciating every word:

"I have no wife. I've been living alone for a year. I live in a room no bigger than a closet in a residence for visiting professors."

"Around here they said you were about to get married."

"What difference does it make what they said? I think I said it myself. To mom or someone. I don't remember."

"But you had a girlfriend. You were planning to marry her. You told me so in a letter. Of course, that was more than a year ago."

". . ."

"I'm sorry."

". . ."

"You'll meet another woman . . . someday . . ."

"I suppose so. She's already gotten married . . ."

"See? Why couldn't you do the same thing?"

Andrés pulled out a pack of cigarettes from his jacket and offered it to Sergio, but his brother rejected it with a gesture. He brought a cigarette to his mouth and lit it, blowing a long stream of smoke into the cold night air.

"Where is Julia, anyway?" he asked.

34

From a chair on the terrace, Sonia observes two silhouettes gesticulating inside a dark halo, an elongated shadow extending the blackness of the foliage across the lawn. She knows that one of those silhouettes is Andrés. She knows because she hasn't taken her eyes off him all night. Inside the house, curled up in the living room armchairs, the others continue arguing, speculating: how could this happen to their house, they were so happy, says Marcela's voice. What can they do now, what a shame to lose everything they invested in the remodeling, and now it's Cristián speaking. Why would they have to lose it, Julián was saying, and that voice coincided with the opinion she would have attributed to him even if Julián had never opened his mouth, there was no reason to leave such a lovely house, while others swore they wouldn't keep living there for all the money in the world. Marcela said she wouldn't be able to sleep in a bedroom that had been a torture chamber, and Cristián hesitated, it *was* a considerable investment; in time, they'd forget; and besides, they couldn't be sure everything Julia had told them about had happened there.

And anyway, where *was* Julia? Apparently, she was still sleeping in the master bedroom, nestled in the couple's bed, especially considering the Dormutal that had plunged her into a slumber from which she wouldn't awaken till much later that morning. And where did Manuel go? He's in the kitchen, on the telephone. He must be talking to Cecilia. No, not to Cecilia, as they discovered immediately, when she rushed into the living room looking for Sonia, where's Sonia? Have you seen Sonia? Yes, on the terrace, Marcela says, thinking she's wherever Andrés is, that's how it's been all night, and she wants to say so out loud to Cristián, but it's better not to, better not to make him jealous, better not to have him think she's the jealous one with Sonia's attacks on poor Andrés . . . Poor Andrés, an expression that was more justified than ever now: now it not only referred to a person in exile but also to someone who had returned to his childhood nest, now turned into shit, transformed into a hell for defenseless women, blindfolded, tied to those electric beds, raped, plunged into horror and death. Yes, poor Andrés, who at this very moment is a shadow clinging to a tree on the patio, something barely darker than the black outline of the trunk, and then Manuel shouting from inside the house: Sonia, telephone, te-le-phoooooone, the way people always shout "telephone" from one room to another, stretching out the vowels, giving the word the magical air of a mysterious, faraway signal. Sonia stands up as though struck by electricity, runs inside the house: who could it be? Estela's the only one who knows we're here, what could have happened? In the kitchen Manuel tells her as soon as he sees her come in, and leaning over the black device, she lifts the receiver and, bringing it fearfully to her ear, asks herself: Has something happened to the kids? Hello, Estela, what's the matter? Are the kids okay? Oh, what a relief . . . Yes, we're okay, too, listen, didn't I tell you not to call me unless it was very urgent? Who? What did you say his name was? Did you write it down, or are you trying to remember? It's just that I don't know anybody by that name. About his daughter, he said? One of my students? Oh yes, now I know, tell me exactly what he said. That it was very urgent? Upset? He was shouting, you say? Oh, so he wasn't shouting because he was angry about anything . . . he was flustered . . . Yes, that's what they say, flustered. Did he leave a number where I could reach him? He doesn't have a phone . . . Is he going to call back? Yes, but if I'm not there, just give him this number, let him call me here if it's as serious as you say. Yes, fine, as serious as *he* says. No, it's all right, Estela, it's all right, there was no reason for you to give him this number, but now I'm going to hang up, yes, just give it to him, I'll be here quite late, it doesn't matter what time it is. The party? Yes, it's lovely, Estela, we're having a very good time. Good night . . . oh, go look in on the children, please, make sure they're sleeping and cover them, I don't want them to catch cold, it's freezing tonight. See you later, Estela."

And now let's go out on the terrace again even though the air's grown very cold, there's even some fog, of course, it's after one o'clock, how the night's flown by, no wonder I'm so hungry, how stupid of me to have drunk so much on an empty stomach, but I'll just pass through the dining room on my way to the terrace; after all, everything they've prepared for the party is in there, the only thing they haven't done is throw the meat on the fire, no one's even mentioned the barbecue. But the dining room table is covered with platters with salads and sauces and even pieces of different kinds of cheese and thin slices of bread, and fruit, and the pound cake she herself had brought, which no one's touched yet. Then she takes a medium-sized plate, places a couple of slices of bread on it, a few pieces of cheese, and she pours herself some red wine in a tall glass that looks like a flamingo, the glass is pink, too, that's the reason for the uncontrollable association with that lovely animal she's never seen except on television. Carrying her plate and her glass, she returns to her chair on the terrace, her vantage point, the magnificent watchtower from which she can monitor Andrés, who hasn't yet become aware of her presence, that's the good thing, the other good thing is that everyone's inside because of the cold, and she's the only one watching the brothers from the terrace. The good thing is that now she can observe without being observed. That Marcela, who hasn't taken her eyes off Sonia since she arrived, and Cecilia, whose stupid idea it was to invite Julia. Where could Julia be? Yes, that's the reason she's felt so alone all night, spied on by her girlfriends, practically attacked by them. Was that the only reason? Or was it on account of Andrés's surprising indifference? Or because of what happened in the house that night? Everyone's nerves are on edge, but no one is leaving because something's going to happen when Julia wakes up, if she wakes up; or when Cecilia comes back, if she does.

Or was it the phone call? Hadn't she been waiting for that call for days, worried about Angélica, watching her in the school-yard at recess, just as she's watching Andrés right now? Searching her out with her eyes among so many uniforms, just as she's been searching for Andrés among the glances that search for her, reproaching her with their eyes. Where did it begin, this thing she's been living with for days? Where did her uncertainty begin, her insecurity, her fear? Yes, that was it. The call she'd just received, the flustered voice of that man who was looking for her at midnight, that voice she hadn't even heard, for which reason alone he sought her with greater desperation and greater anguish. That imaginary voice: that was fear. That's why it's so difficult for her to swallow the bite of cheese she's put on the slice of still-fragrant bread; that's why she can drink the wine only in tiny sips as the glass grows warm between her hands, which aren't cold in spite of the cold night air; heat radiates from them, fear is a kind of heat, the premonition of another misfortune; fear is a kind of heat that comes from her hands, clouding the pink glass and its long, delicate, artistic stem, how strange to call this thing staring at me from my hand a stem, realizing that I'm afraid, that behind that phone call misfortune lurks in wait for me, stem, that's also part of a plant but not of a tree, that's the trunk, and the crown is the shadow overhanging the neighbor's roofs, the sleeping giant's body that barely sways, rocked by the breeze; the crown is the dark culmination of the tree beneath which Andrés still clings to the wood, talking to his brother, his arms crossed over his chest, his head also leaning backward, resting it on the bark, and she, watchful, alert to every movement, much more alert to him than to his brother, who, when he crosses the wall that she invented by disdaining him and that also exists in her mind's eye, appears submissive, gesticulating like someone who's making excuses for himself, trying to explain himself, wanting to be heard, wanting to be. Then she thinks that Angélica must have appeared much the same way at the principal's office, offering explanations, begging to be heard, asking for forgiveness and knowing she wouldn't be forgiven, asking them to let her be a mother and a student, knowing that under those conditions simply being would be very difficult. And once more the involuntary parallel: the shadow beneath the tree and the image of Angélica laughing at recess, huddling in little groups, whispering secrets . . . telling them? And if that were true, what if they all knew? What would happen now? And if they all knew, what would happen to her now, if something serious had changed things? And the parallel between the two figures extends itself in a parallel of voices, Andrés's voice telling her that nothing would make him happier than being with her forever, how wonderful it would be if life would give them a chance after so very long, how nice it would be if she could have faith in him again, just a few months and he'd be back forever, and the voice of Angélica's father, which she still hears in her memory, asking her for a chance, a couple of months, to have faith in him.

Could that be what the call was about? Could it have been to find out if she had given him that vote of confidence, if she had granted him the few months that the man was asking of her, that the girl was asking of her, that the child growing in her womb was asking of her? Or had something suddenly changed their plans? The other fear, of losing Andrés forever, was again a co-incidence; his behavior that night was also surprising: exactly four days ago he had asked her to wait a couple of months, there was no reason to lose hope, and now she had the feeling she'd lost everything. It was a different Andrés who had spoken with her on the patio, evasive, suspicious, inhibited by Julián's presence. And where was Julián right now? Had they perhaps solved the mystery of the empty house? Now I understand why such a lovely house was vacant for so long, Cristián and Marcela, Julián and Manuel, repeat again and again, and their voices reach Sonia as if from some distant memory. The reality is all right there, concentrated in the shadow that blends with the tree, and that other shadow, the memory of Angélica at the last recess, the little group fluttering around at one corner of the schoolyard and the first nervous little bursts of laughter, and then some secrets, and finally the girl's eyes meeting her own as if the contact of their glances might produce a flash, a spark, a strange fire. A fire in which the last night was consumed by insomnia, pierced by the vision of the girls laughing in the schoolyard and by Andrés's promise, the voice she can still feel resonating in her ear, still blended with the sound of the sheets and the traffic that pene-trated the hotel from the street. Yes, just a little faith as, sleepless, she listens to Andrés's entreaty, listens to Julián's breathing as he sleeps beside her, listens to Angélica's father's plea. Just a few months. Faith.

Two shadows. Two voices. Two blindfolds.

And now Chelita's voice within Julia's, because Chelita had

told Julia and Julia told her, such a short time ago, before she fell asleep:

How was I supposed to know? I was blindfolded.

Or rather:

In those days they never removed my blindfold.

Or:

Can you imagine what it was like to wear that blindfold for over a month?

To wear a blindfold for over a month. They bind themselves, they wrap themselves in binding so no one will notice their pregnancy, they burst out of the binding, they practically kill themselves: a colleague had told her about it in the teachers' lounge when she broached the topic of pregnant students, feigning indifference, like someone who makes a comment about something that has nothing to do with her, something that's happening far from her own life, that barely even reaches the other bank and not even of the same river. They bind themselves, they kill themselves, they burst. There was another kind of binding, then. And Angélica soon would start using it, it was the only way to avoid nature's notoriety, the rounded display of that which is born, in this case, of clandestine life, forbidden fruit, and she recalled that French film – one afternoon of ditching classes with two school friends – at the Toesca Cinema, while her classmates were doing math-English-biology, forbidden movies forbidden afternoon, walking furtively along the downtown streets, we're almost there, dummy, don't let anyone see us, clinging to the walls, clinging to the shadows of the doorways, frightened, forbidden. *Forbidden fruit*, the binding forbidding the natural exuberance of the fruit, the parallel binding, the blindfold, the binding at school and the blindfold in the house, bound womb and bound eyes, the binding that conceals from the eyes of the other girls and the blindfold that conceals the eyes of the other women, and Chelita's eyes, and all the Chelitas who lived in that house, those who were tortured till they bled, the blindfolded ones, those who were shoved into the horror of the basement, the horror of fear, and the binding into which Angélica is descending, poor Angélica, so young and already fallen into hell.

It wasn't good to drink so much *pisco*, she thinks now as she feels fear like a void in her stomach, in her womb, and in her head, full of voices and visions that overlap, intermingle, become confused, and confuse her. She no longer knows if she should go home, wait for some reaction from Andrés, or wait there for Angélica's father to call back. Or if she should run off, just as Cecilia had run off, or numb herself with a Dormutal as Julia did, or bind herself up, bind her imagination so that she would never be so stupid again, and the image of the hotel, the faint, chaotic noise of the city that reached the bed through the heavy, closed shutters, *you'll have to wait for me for a couple of months, have faith, I want to believe him*. And she did want to believe him, and now she wants to bind all the tenderness up inside herself so that she'll never again fall for an appeal that might connect her to her student in such a risky way, or to that father who called her house practically at midnight, to that man who also asked her for a couple of months, a little faith, you've got to believe me.

35

"And the fear, Chelita? What was the fear like?"

In the couple's bedroom Julia, dazed by the Dormutal, noticed the noise about which she had heard so much recently, including that very night, noise from Cecilia's nightmares, different from her own but identical on this one point: the barely audible moan, which she now knew was just the brushing of the walnut tree's leaves against the windowpane, devastating in its unbearable repetition, each time more like a human voice, like the distant death rattle of someone crying somewhere. She also perceived voices coming from faraway, blending into a single voice as they drew nearer, Chelita's unmistakable voice – her words enclosed in the folder that's lying on the dining room table now, a folder she heedlessly left on the dining room table in her house a few hours ago, not suspecting what was coming – a voice she hears now, as if that voice and those words were also lit by the light of the streetlamp illuminating the luxuriant foliage of the tree, and its moaning against the windowpane, and its shadow trembling on the walls.

"The fear . . ."

And then Graciela Muñoz Espinoza – now known to the barbecue guests as "Chelita" – placed her hands on her knees, pressed them against the bones that whitened her plum-colored stockings, and transfixed by her own gesture, lost her way among those poor skulls that exposed her own equally material condition, the vulnerability that obliged her to know and know again, so many times in that house, when it was not yet an empty house. Her knees were touching, and her hands, whose bones repeated that white presence, no longer pressing on the stockings now but on the skin itself, connected with that bony substance, forming a strange structure made of knots and protuberances, and skin and wrinkles, and folds, and little scars that were like reminders of childhood, and tremors remaining from a very recent past, which Julia observed, unembarrassed, attracted by the way in which the bones and skin of those knees resembled their almost identical relatives, the joints and skin of the hands, tense now, pressing the traces of pain in order to remember her fear.

"The fear was just that: fear."

And then to realize that the worst was yet to come. To feel it in her heart, in her skin that was beginning to sweat, in her eyes, which she squeezed shut from behind the blindfold in order to make the world disappear. But what she really wanted was something else: to make time disappear, what was coming, what was about to come, regardless. And it wasn't exactly that she wanted to make time stop, to prevent what was coming regardless, what had to come. No. It was that she couldn't or didn't want to think about what would come. Her heart hurt; she felt like she was falling into something that wouldn't end, like in a nightmare, falling, falling, falling; more and more drenched in her own dampness, soaked through, but her mouth became more and more dry, more bitter. And all that was the result of the effort to stop time from passing. She knew they would arrive in five minutes, she would hear them walking down the steps, she would feel them approaching and then she would hear their voices, she would feel those hands on her face, pressing on the blindfold or making sure it was on tightly. She knew all that, but when it finally came, it was no longer fear.

"I could shout there, and then they would hit me; all those things happened that you told me I didn't have to tell you about. The fear, what I discovered in that fear, happened before I heard the door opening and the footsteps approaching, step by step, until they were right next to me. The fear was that horrible need to make time stop. It was what happened before the footsteps. It was that moment that kept on happening even though you wanted to stop it. Fear was knowing that the worst was yet to come. That it would come at the next moment. Yes. I think that's how I could describe the fear to you: trying to hold off the next moment and realizing that was impossible."

"Always the same way? Without any hope? Didn't you ever think about anything else?"

"I didn't think. I was just terrified."

"And did you ever talk to anyone in the basement? While you were enduring that wait, I mean."

"Not when we knew they were about to come. You feel so alone, really."

"On account of the blindfold, of course."

"Of course, on account of the blindfold. But not really so much because of the blindfold. Much more because of fear. You never know if you're going to be able to take it. And they didn't always come with the doctor."

She continued squeezing her knees, with her fingers wide apart. She fell silent for a moment, and Julia knew she couldn't invade that silence, that strange materiality that the total absence of words had produced, that thing which floated over the narrow desk at the Vicaría, that kept floating there right now, enveloping the shadow of the objects whose outlines were accentuated by the bluish light of the streetlamp that penetrates Cecilia and Manuel's bedroom from the street, illuminates the design on the bedspread, lies down beside her, accompanies the tree's moaning, Chelita's silence.

"That's what fear is like, Julia. That thing that isn't you."

"Have you ever felt it again?"

"Never like that. I always have nightmares, but now I wake up to something else. If I ever felt the same thing again, I think I'd kill myself."

36

At that point in the evening Andrés wanted to find out what was happening with Julia. He imagined she was trying to compose herself in an upstairs bedroom, but the problem was to get to the staircase without Sonia's finding out. And since Sonia had been watching him for a long time, he decided to wait for the opportune moment; he knew that if he passed by where she was, Sonia would follow him wherever he was heading. When Julián approached Sonia with a dish of salad and sat down beside her, Andrés advanced from the garden to the living room, skirted around the couple, flashing them a smile, and strode quickly upstairs.

The second floor was dark, but he knew how to negotiate the space, with which he had been familiar since his childhood. From the master bedroom a cone of light filtered through the half-closed door. Protected by the darkness, he stopped to listen and determine if someone was there with Julia. No sound could be heard. He approached that crack of light exposed by the nearly closed door and regarded the space where his parents had slept for so many years. It had been transformed into something very different; enveloped in that semidarkness, he received unfamiliar data transmitted to him by reality. The headboard of the bed was a bronze frame that gleamed in the light of a bed lamp. It was a faint light that barely outlined Julia's motionless body on top of the bed. Was she sleeping? He pushed the door in carefully, slowly. Now he was inside the bedroom. He paused there, trying to match the weighty silence. He sensed that Julia wasn't asleep. There was an alert presence that accentuated the darkness with something resembling heaviness. He took two cautious steps forward. He didn't want to invade whatever was happening there. The faint light of the bed lamp outlined the contours of a peacefully recumbent body. Julia didn't move. She didn't even seem to be breathing. And in that position, lost at the edge of an enormous bed, she seemed to him like the very image of vulnerability.

He was awed by her fragility and, at the same time, by her strength. And he was especially awed to realize that the fragility was the result of an obstinate determination to fulfill what she had decided was her mission, and that somehow that same fragility was the primary reason for her obstinacy. The vulnerability was compensated only by the risky execution of the most difficult acts; these had become her only way to cling to a strength she feared she was losing day by day. Suddenly, Andrés felt astonished by the clarity of a paradox that described his friend better than anything else. And this paradox astonished him beyond words: her displays of strength made her more vulnerable every day, but that vulnerability – and he began to think that Julia already guessed it – was the wellspring that nourished her selfless acts. He understood that her disproportionate struggle to save the most essential thing, everyone's dignity in the midst of the insanity hurling them all into chaos, was an effort sustained by thousands and thousands of fragile beings, beaten, cornered in their final hiding places, and that the fate of what truly mattered depended on that humanity and that last-gasp effort.

"Andrés?"

He was surprised that she noticed him in the darkness, without turning her body to look at him. Taking a few steps he sat down on the bed. He placed his hand gently on Julia's forehead.

"How do you feel?"

"Better. I took a tranquilizer."

"Sleeping will do you good."

"I hope I can."

"You have to take care of yourself."

"I'm not crazy, am I?"

"Why do you say that?"

"Sometimes I think I'm crazy. If I fall asleep, you can leave with Sonia."

"I can stay till you wake up."

"The pill turns me into Sleeping Beauty. You'll have to wait several years."

"Don't worry, I'll come looking for you."

"If I fall asleep, it would be better for you to leave with her."

"With whom?"

"With Sonia."

"Sonia?"

"Yes, don't make that face."

"What are you trying to tell me?"

"You know."

"Well, if you stay here, somebody will have to take me home. I don't know why it would have to be Sonia. And in any case, I wouldn't leave with Sonia, as you say. I'd go with her and Julián. Why are you telling me I ought to leave with Sonia?"

"I didn't say you ought to."

"I don't understand what you're trying to tell me."

"Yes, you do. And what difference does it make? I'm very tired. I'm falling asleep. Can you do me a favor? Don't let go of my hand till I fall asleep. Maybe that way I won't have the same dream."

"I'll stay here with you."

"Just till I fall asleep. It won't be long . . . I hope."

". . ."

"I spoiled the party for all of you."

"Don't say that. You didn't spoil anything."

"They must think I'm crazy."

"Nobody thinks that."

"Chelita must have been right here. And so many others. In this room. I can't get their voices out of my head."

"Do you still talk to them?"

"I haven't talked to them for nearly a year."

"Then it won't be so hard for you. You've got to make an effort. It's not good for you to keep living with that."

183

"Here. Do you realize that? You can't imagine what they did to them."

"Yes, Julia. I can imagine. And I know it's awful. But now you have to rest."

"It worked like an office. They showed up punctually, like bureaucrats who knew full well all of us were paying their salaries. And most of them tortured for eight hours. There were lunch breaks. Did you know they ate lunch right here? They had a guy who cooked for them. Or a woman, there are different versions on that point. They also had switchboard operators, secretaries, doctors, electricians, dog trainers. A multidisciplinary team, very efficient. I can't stop thinking that all those people showed up here punctually at eight o'clock to abuse some poor, terrified, blindfolded women crazed with fear. Every day, all those people. And in all the houses that were occupied for that purpose. Imagine, besides, in every one of those houses there was a staff as complete as the one that was operated right here. Hundreds and hundreds of Chileans punctually collecting their salaries, building up years of service, receiving awards, receiving bronze plaques in front of their children. People who seem normal. People who could be sitting next to you in a restaurant, in the movies, or walking down a deserted street at night. People who will always be there. Always."

"You have to rest now. You won't be able to sleep if you keep thinking about that."

"I knock myself out with pills, Andrés. Now I've done it again. I do it almost every day. It's called Dormutal. Sometimes I think this country can only fall asleep with Dormutal."

"It's going to change."

"How?"

"With the things you're doing. People like you will change it."

"Do you really think this could change someday?"

"Yes. That's what I think."

"I don't need for you to pacify me. That's what the Dormutal is for. I want you to understand me."

"I do understand you."

"They think I'm crazy."

"You're not crazy."

"I know."

"You've got to take care of yourself, Julia. Rest."

"How? How do you do that?"

"Don't talk. Try to sleep."

"Here. They tortured them right here. Right here is where they killed them."

PART THREE

The Collapse

And at last the house opens up its silence,
We enter, tread on its desolation,
the dead rats, the empty goodbye,
the water that wept in the pipes.

It wept, the house wept night and day,
left ajar, it moaned with the spiders,
from its dark eyes it came undone,

and suddenly we bring it back to life,
we dwell in it and it doesn't know us:
it has to blossom, and it doesn't remember.

Pablo Neruda, *One Hundred Love Sonnets*

17

37

The night preceding the afternoon when they saw the new house for the first time, Cecilia had visited her father, convinced that her drastic decision required his consent. She recalls how she felt the urgent need to tell him about it that very night because she wanted to take the first step of the decision immediately: Manuel had to leave. At least for a while. Later, everything could be worked out differently. He could even stay in the apartment; she'd find someplace bigger, a house would be much better for the girls. And since she wanted him to leave that same night, she thought she needed to inform her father of her decision before putting it into action.

She arrived at the house on Ricardo Lyon Street – the same house she's heading for this Saturday night with her two daughters asleep in the backseat of the car – just as the old man, after having tea in his library, was getting ready for the bath to which he meekly submitted every winter afternoon before going to bed. Don Jovino enjoyed that twilight bath. He capped off the rituals of the day by slipping into a tub full of warm, fragrant suds, anticipating that by the time it got completely dark, he'd already be in bed, making progress with his bedside reading, that week a biography of Field Marshal Rommel.

When she arrived, Cecilia noticed an uncommon commotion: María's excessive skittering, Iván's more than normally severe expression.

"What's going on, Señora Cecilia, is that Don Jovino's in a terrible mood."

María and Iván were more familiar than anyone else – even Cecilia – with the fluctuations of Don Jovino's temperament. They had been his household servants ever since Cecilia was a child. They had witnessed not only the old man's stormy mood swings, but also the young lovers' initial eagerness, and the promising amorous posturing of the love that now generated only frantic movements, badly timed visits, recriminations, tears Cecilia could no longer conceal. They had borne witness – it was María who opened the door that afternoon – to Manuel's appearance in the house, much skinnier then, sporting a black leather cap and a cartoon-like Bolshevik appearance, precariously balancing a stack of books under his right arm and asking in a timid, nervous, miserably reedy voice, from outside the wrought iron gate of the front yard, if he might see Cecilia. Many times María and Iván had occasion to observe the first embraces, disguised as shoving and playing, that Cecilia and Manuel gave one another as they emerged from the swimming pool, surrounded by a halo of water, drenched, dripping on the warm tiles with that other heat in their bodies that not even frequent dunking could relieve. And they were witnesses, too, to the first kisses and the bolder gropings beneath the trees in the backyard, or sheltered by the warm shadows of the library, illuminated only by the fire in the fireplace. Loyal, discreet servants, they rejoiced at the couple's new happiness, just as they were troubled by the desolate expression Don Jovino's face acquired as he acknowledged his capitulation. It was then that, with astonishment, they began to notice their employer's frequent appearance on TV panels and news broadcasts, and later the increasingly frequent visits of other real estate and construction executives, who would arrive at the house with worried expressions, rushed gestures, and alarming phrases. They've just broadcast the latest news, they announce, emerging from the car, hurrying toward the iron gate in the front yard. Have they all arrived? they ask. There are several gentlemen with Don Jovino, María replies, and once inside they rush into the library, whispering: Did you hear the news? and inevitably that mournful expression might grow more severe at some new misfortune, a new bankruptcy, another government takeover, a new seizure, another embargo, a new expropriation.

Witnesses of such a dramatic history from such a humble vantage point, María and Iván continued coming and going with coffee pots and tea services, opening and closing doors and gates, turning off lights when it all seemed to be over. And so they watched Don Jovino's power grow every afternoon within the four walls of the library. First they brought the trays carrying tea in Limoges porcelain cups, and two hours later, when they surmised that the gentlemen were about to depart, the Val Saint Lambert crystal, refinements that Don Jovino preserved as his dead wife's most precious legacy. They offered whisky, soda, and ice in complete silence, stamped with the funereal ambience of those meetings that seemed more like wakes every day. And everyone knew those meetings took place there because of the leadership Don Jovino was consolidating day by day among that group of entrepreneurs. That's what the early edition newspapers said and what the TV commentator repeated at the close of the day, when the gentlemen had already left with even more worried expressions; that's what César, the chauffeur, heard, and what María and Iván in the kitchen heard from him as they drank the same tea they had served in the library.

Although it seemed odd in those days, the leadership Don Jovino had achieved was, at least for a while, more the result of his restraint than a product of intolerance. And Cecilia in particular knew it, more concerned than anyone else by the imminence of an earthquake whose underground rumblings she could hear growing louder every day. She knew it quite well, and for that reason she couldn't help being amazed each time she heard a comment to that effect. It was evident that, despite her father's mania for correction, his final acceptance of her courtship was yet another sign of Don Jovino's conciliatory spirit.

This advantage was great, however, probably greater than Cecilia had calculated, a direct benefit of the old man's restraint. The mood of the country – strictly speaking, not just its mood but also its material condition – was frankly deplorable. There was a great deal of desperation and, as an outgrowth of that desperation, a growing anger, a rage that grew with all the leavening that didn't reach people's tables in the form of bread. There was a

spreading feeling of uncertainty and insecurity, but also a growing belligerence, for in truth, very few people sincerely wanted
peace. Everywhere, and with ever-increasing hatred, paralysis,
intransigence, permanent blame, and confrontation. Rarely had
so many logs been piled on the fire in such a short time, loudly
warning of the conflagration that would consume the last corner
of a house many people could already see in flames.

Serving tea, removing the cups from the library, or entering
with a tray of whisky, María and Iván, and sometimes even Cecilia
– who would never have interrupted one of her father's meetings
but who did keep him company in the library when he was alone –
heard expressions such as "If we try to recover everything, we'll
never recover anything" or "If you want to get something, you
have to give something," a phrase Cecilia would recall the afternoon she came to confess her decision to break up with Manuel
to her father, the eve of the day when she visited – paradoxically,
with Manuel – the new house for the first time.

38

Cecilia had gone to see her father for the purpose of telling him
about her decision, perhaps in the hope of getting his support,
probably wanting him to take the rudder; she, then, would allow
herself to be steered, like so many times before, toward the safe
harbor of whatever determination the old man might dictate. She
remembers this now, several months later, after traveling the distance between the newly renovated house, already lost, and the
old house, the one where she spent her childhood and left the
day of her wedding.

This time she arrives with the two little girls wrapped in blankets that protect the deep sleep that neither the trip nor the nighttime noises of the city nor Cecilia's sobs have managed to wrench
from them. She remembers how that other time – it's hard to
believe, but it's been only three months – she had opened the
wrought-iron gate to the front yard just as hurriedly, run just as
quickly over the tiles that divided the peaceful, oak-shaded lawn
into two swaths of green, climbed the steps of the broad stair-

case with identical anxiety, until she reached – just like tonight, this night from which she thinks back – her father's bedroom door. At that moment she saw María approaching, drying her hands on her apron, frozen beside the bathroom door. Cecilia noticed, as though it were a discovery, her tired appearance, a few more noticeable gray hairs, and a less straight spine, and she stood there staring at that familiar face across which long-vanished laughter and all the possible expressions of misfortune had passed. She had seen the same bewilderment in María's eyes the afternoon she told her – in that same bathroom, brutally, like a brusque phrase, something that sounded like a gunshot to both of them: "I'm getting married," as she finished applying her eye makeup and as María began picking up the clothing that had been abandoned in a heap on the floor, the morning when the poor woman stood there staring at her with the same incredulous eyes with which she's looking at her now, twelve years later, I'm getting married, and then, from the depths of María's eyes, her astonishment at the first transgression she had ever witnessed in that house since her arrival, when she was still practically a child herself. I'm getting married, and it was unbelievable; hadn't she just heard Don Jovino shouting his stubborn opposition from the kitchen? Hadn't she heard, from the same bathroom where they're both standing now, Doña Leonor quietly sobbing in her bedroom? I'm getting married, and then, what was really going on in the house and everywhere, if shouting had no repercussions and tears had no real cause? Because ever since Cecilia's announcement the household began to live for the wedding; all its inhabitants and its every newly adorned corner transformed, just as Doña Leonor's spirits were transformed, although she was already very ill. Iván told María that when he took her outside to sun herself on the terrace facing the gladiolus garden, he could hear her sad wheezing growing more pained all the time. But María was confident that Doña Leonor would be there for the ceremony, perhaps not well enough to enjoy the tinsel and festivities or even to watch it from her wheelchair, but enough to register that the wedding had taken place, for which reason she rejected all suggestions to postpone it, which clearly spoke of something no one dared say out loud: let's just wait until Doña Leonor leaves us, and after a few months we'll celebrate the wedding. For Doña Leonor, closing her ears to these subtle suggestions that were almost always made behind her back, whispered in corners, was a way to stand beside her daughter, supporting her in her decision. There's absolutely no reason to postpone the ceremony, she would say with a bright smile, and then she would ask them, or is there some reason, in your opinion?

The first invitations to the wedding were just arriving at their destinations when another announcement shook the country: the Chamber of Deputies had declared Salvador Allende's government unconstitutional. The family chose not to change their plans: the ceremony would take place on Saturday, September 8, with Doña Leonor already taken to her sickbed, awaiting only the consummation of the marriage in order to die in peace. The entire nation awaited another consummation, less private but more disturbing, one that would have even more decisive consequences in the lives of the newlyweds: the coup d'état of 1973.

The morning of September 11, 1973, caught Manuel and Cecilia enjoying their honeymoon in a hotel in Rio de Janeiro, from which they would return to their apartment on Pedro de Valdivia Street – made ready for them the night before the wedding – on the following Saturday. Stated differently: on Saturday the eighth they were immersed in the hubbub of the wedding reception, the embraces, the sumptuous dinner and drinks, the peaceful kingdom of the wedding cake and the bride's first dance with her father beneath the enormous tent that had been set up in the garden. On Saturday the fifteenth, timidly opening the curtains of the sparkling new apartment, they saw the shadow of a city conquered by silence and death. The only sounds reaching the apartment were those of the military trucks patrolling the curfew-silenced streets, the monotonous whirring of a helicopter patrolling the city from the air, and from the National Stadium, the echo of gunfire.

Doña Leonor died at the end of October, accompanied by Cecilia, who didn't move from the foot of her bed until her mother breathed her last sigh. She was aware that, thanks only to her mother's support and willful determination not to die until the wedding took place was she able to impose her wishes so firmly despite her father's opposition.

In one of her more lucid moments, relieved from pain by the morphine her doctor had just administered, her fever broken by the tablets and cold cloths that María draped across her forehead, Doña Leonor sat up in bed as well as she could, grasped Cecilia's hand between her own, and looking her in the eyes, asked her if she was really in love with Manuel.

"If I weren't, why would I be marrying him?" Cecilia replied, taken aback, bringing her lips to her mother's ear. She wanted to buy time and figure out what her mother was really asking. But she didn't have to wait long. The next question contained, intact, the enormity of the assertion:

"Didn't it matter more to you to go against your father's wishes?"

"And what would I gain by doing that?"

"You know what you're gaining."

"Lie down, mama; this is too much of a strain on you."

"You've got to get this straight. You don't know how hard it is to oppose your father. You don't know what lies ahead. Or the power he has. Or how stubborn he is. You don't even know how much he loves you. And how much he loved me. Now I want some water. And turn out the light. I want peace."

39

"What do you want?"

"For you to help me."

"What's happened now?"

"I'm getting a separation."

"The same thing again?"

"No. This time it's for good."

"What did he do to you this time?"

"Nothing."

"So?"

197

"I don't want to give you any explanations. I want you to help me."

"How?"

"By understanding me."

"Understanding what?"

"That what I'm doing is right."

"Then tell me why you're doing it."

"It's just that I can't stand it anymore, papa."

"What happened now, Cecilia?"

"Nothing new. But I can't go on like this."

"What do you want me to do for you?"

"I want to stay here for a couple of days. I don't want to throw him out into the street."

"And what will you solve in a couple of days? I think you've lost your mind."

"Why do you say that?"

"You come here to ask me to put you up for a couple of days, and you can't give me any reason for the separation."

"I don't think I have what you call a reason. And what might be a reason for me, you wouldn't understand."

"If we can't even have a conversation . . ."

"Papa, it just burned out. Something burned out and I don't want to live on those ashes anymore."

"What do you mean, it burned out? Something burned out in you or in him?"

"In both of us."

"And when did it burn out in you? Tell me."

"I don't know how to describe it."

"And what about him? What burned out in him?"

"He curled up inside his shell like a snail. He shrunk into something I don't recognize. He lost his enthusiasm, his words, his desires."

"Did he cheat on you?"

"In what way?"

"With another woman, I mean."

"No. I don't know. I don't think so."

"So then, why? What has he done to you? You should have helped him if you saw him looking so . . . burned out . . . as you say."

"It's not just that he's burned out, papa. He seems so distant to me. Maybe I've become distant myself, and that's not his fault."

"It's your fault, then."

"Fault? No, papa. I'm not going to keep talking if this is going to end up being a question of fault. I won't fall into that trap anymore. If you want we can talk about nights without love, without closeness, without desire. About mine and about yours with mama, in case you ever wondered about that. About mine and my mother's, since you seem to think this has to be a woman's business, a 'woman's sensibility,' as you put it. Did you ever wonder about the hours my mother spent alone? Did you ever wonder about her loneliness? Hers and yours, papa? Did you ever wonder about that distance that starts to grow without your noticing it? Separation doesn't begin, at least not in my case, with anything other than that simple, terrible, distance."

"Did he hit you?"

"Never. How could you even think that?"

"Has he stolen from you?"

"What?"

"Has he taken anything from my allotment without telling you?"

"He doesn't even know about that. Sometimes I think he doesn't even know we live on what you give me."

"So then?"

"So then, what?"

"He doesn't cheat on you. He's never hit you. He hasn't stolen from you. Why do you want a separation?"

"Well . . . maybe because those reasons aren't enough for me. I want much more than that. I want to be part of a couple."

"Do you know what being a couple is?"

"I don't know what you expect me to say."

"Being a couple is what you discover when you lose it. Just look at me, all alone! Aren't I just a shadow of what I was when your mother was with us?"

"Now I'm a shadow, papa. I feel like I'm what you call a shadow. Maybe because Manuel died for me a long time ago."

"Then we're alike. We have something in common. Maybe now you'll listen to me."

"Yes, I'm listening. I'm so tired!"

"I've been a widower as long as you've been married. The number of years I've been alone is the same as those you've had a companion."

"Assuming I really had one all those years."

"Yes, assuming. We're assuming here. But you got married right before your mother's death; that's what I mean. How long has it been? Eleven, twelve years? In a few more days it'll be twelve years. Your mama died on October 27."

"Yes, I know, papa."

"Life is very cruel. I . . ."

"Papa, I didn't come here to . . ."

"It's very cruel, but not because of what you think I'm about to say. The worst cruelty isn't death all around us. It's that other loss . . . To live with love, to think nothing more important will ever happen to us . . . and then one day, to find yourself crossing the street so you won't even have to talk to the woman or the man who was the love of your whole life."

"You're right. Maybe we *are* talking about exactly that kind of cruelty. But what can I do if it's already there? I didn't come here so you could tell me that what's happening to me is cruel. As if I didn't know!"

"I didn't mean to say that. If that's what you thought I meant, forgive me. I meant to say that it's so cruel, that if we could do something to fix things, to retrace our steps, to erase what was done against our wishes, then we'd have to do it . . . Yes, we have to do it! Because if what we're talking about is cruelty, the most terrible thing is when you want to fix things and you can't, when you want to start over and time has run out, when you want to keep on living, and then it happens, just like it did with your mother, and one day you realize that in a matter of months or weeks you won't be here anymore. And all that loneliness you're talking about, and that she surely felt once . . . or many times . . . has no solution anymore."

". . ."

"Something needs to be done. Sometimes that distance, that loneliness, starts without our noticing it and sometimes it starts because of some dissatisfaction, because something is missing . . . and not necessarily affection, either. Are things very tight for you?"

"What?"

"A very tight budget, I mean . . ."

"We've always lived like that, papa. Things aren't very tight . . . I don't know. I don't know what very tight means to you."

"Things haven't been going well for him since he left the real estate firm."

"But he couldn't stay there either, papa. That wasn't his life."

"And what's he doing now? Is that his life?"

"Papa, now that is cruel! You know he's not doing anything right now . . . There's nothing . . . He can't find anything."

"That could be the cause of everything. Or at least the main reason. How can a couple function under those conditions?"

"What time is it, papa?"

"It's late. Do you want to go? You told me you wanted to stay for a few days."

"May I?"

"You may. It's your house. You can stay as long as you like. But I'm going to ask you for something in return. I'm going to ask you for a favor. Do it for me. Do it for your mother, who would surely ask you the same thing, and for those poor little girls . . ."

". . ."

"Cecilia?"

"Yes, papa?"

"Try again. Let this be the last time, if you like. You have to give things time . . . when you can. I want to give you a gift. Since you're a little crowded in that apartment, I'm going to give you a house. What do you think?"

". . ."

"A new house. A house where you'll have all the space you need. A house with a yard for my granddaughters to play in. A house to make a new start in. A house so you can leave all the tough years behind. A house that will see you come together again, love each other, and not feel alone. What do you think?"

". . ."

"What do you think, Cecilia?"

". . ."

"Do you like the idea?"

"I'll think about it, papa. But . . . can I stay here for a few days?"

18

40

Just as the moth flutters around the light bulb on the terrace, they seem to spin around in a dark void they're incapable of noticing. Because although they were aware of how their lives had deteriorated, they didn't understand – with the possible exception of Sonia – exactly what that thing was around which their lives were condemned to keep spinning. Sonia, the most lucid of those affected, thought her mistake was having married Julián even though she knew that a possible, imaginary life with Andrés much more closely resembled her concept of happiness. Andrés toasts her from the patio now, raising his glass, and she senses that the banality of the gesture hides the complete lie, which would have been senseless for her to accept. That long-distance toast, that toast to nothing in particular, was a cover-up for his inability to approach her, to walk those thirty or so feet across the lawn and tell her straight out what had changed since the previous evening. In any event she continued to flutter around the hope. It was no longer the hope that he would repeat what she had heard in the hotel, spoken so softly in her ear, "have faith, our opportunity will come," but simply, "everything's changed; it was an illusion; I made a mistake." Yes, that's what she was expecting to hear now, and it was so different from what she had hoped for the past few nights, so different from what she wanted to hear now, so different, really, from what she dreamed of hearing so many times over the last few years. Nonetheless, she responds to Andrés's toast by raising her glass, too, giving him a smile, and thinking that what he really wants is to identify his homecoming with a person, to feel his return just as he felt her in the hotel, to kiss and bring his ship to harbor.

Marcela, too, flutters around the evening's mysteries, revolving around Andrés's sigh, a sign of vulnerability that stirs something strange and almost perverse in her, a sea of unknown depth, the piercing moan that diverted her from the bathroom toward her son's Matías's room to discover that it was none other than Andrés – so distant the night before and tonight, as well, standing under the tree for such a long time, glass in hand – who had dissolved into tears, concealing his sobs in Matías's sneaker, stuck to his face like an extension of his skin, like a mask, different from what she sees now as she observes Andrés's long-distance toast to Sonia and thinks that this attention he's giving her friend – her friend? poor, foolish Sonia, she thinks – is a real insult, a defiant act that Andrés shouldn't permit himself in her presence: for whatever it's worth, she is the mother of his child, after all. What is Marcela revolving around, then? What dark axis? What is she whirring around with that annoyed air, at the edge of irritability? Jealousy? Is Marcela spinning around a feeling of loss? Does it bother her that she's no longer the indifferent sun around which Andrés's little emotional planets revolve? Is jealousy that dark light around which her growing displeasure turns?

And if that's the case, what is Cristián revolving around, so confident when he arrived, so confident he will "arrive," so self-assured in his halo of success; even though his wife hasn't stopped tracking Andrés's every move, Andrés, whom he's hated ever since three nights ago, in bed, when Marcela called him "poor Andrés": "Andrés is back, poor thing. Cecilia told me. We're invited to a barbecue on Saturday." But Cristián is spinning around something different from jealousy. The thing that sets him off is a deep contempt for these friends of his wife, mediocre people, in his opinion, with no victories to proclaim, no awareness that today, as never before, the dividing line between success and failure is clear, tangible, can be measured and even corrected, and coincides completely with the boundary between good and evil, placing us with the righteous or the sinners. All their embittered sniveling is useless now: the country has finally changed, and it will change a lot more. At last there's no more room for those "poor Andrés" types, for easy pity, for the sentimental solidarity that was always phony anyway. He can't stand it anymore; we should leave right away, let's go, Marcela, I'm sleepy . . . and she replies yes, let's go, but he sees her hanging on Andrés even more. All right, we're leaving, Cristián, but wait a minute! I want to find out what's going on with Julia, let's wait till Cecilia comes back, what happened is so terrible. And he thinks: what happened is what had to happen. You can't make an omelet without breaking eggs.

And around what light – or what unknown shadow – does Manuel revolve, looking like a waiter by the end of the night, half drunk, carrying dirty plates into the kitchen – Berta's been asleep for a while now – bringing another bottle of wine, something to make up for the roast, what a shame the meat ended up like this: an enormous hunk of red, cold meat, stuck on a skewer beside the barbecue pit, unmistakably far from the fire, which has turned into ashes. Cecilia should have come back by now, he thinks from inside his own personal fog, looking at the fog that's descended on his lovely garden. Yes, she should have come back. Why the kids? Why did she take them when it was so late? And he sees Marcela and Cristián arguing, sitting on the living room sofa . . . his living room, goddammit. Would anyone care for a nice little '73 wine? And Marcela looks at Cristián, lowering her eyes. Cristián stands up and heads for the window facing the garden; so they didn't appreciate the joke, tough shit. Why the hell did she go to that fucking old man's house when he was the one who got him into this trap? Was it possible he knew how it would all turn out? Was this his masterstroke? His checkmate?

In order to compose himself, to focus on something else, to keep doing the same thing he did every night in the kitchen in their apartment and later in the kitchen of the newly renovated house, he poured himself another drink, fussed around lighting a half broken cigarette that he pulled out of an equally battered pack, anticipating the next sip, that other farewell, that repeated form of self-eradication. It wasn't a bad little wine, he thought, not bad at all.

41

The house seemed abandoned again. Not a single sound, not a single voice, could be heard.

Julia slept, thanks to the Dormutal she always carried in her purse, or possibly lent to her by Cecilia this time, unaware that Julia knew how to help herself in her crises, as did Sonia, Marcela, and all the rest: the little bottle in a purse, on a nightstand, in a hard-to-reach corner of a closet, according to the addiction, the level of trust between husband and wife, the degree of fear. They were the "irritable-bowel chicks," as Julia used to joke, and then they'd laugh at her wit, wonder where the poor thing is tonight, so immersed in that deep sleep, that self-eradication so much like death, that close-your-eyes-swallow-and-take-off-for-oblivion, that disappearance. That escape she seeks more and more often now.

Cecilia, the hostess, was far away, and it was hard to imagine she'd be returning.

Manuel, sitting on the sofa, had given up trying not to fall asleep and produced regular snores that, at that hour of the night – early morning, really – were excusable. How could anyone guess what he was revolving around in his sleep? What was the black light of his nightmare? Why did he startle each time he abruptly stopped snoring to take in a breath that made his mouth hang open even wider?

Cristián and Marcela couldn't take their eyes off him, held rapt by this strange respiratory demonstration, as though they were witnessing some rare species that unwittingly fascinates us from inside an aquarium.

"Look how his mouth is hanging open. He looks like a fish out of water," Cristián said to his wife.

"Poor Manuel," said Marcela, without thinking twice, as in a continuation of the *mare nostrum* imagery, she imagined Cristián, standing beside her, turning into an offended sea urchin, spines all aroused. She realized at once that this was the worst possible comment she could have made; after all, her spouse's insight wasn't such a frequent occurrence.

Andrés loped up the stairs to the second floor. He wanted to find out what was going on with Julia. Upstairs, everything was dark, but it pleased him to confirm that he could move about up there in complete darkness. It was a strange feeling of belonging, now that the house didn't belong to anyone. He felt his way over to the bathroom door, opened it, and turned on the light. A yellow brightness spilled out into the hallway, growing fainter toward the interior of the bedrooms. Andrés went over to the couple's bedroom and adjusted his eyes to the furnishings. The mirror over the bureau duplicated the light of the street lamp on the light blue double bed. He glimpsed Julia's body lying on top of that brightness, weighing on the left side of the bed, one arm at her side, her pale hand about to graze the small rug covering that portion of the wood floor. He held his breath and then he heard Julia's breathing, very faintly, growing heavier in the silence. It wasn't just that she seemed to have fallen asleep forever under the influence of the sedative. She seemed, rather, to have abandoned that house in a final gesture of farewell; she had erased herself from that place. She had disappeared along with all the voices and memories that tortured her that evening, that had been stealing her sleep for years. Andrés took one step toward the bed in order to see if Julia would react, but there was no change in the intensity of her heavy breathing. Then he turned toward the door and closed it gently so her apparently peaceful sleep could continue uninterrupted.

As he left the master bedroom, he saw the beam of light from the bathroom filtering like an invitation into the girls' room, the room that had been his bedroom so many years ago. The scent of sleeping children still floated through the room. The moonlight illuminated two glowing, bluish rectangles, rumpled sheets, the traces of flight. Andrés decides not to turn on the light. In that faintly lit darkness, he looks for recognizable angles, familiar spaces. But everything has changed. When he was a boy, there were two narrow beds in that bedroom, flush against the walls that formed an angle opposite the intersection of the window and the closet. The middle of the room was an empty square that had seemed very wide to them back then, divided by the parquet into a number of other squares. Here, in this space that seems so insignificant to him now, there was room for so many games and fantasies. There were no electric trains – in fact, there were hardly any in the neighborhood – in those days, they were an expensive, exclusive form of entertainment; they had to improvise with an imaginary train made of any kind of rectangular object that could be linked to another; but there was an entire stadium, with bleachers and a field with official dimensions, with arches and nets, with playing areas and a central circle traced with chalk, and little cardboard players they carefully drew and then painted with watercolors, cut out and pasted on bottle caps they collected by the hundreds at the corner grocery, which in one corner had a soda fountain where they even sold clandestine beer and wine in ceramic jugs. In that room Andrés and his brother had dreamed for hours on end; they had passionately infused it with their part of the world: they yelled out goals, imitating radio broadcasts, rapid, loud announcements of plays that happened more in their imagination than in the stiff trajectory of the bottle caps they propelled with an index or middle finger, according to the distance from the button that served as a ball and the dexterity of the finger selected to execute the miraculous goal. Yes, all that wonder fit into that small space. Just as the astonishment of the world fit on the walls, which they covered with posters and photos of team banners and emblems. Soccer clubs. Andrés put up a huge picture of the Colo-Colo team, and Sergio added an equally gigantic University of Chile banner. Then came Elvis Presley, a shared passion, and later Claudia Cardinale, assailed by the brothers' not-so-innocent leers and the palpitations of a single heart. And afterward the unforgettable image of Che, the beret with a star, the sparse beard, and the firm gaze of an enlightened Christian, that icon at the head of the young men's beds, inciting all sorts of rebellions. And just as if Cardinale had decided to jump down from the wall and make herself comfortable on the bed, one day the first girlfriend appeared, with the same sixties hairdo, the identical white dress, because from there they were going to a party, a Saturday night dance (another Saturday night party, of another era), and a few months later Sergio's girl, shyer, cuter than the younger brother's. It seems the room was getting too small for them; it was much more apparent when one of them wanted to smoke and the other didn't, or after the first, inevitable binge, with its unfortunate consequences, and later the first serious illness, when Sergio slept on the sofa while Andrés recovered from a bleeding duodenal ulcer, and now, the memory of his brother's gestures: Do you want me to bring you a glass of milk before I go to bed? Do you want me to take a letter to Silvia? Do you want a smoke? The same brother who, a moment ago, under the tree, tried to close the gap of time and of so many other things by telling him that everything had changed, that he had to go, that the house wasn't the same, and they weren't the same brothers, either. And after, the first experience of prostration and weakness of the flesh, the first experience of death. They had to give up their room to their grandfather and move to the living room, putting the sofa and chairs together at night, improvising a bed where they couldn't sleep, not just because it wasn't a normal bed, but also because they could hear their dying grandfather's terrible moans from the expropriated bedroom. They finally got their room back, but with the feeling that something much more important had been lost forever. It was then they understood that there is no more absolute innocence than that of a life in which no one dear has yet died. They also learned that that selfless dedication to their grandfather's care (it was their paternal grandfather, and their mother devoted all her time and attention to him) was something different from everyday human behavior; it was a force and a will seemingly demanded by something beyond people's habitual customs and range. And so, when a year or two later, he suffered a second bout of hemorrhaging that placed him face to face with death, Andrés realized once more that everything in that house would acquire another dimension, would rise above the habitual and familiar and would achieve the generous proportions demanded by exceptional circumstances, as he already knew. His brother would walk around the patio until quite late, in order not to violate his privacy in their room, his room, too, from which he had been exiled for the third or fourth time. Their mother lost weight through fear and hard work. Their father gave up smoking in order to pay for the medications. They did everything possible to drive death away. Especially if it was the death of a resident of that house. Everything was performed like a ritual, a silent homage to life. He remembered what his brother had said: "Don't tell him you're leaving; he needs you more than ever." And in one instant – as he recalls all the illnesses that disturbed that room and the nervous pacing of the she-wolf within it – he understood the meaning of his brother's invitation and wanted to go downstairs to make up with him, to explain things to him, to have a drink together before they went their separate ways again. Wouldn't his father secretly wish for something like that, to ennoble them in a gesture of real love?

The wind rustling the leaves creates a movement of shadows that can be perceived more intensely on the walls and bright rectangles formed by the girls' unmade beds. The tumble of slept-in, tousled beds; a tangle of sheets catching on their feet; the sound of clothing on its way to an initiation, an opening night, that first night, the night Marcela spent with him when his parents had to go to a wedding in Valparaíso.

They were in their fourth year at the university, studying philosophy. Six months later they decided to get married. The way it's done in Chile: in order to escape from home, to leave the nest, to fool around, to do a perfectly normal thing that isn't normal for the family. What's happening to Marcela now? What's happening to his son, that oddest, most endearing of creatures? His son was four when Andrés realized he couldn't go on living with Marcela. What's happening to his son now? Is he part of this room's history? Is he the continuation of that history? Of that corner of the house where Andrés slept until he was as old as his son is now? And when did violence become part of that history?

Now he feels it very clearly: every since he arrived, everything's seemed abnormal and violent to him. That was the reason for an underlying, continuous annoyance, a rancor he didn't want to accept, a feeling of incongruity between his being and the irreconcilable recreation of a past that refused to die in his memory. He hadn't even been here three days when he found out about a crime, and the following day he thought he saw the perpetrator in an elevator. Tonight was witness to the multiplication of the crime. But he also remembers that his uneasiness had begun before he learned of those deaths. It began by reading a large sign outside the airport, promising the opposite of everything he's seen since he's been back: *Chile moves forward in peace and order.* Now he understands that a boy's bedroom says much more about peace and order than the signs that have been put up along the highways.

A few hours ago two little girls slept soundly in this room, on top of a restored parquet floor, cleaned of all traces of horror. The girls slept over what had been some black stains etched into the wood, stains that, according to Cecilia, looked like burns. And so it was: there had been burns there. Flogged women. Torture and death. That's why the stains looked like burns. And there, a couple of hours ago, Cecilia's daughters were playing and laughing, just as he and his brother had done.

He had the feeling of having lived through the same thing he was experiencing now at some previous time. Or in any event a clear sensation of being expelled from some space of his own. He imagined that the ancient space was his childhood and his youth, lost forever. He recalled a discussion, equally ancient, in Los Cisnes, outside the Pedagógico, a discussion about the legitimacy of looking for hidden meanings in a Cortázar story. They had read *House Taken Over* in class, and the discussion spilled over into the café. Some of them maintained that it was useless to theorize with closed interpretive readings. It's like hunting butterflies; I like them better in the air, Manuel had said. It's like nailing them into an album, Cecilia added, and the final expression at which they arrived was a common patrimony that satisfied all of them by the time they paid for the beers: it was like taking that enormous dragonfly with wings extended, which resembled Cortázar only in flight and never in empty phrases, and tacking it into an album with symbolic pins. But nevertheless, now he believes that the house taken over in the story is like this childrens bedroom, like those other parts of the house that were also occupied, taken over, and from which he was expelled. And it wasn't just the fact that he was thrown out: after all, that wasn't the most important thought crossing his mind, but rather everything that has or had to do with him and his house: his way of feeling, of evaluating, of being.

He ought to leave right away, he thinks; the sound of death here is frightful; he ought to head for the street immediately and throw the key into the first sewer he passes, so that no one will wander in here by mistake and find all this.

He walked downstairs to the living room. When he reached the last step, the first thing he saw was the light glowing in the full-length mirror at the end of the hallway, and then his own reflection. That replica of his desolation was he himself, that body, already slightly stooped, for reasons he doesn't understand: because it's gotten too late, perhaps, or because the years have grown too long. He recalls some Neruda verses:

They've all gone, the house is empty.
And when you open the door there's a mirror
where you see yourself full-length and feel a chill.

He wants to speak to his brother, remember their games, the old house, that other time. He wants to have a drink with him, to clink glasses, to let the toast ring out, to let it be an embrace like the one Sergio had sought standing by the tree trunk. When he reaches the middle of the living room, Sonia – momentarily interrupting that muted argument with her husband – tells him that Sergio and Ivette have left. Manuel, quite drunk by now, is out on the terrace, freezing, shirtless, struggling to bring another glass to his lips, his gaze fixed on the enormous hunk of skewered meat, so close to the grill but already so far from the fire. Then Andrés decides to leave without anyone's noticing. He goes to the kitchen, followed by Sonia's eyes; as he passes, she asks him for a glass of water. Andrés knows that in the kitchen, there's a side door that will let him out by the side of the patio, and from there to the green door with the peephole, and from there to a street that also seems to be immersed in silence and death.

He thinks: Julia will certainly sleep till noon. Tomorrow I'll phone Sonia. We'll get together somewhere more neutral than her house or that Chinese restaurant. Yes, a neutral place, without memories. There I'll tell her I have to leave in a few days. And that I've decided not to return.

19

42

She entered the old man's room wrapped in a forty-year-old aura of fear. She was facing her father again.

Don Jovino, propped straight up in the wide double bed as if he were sitting at the executive boardroom table, looked as though he had been expecting her visit. But in truth Cecilia's sorry appearance was the last thing he had expected at that time of night, which had for many years been his bedtime. And yet he was wide awake. The bath salts and fragrances applied to his body by María and Iván's hands, invisible beneath the suds, hadn't produced their usual effect tonight, although fatigue and wakefulness weren't enough to overcome Don Jovino's erect, stern demeanor. He fixed his eagle eyes on Cecilia's tearful ones, wondering what new disaster had brought her there at that hour; they must have had another fight, now it will be harder to get things patched up.

What am I doing here? Cecilia wondered, trying to brave her father's inquisitorial stare. She had come looking for refuge but found the same stern patriarch, the implacable judge, the corrector, now glancing at the clock – she shouldn't have come at that hour without warning him; calling ahead would have been the proper thing to do – apparently equally annoyed at her disheveled appearance, that old, stained suede coat, her hair uncombed, until at last he focuses on his daughter's face, still bearing evidence of tears, and now, for the first time, an expression resembling concern darkens his own face.

A feeling of displeasure overwhelms Cecilia; she feels guilty; she anticipates disapproval. She stands at the foot of the bed, pressing her knee against the metal footboard, feeling that cold contact with her naked skin like a replica of the stare that strips her of her possible defenses and prevents her from doing what she would like to do: draw closer, sit on the bed, take his hand and squeeze it in order to transfer the metallic coldness to the warmth of another body, make him look at her differently, ask her, rub her head, comfort her, tell her everything was all right, calm down, it was a bad dream, those words she wanted to hear when she was a child, words she would love to hear more than ever tonight.

"Tell them not to come up," he said, referring to Iván and María, who were on the landing, awaiting his orders. "I don't need anything; you can go to bed."

He doesn't need anything from me, either. He puts up with me. He wants me to leave right away, Cecilia thought. He thinks he doesn't need anything from anyone. Thinks nobody should need anything from anyone else. And how I need him now! Where do I begin? How do I tell him?

She looked at the bed again. Everything was clean, pale, and fragrant. She recognized those scents; she learned to recognize them on her mother, to recognize her in the darkness of the room when that perfume approached her for the good night kiss. And much later she recognized it on her father when he came near to inspect her homework, as she anxiously awaited a word from him, a kiss, a hug, instead of the usual correction. Write more clearly; no one will be able to understand this. It's better to leave a margin for corrections. And the first correction had already been made, the one that always came from him, the one she was supposed to be grateful for, "so you'll do better next time," before receiving a grudging pat on the head that she treasured for days, waiting for next time, because next time there'll be no mistakes, she'll try hard, she'll work hard, and she'll finally be able to feel the warmth that goes with the perfume, the fragrance and that warmth which, along with her mother's "good night," she learned to recognize from childhood.

That fragrance subtly invaded the room, mixed with the cologne that María and Iván had rubbed on his body during the final stage of the evening ritual: helping him out of the tub, drying him, dressing him in his pajamas, and laying him on the double bed, the solitary bed where he now rests. Cecilia imagined that the fragrance was the natural aura of her father's tidy, well-cared-for, correct person. She even came to believe it was the scent of Don Jovino's huge, dark eyes, riveting her own before she could reach the edge of the bed.

"Is the party over already?" the old man asked.

"No, papa. The party's not over."

"What time is it?"

"Around twelve."

"Are they planning to celebrate all night long?"

"I don't know."

"Did the house look nice?"

"Why weren't you there, papa? Why not?"

"Wine out?"

"What?"

"I was remembering an old joke from my youth, when I used to go out celebrating with friends. Like all of you tonight. For example, if someone asked, why not?, you had to answer right away, wine out? Who's out of wine? Bring more wine!"

Don Jovino tried to laugh at his own joke, or rather allow himself to be carried away by the warmth of the image it evoked, but his laughter degenerated into a cadence of sharp coughs that rattled his lungs, eroded by tobacco and time.

"How are you, papa?"

"Just as I look."

Cecilia remained silent.

"And how do I look to you?" Don Jovino asked.

"Fine, papa. You look fine. Why did they give you your bath so late tonight?"

"Because I woke up feeling a bit nervous, and I asked for a second bath. And what happened to you? What are you doing here?"

"I'm not alone. I came with the girls."

"Where are they? Why don't you bring them in?"

They're sleeping, papa. I didn't want to wake them."

"You brought them over asleep?"

"Yes."

She didn't want to add anything else. The old man waited a few seconds and then underscored Cecilia's silence with an even more penetrating gaze from his birdlike eyes, a gaze from which the seeds of his fear kept bursting forth: if she left her house at this time of night, with the girls sleeping, something serious must have happened. Cecilia felt she would finally have his complete attention. Besides, he had already asked her about the house twice. But how could she tell him? All the way over she had thought about how to be tactful, but now she found it hard to contain herself.

"Did the house look nice?" the old man asked after the long silence. And he added, so that Cecilia would speak, "I thought maybe you came over to tell me about the housewarming."

Cecilia struggled to find a way to tell him. She sensed that this was the right moment.

"It was horrible."

"Horrible? What was horrible?" he whispered.

Then Cecilia noticed he was falling asleep. "Everything."

"You had another fight."

"No."

The old man's silence indicated that if she wanted to talk to him tonight, she'd better hurry, before he fell asleep. She came over to the edge of the bed, sitting on the wide, empty space where for years her mother had slept, dreamed, loved, and finally died. She placed the palm of her hand on his forehead; it felt cool; it was the peaceful head of a healthy man about to fall asleep. Then she asked him:

"Where did you get that house from, papa?"

"The house? What's wrong with the house?"

"Don't you know?"

"What?"

"Open your eyes, papa. I need to talk to you."

"Go ahead. But I'm tired."

"Me too, papa. I'm very tired. I don't know what to do anymore . . . I don't think I can stand it anymore." And she rested her head on him, took the inert hand that was already asleep on top of the covers, kissed it, and held it in hers, trying to revive it, to make him wake up.

"You didn't have a fight?"

"No."

"It has to do with the house, then?"

"Yes. The house."

"It turned out very lovely."

And she noticed he was once again falling asleep.

"It's horrible, papa."

"The house? What happened?"

"Tell me how it came into your hands!"

"The house?"

"Yes, the house! That's what we're talking about! About the house!" she shouted, not even trying to hold back.

The old man opened his eyes, which looked enormous but devoid of questions. Eyes without sight and without curiosity.

There was a long pause. Now she knew that he knew, too.

"I thought it was a good house."

"That house?"

"Once it was renovated, it was a magnificent house."

"That house, papa?" Cecilia persisted with the same question, in the same tone of voice: maybe they weren't talking about the same thing.

"That's what I thought."

"Then you knew what that house was?" and she released his hand, which again fell inertly on the sheets.

"Knew what?" the old man asked from somewhere that no longer was merely a descent into sleep.

"What they did in that house," Cecilia said firmly.

The old man said nothing, but now he was looking directly into her eyes. Cecilia called upon the bruised remnants of her former strength, because it was so hard for her to repeat the question.

"You knew, didn't you?"

She realized that the new silence was a confirmation.

"Why didn't you tell me? Don't close your eyes, papa. Don't fall asleep. I need you to tell me what happened. And I need you to tell me now."

There was a strange expression on his face, something she couldn't quite define. The old man remained silent, and yet he wanted to tell her something, something he finally spluttered out, confusedly, choking on his own saliva, spitting the words out, suffocating as he reached a high-pitched shout.

"You're crazy! How can you believe those stories! What right do you have to tell me this, when I gave you that house so you and Manuel might finally learn to live like normal people! But still you go on fighting like cat and dog because of all those damned people who've poisoned your minds. And don't even think of going around repeating that stuff! It's very dangerous! Let's see, tell me, who brainwashed you? Your grateful guests, your fancy friends from the Philosophy Department? You never should have studied that junk, they've filled your head with ridiculous fantasies and bitterness . . . bitterness and hatred . . . they're just a . . . bunch of bitter misfits who brought us to the brink of hell . . . what am I saying, to the brink, to hell itself . . . Or don't you remember? A bunch of social misfits, that's who your friends are! That's why I didn't go to your party!"

In his rage Don Jovino knocked over the glass of water on the nightstand that he was trying to reach for to quell a sudden bout of coughing. The water spilled all over his pajamas and on the sheets, which took on a darker, slightly bluish tone. Cecilia stared at him incredulously, unable even to pick up the overturned glass from the bed. It was difficult for her to believe what she was hearing. When their eyes met, there was a flash of revelation. Deep in her father's eyes, which were peering at her intently, Cecilia discovered the rage of the persecuted, the rage of the guilty, that other face of fear. Don Jovino, mute now, unable to open his mouth again, soaking wet, shivered with spasms that rocked him in the drenched bed.

She stares at him resolutely, without saying a word. They remain silent for a long time. The old man is shrinking, sinking down into the bed as if seeking refuge.

"How did that house come into your hands, papa?"

Don Jovino squeezes his eyes more tightly, compressing his

eyelids, and in the angle where they meet his forehead, the first tears begin to fall.

"Tell me how it came into your hands!"

". . ."

Cecilia stubbornly insists, enraged now, accentuating and separating each word.

"Tell me how it came into your hands!"

"The house?"

"Tell me how it came into your hands, papa!" she says, now in the threatening tone one would use with a child who refuses to confess to wrongdoing. "Look at me, papa!"

Without realizing it she finds herself sitting on the bed next to him, and now she feels the damp sheets on her legs but also the last trace of warmth in her father's body. She seizes him by the shoulders, firmly, almost violently, forcing him to look at her. For the first time, she feels that body, and also for the first time she realizes she's stronger than that fragile body about to yield.

"Papa, did you know?"

"I don't know what you're talking about!"

"Papa, you knew."

Perhaps because now she's making an affirmation, Cecilia's voice is so weak she can hardly hear herself.

"I don't know what you're talking about," the old man repeats, pressured by his daughter's gaze.

"Papa, did you know?" Cecilia insists, recovering her tone of voice and the question.

"I don't know what you're talking about," Don Jovino implores. And his eyes plead with her not to open a door that's remained closed for so many years. He asks her to let him keep his world intact for the short time he has left, because he can't live in a different kind of world anymore.

Seeing him so totally defeated, Cecilia understands she must accept what her father asks of her. He has no other way to live, that's true. And she also understands, seeing him numb and trembling on the drenched bed, that he has no other way to die, either.

She heard footsteps in the hallway and then a few discreet knocks at the door.

"What is it?"

"It's me, Señora Cecilia."

"Come in."

María opened the door cautiously, as if she knew something she shouldn't know about was going on in there.

"What is it?"

"Would you like me to bring you something? May I go to bed?"

"Go to bed, María."

And as the door closed, "Leave some hot water in the thermos."

"Would you like some coffee?"

"I'll help myself later. Go on, go to sleep. Good night."

"Good night, Señora Cecilia."

When she heard María's footsteps going downstairs, she took her father's hand, but this time she squeezed it without warmth because hers were cold, too.

"I want to sleep," Don Jovino murmured.

Cecilia saw a darkening in his eyes, a beaten look, but also something resembling night, something like repose. She had put her finger on something much more serious than all the errors he had corrected since her childhood.

Without knowing exactly what he was trying to tell her with that look, but understanding that it was precisely what she had feared most – a confession that had been growing as she drove to her father's house with her children – Cecilia had intuited the whole story. Everything that might follow would only be a confirmation of that suspicion, even if she never learned, or wanted to learn, the details. She had discovered the crime and also the difficulty of the confession. She had suspected her father's guilt and also the seeds of reparation in herself. She'd have to begin reconstructing the rest of it from the foundation up. And on that very long night, she understood that obligatory silence and calm humility were part of that foundation.

In the middle of the huge, old double bed, Don Jovino was an insignificant lump, a tiny mound of matter, hiding from death under winter-white blankets. That head, whitened by the years, a pale collection of wrinkles and white hair barely grazing the starched whiteness of the pillow. Cecilia suddenly realized she was crying at the very moment she most needed to keep a cool composure; and without knowing how, she was crying on her father's chest, a warm smallness, a tiny torso. She felt her father's rapid heartbeat in her ear, she smelled that familiar cologne of her childhood, as well as the bodily effusions of a man who was about to die.

She yielded to that repose on the only chest she never dreamed of feeling against her cheek, or at least had never felt before. She rested there for a long time, her entire lifetime. What she had begun there would end there, too: that inaccessible chest and that secret caress; that peaceful pain over her father's final, troubled breathing.

She sensed that Don Jovino's hand was not asleep. It was clasping hers. And then she surrendered to that first, only, and final caress.

20

43

As they rounded the curve leading to the passenger drop-off at the airport, Andrés again saw the sign promising order and peace. He looked at his brother, imagining that he, too, had caught the irony of the situation, but Sergio was already getting out of the car, now parked at the curb. They headed for the cart next to the man who was approaching to carry the baggage. Sergio closed the trunk and got back into the car to park it. Following the man with the luggage, Andrés again found himself at the Lufthansa counter.

The airport was packed. It looked to him like Paseo Ahumada at noon, although there was no gray army of street vendors here, or improvised shop windows made of paper, or alarms, or even the assault of the green army's whistles and nightsticks. There was no place for the long, absurd war of the Paseo here. And yet it seemed to him that this space, designed for journeys to distant places, was somehow a street, a place where you don't recognize anyone, from which you can head in any direction, from which you can see life as an adventure once more, or at least a possibility. He joined the line, excited by the imminent adventure, of being part of a whole whose substance he couldn't determine and didn't even know, but that would affect him in a way that was also part of that randomness, that game, always different, always unpredictable. And now that randomness had assumed the form of his traveling companions on this flight, his serendipitous comrades standing in line ahead of him. In front of him was a family that gathered every so often around their suitcases and the tedious wait: the woman, a Chilean dressed for a long journey, in jeans, tee shirt, and a sweater tied around her waist; three children who clung to her legs, ready to cry; and a husband who kept their place in line, immutable beside the suitcases, which he pushed along with his foot each time the line advanced.

Behind him stood a woman, no longer young but dressed and made up as if she wanted to be. She was no beauty, but she had the look of someone who had been really lovely at one time and who took pains to prolong the aura of youth and seduction she had maintained successfully through the years. How beautiful she was, Andrés said to himself, attracted by the replica of her former splendor. And how interesting she still is. He cast a glance in her direction, trying to be discreet and obvious at the same time, while he checked over his ticket, passport, and the bills he had tucked inside it to pay the airport tax.

Here I am again, Andrés thought. In line again, about to leave. It was so congested that the line moved slowly. It had advanced only a few feet by the time Sergio came over and stood next to him, after parking. He still had a long way to go to the ticket counter. Andrés realized that this was the last time they would be together for a long time. He remembered the harsh conversation beneath the tree, his brother's frustrated embrace, the mutual accusations.

"Write to us," Sergio said, searching for words that would conceal the uncomfortable silence lying beneath the din of the airport.

"Sure."

"I mean it. The old man lives for that."

"Don't keep telling me what the old man lives for. I'll write. I promise I'll write you more often this time."

"I'm not saying it for my sake, Andrés. Even though I'd like to know how you're doing, too. It's only normal, right? But I'm really worried about the old man. And mama, who's so happy when your letters come."

"They'll come."

"Don't take it the wrong way. It's not a demand."

"I suppose not."

"It's not an accusation, either, if that's what's making you so crabby."

"I didn't think it was an accusation."

"Then you'll write."

"That's exactly what I just told you."

There was a garbled announcement. The loudspeaker transmitted the nasal ambiguity of a woman announcing something or other.

"Is that your flight?"

"Did you hear it? Did you understand?"

"Not a word."

"I don't think they were calling my flight. It's not for another hour."

"Look," he said, pointing to the electronic board where cities and flights rapidly changed position. "They're calling your flight."

"I don't think so. Look at the line, all the way up to the counter; they can hardly call for boarding when they haven't even taken care of half of the people waiting to get up to the ticket counter. But if you have to leave, go ahead. I understand you have to get back to work."

He regretted it immediately, because his display of consideration seemed hard, scornful, and he understood that everything he might say was threatened by the possibility of a misunderstanding that could undermine his words and gestures, and it was always there, always present since that irreproducible night, that frustrated embrace beneath the tree.

"I came to see you off. I'll leave after you've gone through security."

"Okay. It's much better if you stay."

He realized then that the mending hadn't changed the tense echo of their silence. They stood there not saying a word. They hoped that time would pass as quickly as possible, but the long line emphasized an agony of stopped clocks.

"Don't you have anything else to say to me?" Andrés asked.

"What else? Tell me what else you want to hear!"

"Are you happy I came?"

"Yes, very happy."

"And about what happened in the house?"

"Not very happy," Sergio said.

"And what else?" Andrés insisted.

"Nothing else. I have nothing to do with that. Or don't you believe me?" Sergio replied harshly.

"Yes, yes, of course I believe everything you told me."

"What are you trying to say now?"

"I believe that you rented our house to those people. That you knew what you were doing. That you never told me what it was all about. You excluded me from your decision, from something that belonged to both of us."

"What do you want me to explain first?"

"Nothing. There's no time now. You heard them call the flight."

"I didn't want things to turn out like this."

"I suppose not."

"I know you've had your problems, but things were tougher here. Here they were a matter of life or death."

They called the flight for the second time while Andrés was at the ticket counter, checking his luggage and handing his ticket to the attendant.

"Good morning."

"*Guten Tag.*"

"Do you speak German?"

"*Ja. Ich spreche Deutsch.*"

"*Schön. Raucher oder nicht Raucher?*"

"*Raucher.*"

"*Gute Reise. Der nächste, bitte.*"

"I never heard you speak German before. Nice," Sergio said, taking Andrés's hand luggage.

"No, leave it. I'll carry it."

"Okay. I can't go past here," Sergio said, at the line marking the entrance to International Security.

The brothers stood face to face for a long time. When their eyes met, they immediately tried to avoid contact, looking for some pretext: it helped to look up at the electronic board, to check the sturdiness of the suitcase handle, to glance toward the window where the security agent awaited the next traveler. Each of them hoped the other would initiate the embrace. A flight attendant walked by with a sign calling for delayed passengers. It was a yellow sign with black letters, written in English and German. Maybe they thought that the garbled loudspeaker would be even less comprehensible for those who didn't speak Spanish.

"I'll send you your share of the sale of the house," Sergio said. "I guess I'll deposit it into the same account."

"I don't know."

"You don't know what? Do you have another bank account?"

"No."

"So?"

"Why didn't you tell me you'd already sold the house?"

"I was hoping to get it back someday. I didn't want you to know what had happened."

"Can you get it back?"

"I think so. I'll have to talk to Cecilia's father."

"Cecilia's father? Why?"

"Because he's the owner."

"Why him?"

The flight attendant who had moved the boarding process along appeared again, announcing:

"Flight 704 to Frankfurt is now boarding."

"And did he know what they'd done with it?"

"Of course."

"I don't get it at all."

"He bought houses that had been 'burned.'"

"Burned?"

"That were very run down or easily identifiable as torture houses. He bought them for a song and sold them after they had been renovated."

"And he gave one of those to his daughter!"

"According to what he told me, he wanted to give her a different house, a clean house, shall we say. A house in Las Condes, or in Lo Barnechea, or in Lo Curro; a house everyone wanted to own."

"And then?"

"Cecilia saw a photo of our house in Don Jovino's office. She liked it a lot. And when he offered her a gift on condition that they didn't get a separation, she asked him for our house. She insisted so much, she loved the house so much, that her father finally gave in."

". . ."

"He never imagined that after it had been renovated, Julia would come along and tell us what had happened."

"But how could DINA sell a house that belonged to us? You always told me you had rented it out."

"I did rent it out. And six months later, they asked me to sell it to them."

"But you knew what they had done to our house!"

"That's why I accepted what they offered me! For them it was a burned house; for us, it was uninhabitable."

"But you didn't tell me that, either."

"I told you how they pressured me. What I didn't tell you in front of everybody was that when they threatened me with that business about long arms, and that they knew about you and where you were, I had to agree to sell them the house."

"But why did they rent it first? Why didn't they offer to buy it from you right away?"

"Because it was being rented. Only when they saw that everything was working out without problems, that the neighbors didn't protest, and especially when it became completely deteriorated, they chose not to call attention to themselves. If I accepted the offer, they wouldn't have to be accountable to anyone."

"They've never had to be accountable to anyone."

"That's why I thought it was wise to accept."

"It was our house. We were born there. We played there. We grew up there. I suppose the folks don't know anything about this."

"Of course not! No one knows."

"No one knew."

"Julia is discreet."

"That's not what I mean! I wish everyone knew!"

"Just when you've got one foot in the plane, right? And how do you propose they find out? How would you prefer to do it? Do you want me to go place an ad right now? And where? With the military police? With DINA? With the judges? Where?"

"What if there were someplace to report it? If such a place existed, would you do it?"

"I don't know."

"There has to be someplace."

"Would you do it?"

"Naturally."

"Then stay."

"If you tell me where to go, I'll stay. At least for a few days."

"..."

"What are you telling me?"

"What hurts me is that I can't tell you anything. There's nothing to be done. Nothing that would have any effect."

"The system works."

"Perfectly."

"That's why your business at the Stock Exchange is going so well."

"Why do you say that?"

"Because everything works: order and peace. There's security for investing."

"Yes. Maybe that's why."

"And because no one knows what's going on," Andrés said, ironically.

"Exactly."

"Don't lie to me! Not to me! Everyone knows."

"I swear there are plenty of people who don't know."

"But you people know."

"What do you mean by *you people?* Who are *we?*"

"The ones doing big business."

"Don't talk shit. One thing has nothing to do with the other."

"They don't?"

"They're different things."

"They're not different things!"

"People are investing because there's security, harmony."

"Because there's order and peace."

"In a certain sense, there's more order and more peace, if you compare it with the chaos of 1973 . . ."

"And what about what happened in our own house? Doesn't that mean anything to you? Didn't you see the signs of horror all through the house? They even installed electric beds in our bedroom. Was that your order and peace?"

"What happened was horrible. But there's also the other side."

"What other side?"

"What you yourself said. We're moving forward. Economically, the country is better off than ever. You read the papers, didn't you? Those figures are accurate."

"Moving forward in order and peace."

"I didn't say that. I only said we're moving forward, even if you don't want to believe it."

"With torture houses?"

"I don't want there to be torture houses. It's stupid of you to connect the torture houses with growth."

"I'm not the one connecting them! Reality does! We're talking about the facts!" Andrés shouted.

"It's an interpretation of the facts. As stupid and doctrinaire as your former interpretation of other facts. What are you trying to argue? That torture and growth are two sides of the same coin? If that's what you think, then, even if you don't know it, you're thinking like the most fanatical fascist. When I say torture and growth have nothing to do with one another, I mean I believe in growth without dictatorship. And furthermore, I'm convinced we've reached the limit, and from now on development can continue only if the dictatorship ends."

"According to your explanation, it's a kind of *conditio sine qua non*."

"Exactly."

"It reminds me of a scene from *The Days of the Commune*. Do you know that play by Brecht?"

"No."

"In the first scene, on a restaurant terrace, the fat man is talking to the waiter serving his meal, as upstage the refuse of war passes by. It's about the Franco-Prussian war, which, incidentally, ended with the Paris Commune. Men on crutches, with their heads bandaged, hungry, begging for scraps. The waiter cries, 'It seems this war will never end.' And the fat man reassures him: 'Quite the contrary. This war will end very soon.' The waiter asks, 'Why do you say that?' 'Because all the businesses that could be built because of the war have already been built. The only business left is to end it.' "

"I agree with the idea of ending wars and ending dictatorships," Sergio replied, "even if the goal is just to build new businesses. Think about what Brecht himself said. He doesn't automatically associate dictatorship with business. He's more realistic. Sometimes dictatorship and business are contradictory."

"Not here, in the middle of so much order and so much peace," Andrés insisted.

"Agreed. But there's no future if we believe that those businesses are just a continuation of the dictatorship."

"The future of all those businesses, you mean."

"The future for all of us. I'm talking about our house, if you want me to be more explicit. Very soon people are going to understand that there will be no greater obstacle to our development than to cling to the dictatorship."

"Are you trying to tell me that the same people who needed the dictatorship are going to need democracy now?"

"That's right," Sergio replied, unruffled.

"So, under democracy, these businesses won't fold?"

"Not at all," Sergio said calmly, adding, after a pause, "The condition for returning to democracy is the survival of those businesses and many other new ones to come."

There were no more passengers left waiting to go through Security for the Lufthansa flight. The flight attendant had long since disappeared and probably wouldn't return to make another departure announcement.

"You've got to go."

"We'll write."

"Sure. But where should I send the money to you?"

"We'll see. I'll write you. Take care of the folks."

"Your visit did them good. Did you notice that? Did you see papa's expression when you made him a drink yesterday? 'Andrés is making me a German apéritif,' he told me while you were in the kitchen. He thinks you're coming back."

"I have to go."

Andrés opened his arms wide, and Sergio immediately nestled into that promise of closeness from which his brother's worn-out raincoat hung like a old flag. Andrés wrapped him in an embrace, resting his cheek against Sergio's head, which felt warm and heavy. He closed his eyes, and when he opened them again the embrace was still there, but his eyes were fixed on the Security Police, the window, the corridor, the luggage control, the dog sniffing the suitcases, the light reflecting off the tiles. Only the other side remained. The next wait, the next departure, the familiar distance.

21

44

Cecilia decided to forgo Don Jovino's protection as well as her own protective attitude toward Manuel. She finally felt the urge to begin something she should have done back in the days when her amorous posturing with Manuel was – without anyone's possible opposition – leading to marriage, the same marriage that was now ending so sadly and after such a prolonged agony: build her independence. To learn that there are mistakes that can go uncorrected, since even if they aren't corrected, nothing much happens. To begin to forgive herself and above all not to demand of others what she herself couldn't achieve by becoming a slave to her overwhelming guilt feelings.

She began taking classes at the university again: Introduction to Philosophy on Tuesdays and Thursdays from 11:50 to 1:20, and Theory of Knowledge on Mondays and Fridays from 8:30 to 10. She signed a contract to translate three Descartes works and, with the help of a friend, became an instructor for some motivational classes required by an advertising agency. That wasn't enough to live on, but she still could land something else; there was time left in the day, and even if there wasn't, she'd just sleep less. She believed she had recaptured her independence, and sometimes she felt that that was something like solitude. Being freer now opened up possibilities that hadn't even been within the scope of her desires, but it also meant limitations she'd never even imagined. Nonetheless, she knew that being free was like starting life over.

In the afternoon, she left Descartes on her desk, lost amid hundreds of notes and crossouts, and went out to look for what would be her new home. She was living in a small apartment her father had put up for sale and offered her as a final gift, since his time was running out, but Cecilia had refused; there were some things more important than the house, and she would make no concessions about that. The only problem presented by occupying her father's temporary, frustrated gift for a few days had to do with interrupting her work. Whenever she was absorbed in her translation, the bell would ring and she'd have to show the apartment to unexpected visitors, those anxious eyes, that docile smile, that wrinkled Sunday paper peeking out from under a sleeve. It was a minor, relatively infrequent problem, though, in that nobody would show up at the door for days, and during those times the translation and preparation of her classes progressed splendidly.

One warm afternoon at the end of November, aroused by the unusual fragrance of the flowers and the heady aroma of the recently watered neighboring gardens, Cecilia felt the need to go downstairs and sense those aromas, that life, that invisible pollen, that commotion entering her window, at close range. She left her cigarette, which was making her feel a bit nauseated, left Descartes open to page 114 of the *Metaphysical Meditations*, and also left the distress that had clung to her all that time, like leprosy, and that suddenly evaporated that afternoon like a miracle.

The Sunday paper, with its rental ads highlighted in the same green marker that pointed out problem areas of the *Meditations*, was in her car. Her idea was to look around Plaza Ñuñoa, and if the offers marked in the newspaper turned out to be inconvenient, she'd expand her radius outward from that preferred spot, a plaza as familiar to her as her childhood memories.

Since there was an ad for a just-like-new apartment right near the plaza that sounded like the apartment of her dreams, she parked her car in the building parking lot and climbed the stairs to the fourth floor. Someone might think that a fourth-floor apartment by definition has lost part of the attributes of a dream apartment. However, Cecilia knew that that apparent disadvantage was the secret announcement of other, compensatory advantages. If a building has no elevator, an apartment on the fourth floor generally costs less than one on the second. And she also knew that for her, that price difference, which had nothing to do with the quality of the dwelling but only with its location, meant a great deal and was a sum that would grow in importance with the simple passage of time.

"Hi, how are you? You're really lucky – I was on my way out. Of course not, honey, come on in. This'll knock you out."

The young woman who showed her the apartment treated her with that phony intimacy – from her greeting on – that sitcom language, that false and basically affected familiarity that Cecilia found irritating.

But the apartment itself was enough to placate the annoyance of the grumpiest visitor. It was so well renovated that it seemed brand new. Cecilia left her purse and the newspaper on the floor, carpeted in a color that accented the whiteness of the wallpaper. The living room looked spacious, and the picture window generous. It offered a view of a surprising display of foliage, a tapestry of trees of different colors and sizes, branches and leaves spontaneously displayed under the rays of a sun that was sinking wondrously behind that assemblage of backyards. And there was also a room for the girls, with good light and enough space for their beds and toys, and the floor was covered with pristine carpeting . . . and a closet whose door had stuck when the paint dried . . . and which she opened with excessive force. The closet, the imminence of the defect, the violent yank, and the door's persistent tremor provoked an instant, terrifying memory in Cecilia.

"Be careful, honey. Don't destroy my apartment."

And as Cecilia's silence blended with the last reverberations of the door, the woman lightened her tactless remark with that same tone of false familiarity.

"Don't worry, it's just that paint. I love the smell of fresh paint. It even makes me a little tipsy, look," she said, laughing in a way Cecilia thought vulgar. "Don't you like that nice rubbery smell of paint?"

"I don't know about rubbery. I like the smell of paint, yes. But I don't know."

The room next to it was smaller, a storage room, probably. A little room for her. Like the little lavender room in the house. To be alone in, to translate in, to read, to escape. A house, she thought, was an imaginary world, a product of dreams, and if the dreams took flight, that would definitely be her house, the one she wished for, her domicile. And she began to imagine: I'll put this over here, that over there. This in the girls' room. In the little lavender room they'll have tea with their grandpa. On Sunday, after lunch. Then she remembered that the night before, while watching a program about divorce, she asked herself the question: And what about Manuel? How many times will he be able to see his daughters? He'll see them as often as he wants to. You need to put some order in your life. No. More than that. You need a lot more than order. You need to put more humanity, more freedom . . ."

"Who lived here before?" she asked, struck with anxiety because she loved the apartment.

"Before what?"

"Who were the last tenants?"

"An older couple, dear. That's why the house is so clean. When the man died, the daughters took her to a rest home."

"And before that?"

"How am I supposed to know what was here before, honey? They lived here for over ten years."

"And that man, what did he do?"

"He was a university professor."

"Ten years, you said?"

"Something like that."

And as she began to dream about her furniture set up between these walls and to think about what she'd have to get rid of and would be good to get rid of, and what she'd add, little by little, to the essentials, so that everything would be different, and how then she'd be in her house surrounded by the things she loved, not like a ghost lost among a pile of useless objects; as she was already beginning to feel herself living between these four walls, freshly painted, nice and new, with the smell of paint and glue, but also with the fragrance wafting in from the exuberant backyards of those Ñuñoan houses; when she momentarily lost herself in contemplating those gardens, with no more bad memories, enjoying that long-forgotten tranquility like fresh air, she was suddenly awakened by a well-aimed question.

"What does your husband do?"

"Why do you ask?"

"He's going to rent the place, isn't he?"

"I'm separated."

"Separated?"

"Yes, separated. But I work. The house is for me. For me and my daughters."

"And what do you do?"

"I'm a professor."

"A professor?"

"Yes, a professor. Why are you making that face?"

"Hey, it's the only one I've got. I'm not making any face. But you'll need a co-signer."

"I don't have a co-signer."

"Do you know anyone who can vouch for you?"

"I can vouch for myself."

"Someone who owns property, I mean. Some relative, a friend. All I need's a name, honey."

"My father owns a realty company."

"So why don't you rent from him?"

"I came here about the apartment, not to tell my life story."

"I'm just saying. I thought it would be much easier for you."

"Yes. Much easier. But this time I want to do it differently."

"You're gonna lose the apartment. It's a shame."

But she didn't want her father to be her co-signer. He'll never co-sign anything again. He'll be a father. A grandfather. And they'd never talk about the other thing again.

"It's just that a teacher, sweetie . . ."

"I'm a professor at the university."

"Uh-huh. What university?"

"The University of Chile."

"See? You'll need a co-signer."

"Explain what you mean."

"I want to help you, honey. I like you. But I also have to do my job. Look: put something more convenient on the application. You don't even have to make anything up. You just have to make an X in the right boxes. Where it says marital status, mark number two. See? Single, married, separated. You check *married*. Where it says children, check *one*. Where it asks for the age of the children, don't even think of saying four or six. Say *fifteen*. Where it asks for a co-signer, write your father's name. And where is says co-signer's profession, write what you told me. It's the truth, I suppose. Then you write '*owner of realty company*.'"

"And where it asks for my name, what should I put? Gabriela Mistral or Marilyn Monroe?"

She had already picked up her purse from the floor, leaving the newspaper there, perhaps without noticing it, when she heard the woman's astonished voice behind her.

"What'd you say, sweetie?"

"Nothing. Good-bye." She opened the door, looking for the staircase and the banister to get out of there as quickly as she could.

"Well, ex-cu-u-use me. I just wanted to help you," the woman shouted from upstairs.

"I know. Thanks a lot."

"Listen, don't get snotty with me," the woman shouted again when she heard Cecilia's footsteps stop on a landing and knew that she could hear but not see her. "I only wanted you to have the apartment. I wanted to rent out this piece of shit this afternoon. That's how I make my living."

"Shove your fucking apartment up your ass! I'm sure it'll fit!"

45

She descends the staircase of the building as though pursued by her own annoyance, that unwanted rudeness, that violence she hated. Her footsteps resounding on the stairs tell her: another mistake, another mistake, another mistake. Correct it, correct it, correct it. Will she have to turn around, give an explanation to that woman who perhaps wanted to help her by suggesting she fill the application with lies? Her footsteps on the stairs tell her: another mistake, another mistake, another mistake, you'll never find a place like that, you'll never get a new apartment like that, mistake, mistake, mistake, it was clearly a mistake, as she descended, as she flew downstairs, clinging to the banister, feeling the cold, hard ceramic of the steps, mistake, mistake, mistake.

What kind of world was she living in? Who gave them the right to decide if you were wrong, and why? Don't get married. Don't get a separation. Don't get married. Don't get a separation. Don't say bad words. And never lose your cool. And descending the staircase, she sees, through the gap of light on the landing, a playground with swings, children climbing on painted trains, tumbling on the lawn. And she doesn't think that her girls could have played there, but rather she imagines, she hears something like a muffled song bursting in her ear, like a chorus of children in the schoolyards of her youth, these same words with the rhythm of a children's tune:

Don't-get-mar-ried,
Don't-get-a-se-pa-ra-tion,
Don't-say-bad-words,
And-ne-ver-lose-your-cool

Yes. She mustn't lose her cool. She had to maintain her inner peace and respect the natural order of things. But she didn't believe in those words anymore. And she was at the point of no longer believing in anything, not even in herself. She only believed in the words drilling into her eardrums as she went downstairs. Frighteningly true words, present and clear to the point of desperation.

They repeated like an echo in the woman's syrupy voice:

"Professor?"

"Separated?"

"Write something else here."

"I want to help you because I like you. But you have to write something else here."

And those words intermingled with others, with her father's: "*Try again. I'll give you a house. A house where you can start over. Leaving all the difficult years behind. To love each other in and not be alone.*" Manuel's words:

"*What are you doing? We've already moved in here . . .*"

"*If this house weren't condemned, it might have been the one next door or the one on the corner.*"

"*Why should we have the privilege of our house not being the one?*" Julia's words:

"*Your daughters are sleeping in the room where there were two grills.*"

"Grills?"

"*Yes, grills. A bed that's connected to an electrical outlet, to electric current. An electric bed. Like an electric chair, but longer lasting.*"

And those of Andrés:

"*Now I know I'm not coming back. I couldn't live here.*"

"What about us? Can we live here?"

"*Well, I don't know how you can. If I had stayed here all those years, maybe I could, too.*"

"How I would've loved not to be here all those years so I'd have the wonderful power of not being able to."

And she goes down, down, only four flights, and there seem to be so many steps, the voices, everything that's been welling up in her memory and multiplying her fear, which, along with her, falls into something that never comes, it's pure descent, vertigo, a bottomless pit, a sheer pause in mid-air, but also a vertical plunge. I've never flown, *mijita*, Chelita used to say – Julia said Chelita used to say this – but fear is like a fall, like a fall that has no bottom and no solution. And that spring afternoon, she descends the stairs of a comfortable apartment house in Ñuñoa, on a street with trees and birds, with children's voices, with playing in the playground, with the aroma of fresh bread and coffee coming from the apartments, just as the noise of footsteps reaches her from the street, and the voices, and that warm breeze of a peaceful city . . . Everything seems so normal . . . as if one could live there so simply. And at the same time, she feels like she's falling, like the slope is endless, continuing its descent toward something very terrible that never quite comes, that descends, that keeps descending, down, down, as if she's using up the steps of a basement; descending to the worst part, as Chelita told Julia, and Julia told her, and she, from now on, will tell anyone who wants to hear her, if she can catch her breath after this, if she can find the words. If those words aren't smothered in a cry.

The fragrance of fresh bread coming from one of the apartments rescued her from madness.

46
THE FINAL CRY OF THE FORGOTTEN ONES

We, the last occupants of the house; we who bled here; who were subjected to this horror; we who were led down into the basement, we who counted the eight steps every afternoon, we who shouted, who howled,

the hopeful, naïve ones, we who still believed in pleas and mercy,

we who, already hopeless, continued moaning and crying, extinguishing ourselves with our tears,

we, who still live,
asking ourselves if it's a blessing or a curse;
and those of use who survive, no longer asking,
and those who were disappeared before we could ask anything at all,
we,
the last, forgotten occupants,
devoid even of the peace of mortals
for we keep on dying in this house

47

Made tenser every day by the annoying difficulties she imagined a woman like her would have in renting a house, Cecilia devoted entire afternoons to investigating those that were advertised in the papers. The most serious problem was that she was now less enthusiastic about showing the one she occupied in those days – and they were no longer days, but rather weeks, a couple of months – frightened by the possibility that renting out her temporary dwelling would prematurely deprive her of a place to live in. But since under no circumstances did she want to accept her father's comfortable offer, for she knew she would always end up entangled in that apparent ease, she redoubled her efforts to locate a place that looked less and less like the one she had originally dreamed of: she was being reduced to something that couldn't help but hurt if she compared it with the newly green garden, and the elegant staircase, and the ample space and the lovely façade of the lost house.

One afternoon, during one of her many trips around the city, guided by the ads highlighted in green marker – and although she never deliberately tried to go near that place – she found herself face to face with the empty house.

When she instinctively stopped the car, the house was already quite a distance away. But the street was quiet, and she was able to back up to the middle of the block. She lit a cigarette, rolled down the window all the way, and determined to look at that once-again empty house, now plunged once more into abandonment.

She thought that while it was unoccupied, the same voices would resound between its walls. But if no one heard the forgotten women, it was as if they had never existed, as if they said nothing. There can be no voice without an attentive ear. Nor words. Nor humanity, she thought. But she also knew that those voices were there before the listening ear. They were there because pain was there. And the cries and tears were there; and the moaning that sounded like a hinge emanating from the corners, and the suffocated breathing on the mattress; and the desperate gasping for breath when, for a second, a head emerges dripping every imaginable misery from the depths of a bathtub. Desperate voices, yes. Voices that came from the margins, from the limits, from the end of life and the first throttle of death. Voices no one heard when the house was empty; voices that only they heard that night because one day, waiting for her father at the realty company, she had looked at the photo of such a pretty house, destroyed by weeds and neglect. There was something good in what happened to them then: ears for those voices. It was good that her hand pushed the iron gate, defeated by rust, and for the first time entered that abandoned beauty asking about the reason for that desolation. That's why that night there had been listening ears for those pleas that rose from the basement, and a desire to give refuge to so much loneliness. That ear not only rescued what was still living in that house: it recaptured it for her, as well; for Julia; for Andrés, living in the same loneliness so far away; for Sonia, unresigned to her own solitude right here; and for all those who heard those voices, for they made decisions that perhaps would improve their lives.

Yes, that's how it is, Cecilia thinks, lighting another cigarette: it was good to enter the house and hear what they were telling us from its corners. It was necessary to do it, not only out of respect for the pain of those who had suffered there, but because that pain had a great deal to do with the loss that kept pursuing her outside its walls.

It was necessary to hear those voices. Whoever heard them could find a response to their anguish. Whether they realized it or not, their destinies could never be dislodged from those walls.

If there is no ear for the pain, then there's no real ear for anything.

We are all vulnerable to misfortune. The only consolation is knowing that our cries will be heard by an understanding heart.

Will there be a heart open to the voices of the house?

Who will push open that heavy door?